Tad strolled over to Dawn, trying to look casual about it. "What are you doing here?" Dawn asked, tightening the cinch with a muscular and well-practiced jerk. "I thought today was the day for pinning Allison down. You must be losing it, Taddeus. You aren't irresistible anymore."

"Allison missed the bus, Dawn. She forgot a book or something. I saw her hunting for it. If I'd had the car today, I could have waited for her. Don't worry. I've got her so stirred up she can't keep her head straight."

She stroked the glossy column of her horse's neck, not looking at him. "You thought you'd get her in bed right off the bat, Tadsy. Here it is almost two weeks later and you haven't made it yet. One week more. Or you lose your chance with me." She turned toward him, smiled flirtatiously, licked her lower lip, and pouted at him.

Tad swallowed deeply and chos⬚⬚⬚⬚⬚ ⬚e the focus. "Why've you got it in for he⬚

She thought about this f⬚⬚⬚⬚ ⬚⬚⬚⬚ nostril slightly raised. "I may⬚⬚⬚ ⬚⬚⬚⬚ s stupid school. I may have t⬚⬚⬚ ⬚⬚⬚⬚ people at this stupid school. B⬚⬚⬚ ⬚⬚⬚⬚ ⬚ke her kind of attitude." Dawn⬚ ⬚⬚⬚⬚ ⬚d motion and looked down at ⬚⬚⬚⬚ ⬚ip suggestively. "I don't like her. ⬚⬚⬚⬚ ⬚⬚⬚⬚ she's nothing, but she gets all A's. I⬚ ⬚⬚⬚ ⬚ething disturbs her concentration, that's a⬚

By B. J. Oliphant
Published by Fawcett Books:

DEAD IN THE SCRUB
THE UNEXPECTED CORPSE
DESERVEDLY DEAD
DEATH AND THE DELINQUENT
DEATH SERVED UP COLD
A CEREMONIAL DEATH

A CEREMONIAL DEATH

B. J. Oliphant

FAWCETT GOLD MEDAL • NEW YORK

A Fawcett Gold Medal Book
Published by Ballantine Books
Copyright © 1995 by B. J. Oliphant

Library of Congress Catalog Card Number: 95-90670

ISBN 0-449-14897-1

Manufactured in the United States of America

First Edition: January 1996

10 9 8 7 6 5 4 3 2

1

Shirley McClintock set her coffee cup down with such force that the coffee splashed onto the newspaper she'd been reading. "I don't believe it," she growled.

"What do you believe less than usual?" J.Q. inquired in a mild tone, looking at her over his reading glasses. "The weather forecast? They're predicting rain for today and tomorrow."

"Nothing to do with the weather! I thought I had subscribed to the Santa Fe newspaper, but this is obviously the *National Enquirer*." She sniffed, running the fingers of one hand through her short gray hair. "Who else would devote two full pages of their Monday edition to a comprehensive examination of cattle mutilations?"

J.Q. returned to the Western edition of *The Wall Street Journal*. "There are a lot of credulous people out there."

"We might as well be living in the Dark Ages. Signs and marvels all about us, and no sense at all!"

J.Q. lowered his paper and assumed a patient expression. "I take it there have been cattle killed here in New Mexico."

"Well, of course there have, J.Q. We've had thunderstorms! August and early September, we had thunderstorms almost every day, especially over the mountains where these private cattle are busy overgrazing the public lands."

"Ah." He allowed himself to look slightly puzzled. "Was that a non sequitur, or have I missed something?"

"Cattle are watered at tanks; tanks are filled by windmills; lightning hits windmills, lightning hits water tanks, lightning hits cows that're standing near windmills and water tanks. We lost one or two to lightning every now and then at the Colorado ranch."

Lately Shirley had taken to calling it the Colorado ranch. It was easier than calling it the McClintock Ranch, with all the loss that implied. Determinedly, she went on: "Lightning deaths happen, especially in the mountains."

"There's also rattlesnakes," he said from behind the paper.

"Them, too." She went on shaking her head as she rose to her full six-foot-three and went for a second cup of coffee and a paper towel to clean up the mess she'd made with the first one. "Or perforated stomachs from hardware disease, or being poisoned from eating horsetail or hemlock. Or hunters who can't see straight. There's a dozen good reasons for cows to die, but that doesn't include extraterrestrials taking samples."

He looked up again, one eyebrow quirked. "The morning paper blames UFOs?"

She snorted, laying the paper before him. "Have a

look! The reporter has covered the field for us. He's even tied in giant ovals in wheat fields, circular depressions near the bodies, a strange smell, strange lights in the sky. And goodness gracious me, only the tongues, genitals, and udders gone! And no blood! Idiots. Of course there's no blood. Even in a slaughterhouse you've got to hang carcasses up by the back feet and slit the throat to get the blood out. Drop them dead on the pasture, gravity pulls all the blood to the bottom side. Then the magpies come, and the crows, and the coyotes assemble, and they can't get to the bottom side because there's hundreds of pounds of dead cow lying on top of it. They can't get through the tough hide, either, so they eat the tender parts that are exposed on top—which do not bleed, because all the blood has run to the bottom side—and the tender parts are the tongue and the udder and the rectum and vagina. And what the crows and magpies and coyotes leave, carnivorous flies and bees and ants clean up to make a nice, surgical-looking cut that's dry as a bone."

"We could put an end to all this mutilation nonsense very quickly," he opined, turning the page and burying himself once more. "If you'll authorize the expenditure, I'll see to importing some African buzzards."

"Buzzards?" she asked doubtfully.

"Not like our little turkey buzzards. Some of those African buzzards are big fellows. Strong beaks, heavy talons, able to open up a carcass and get at the innards. The problem is, here in the West, the wolves are gone, the bears are way back in the hills with the cougars, we've only got little old turkey buzzards to clean up the mess. And crows, of course."

She grinned fiercely. "A wolf or a bear would do a

3

better job of it. A good reason for bringing wolves back, maybe."

"Or we could import hyenas along with the buzzards."

Shirley stared upward, lost in the vision of African buzzards and whole families of hyenas populating the New Mexican landscape.

J.Q. turned the page, found nothing to his interest, and put the paper down. "Doesn't the paper quote anyone sensible?"

"The FBI investigator. Well, he says pretty much what you and I just said, but he works for the government, so of course he's considered unreliable. The locals would rather believe in UFOs. Facts are no fun."

He yawned. "Tolerance, Shirley. Tolerance. We've fetched up in the heartland of gullibility, where there's sixteen crystal gazers to the square mile, plus uncounted bevies of psychic healers and channelers for dead Indians—mostly gringos, of course."

"You're talking about our neighbor. Ms. Shadow Dancer."

"Shadow Dancer?"

"That's her name."

"I thought it was Bridget McCree."

"She was Bridget McCree. Last week she got it changed legally. Now she's Shadow Dancer. She sent a notice to all the neighbors."

"Mighty thoughtful," said J.Q., tongue firmly in cheek. "Otherwise we might not have known where to send the men in the white coats when they turn up."

"In Denver they'd turn up. In Nebraska or Texas or Oklahoma or Ohio. Not in Santa Fe."

J.Q. focused through his glasses, preparatory to returning attention to the financial establishment. "Is she still wearing those fringed leather dresses?"

Shirley laughed, genuinely amused. "She was the last time I saw her, couple of days ago. Beaded buckskin and moccasins. It must go over well with her . . . patrons; she seems to keep busy."

"She could be a good-looking woman," he remarked, turning a page.

Shirley gave him a sharp look. "She could, yes."

Shadow Dancer née Bridget McCree was about thirty-five, Shirley supposed. Nice skin and hair, pretty eyes. Kind of hard to tell what shape she was. Fringed leather smocks were like Mother Hubbards, all-concealing. Still, to each his own and all that.

"I shouldn't make fun of her, J.Q. She sends us business. Two or three times this last summer, as a matter of fact. I presume they were people she was healing with psychic impulses from outer space."

"I remember the Williamses, but who else?"

"The whiny guy who wanted his bed moved because entities from Jupiter—or was it Io?—were sending all kinds of healing rays and he had to be aligned east–west."

"Those rays must be what's helped my arthritis in passing," he said, giving up on the paper. He folded it into a neat rectangle and stuck it under his arm as he got up.

"Couldn't have." Shirley grinned. "Your bed is north–south."

"I sit east–west," he said as he went over to the window.

"I think when you're sitting, it has to be in a pentacle with the right crystals in your hands or it doesn't work."

"Speaking of not working . . ." He stared out at the October morning. Rancho del Valle's cottonwoods sparkled gold along the ancient irrigation ditch, the acequia, throwing sunlight in all directions. A summer's crop of young magpies was making parrotlike chatter in the boughs and the sky was a breathtaking autumn blue. "Have you noticed that something's not working with Allison lately?"

When he turned back, he saw Shirley's face had become very tight and withdrawn. He sat down again.

"What is it, Shirl?"

"I have noticed it. Yes. I'm worried about her. I try to tell myself we were just spoiled. . . ."

He raised his eyebrows.

"She's always been so perfect, J.Q. So sensible. We got used to her being that way. Lord, I got used to her being top of the heap, the best kid in town. Even that thing last summer with her aunt and uncle, all that witchcraft foofaraw, she was steady as a rock. When she's not all right, I remember. . . ."

J.Q. put his hand on her shoulder, knowing very well what she remembered: her own twelve-year-old daughter, killed all those years ago but never forgotten; her own son, disappeared and still mourned. He nodded heavily. "I thought it was probably just the new school. New schools are difficult, but it's been a couple of weeks now. I really didn't start worrying until I noticed she wasn't paying any attention to Beauregard. She hasn't groomed him the way she should, hasn't ridden him in weeks. . . ."

"I wonder if it is something from school," Shirley interrupted. "I could ask that teacher she talks about. Mr. Patterson. Jeremy Patterson."

"And the other thing that worries me," he went on, ignoring the interruption, "is she's turned so pretty. And too sexy looking."

"There is that." Shirley hadn't quite been prepared for Allison's being so startlingly pretty. She might turn out to be beautiful, which Shirley regarded as much a curse as a benefit. Ordinarily, she would have talked it over with their white-haired housemate, Xanthippe Minging, ex-schoolmistress and dear friend, who had had years of experience with adolescents, but Mingy had gone east to attend lengthy family festivities culminating in the wedding of a favorite niece. She wouldn't return until around Thanksgiving. Allison's strangely withdrawn behavior certainly couldn't be allowed to go unremarked or unmodified until then.

"You don't suppose it's drugs, do you?" she asked, not looking at him. "These days, that's what you think of."

"No sign of that," he said firmly. "She's not taking anything, Shirley. She's just . . . being unreachable. One of my daughters was like that, thrashed around like a hooked fish for the better part of three years. She's fine, now. Very sensible."

"She's probably forty."

"Well"—his brow furrowed in concentration—"thirty-five? Thirty-seven?"

"I'd prefer not to wait twenty-some-odd years for sanity to reemerge."

"What can we do? Deal with it, I guess. What's the real problem?"

"Problems, plural. Beauregard is one. Her not keeping up with her schoolwork is one. I had a call from her algebra teacher last week. Her not telling us where she's

7

going, or where she's been is one. Her seeming to be somewhere else all the time is one."

"All boils down to distraction. Some boy, you think?"

Some boy. Oh, if it were only that simple. Shirley ran down the mental list of boys Allison had mentioned or introduced. The Brower boy, pleasant, intelligent, a bit spotty. Allison had met him last spring, at a horse show. The Martinez boy, handsome, not at all spotty, macho as they come, brighter than he let on. He was a sort of down-the-road neighbor. Then this fall she'd met the Manicelli boy: football, basketball, body like a Greek god carved out of marble, brain also carved out of marble, pure stone, all the way through. And then that new one who had walked home with Allison a couple of times, Tad somebody. Pole. Tad Pole. A nickname. She said, "Could it be what's-his-name, Pole?"

"The one they call Tadpole?" asked J.Q.

"I was just thinking about the boys she's met since we've been here. She hasn't talked about that many; four I can think of. She said Brower was a nerd. She said Matteo Martinez came on too strong, scared her a little."

"The football player had nothing to talk about," J.Q. mused.

"Which leaves Tad Pole."

"Or somebody else. Somebody we don't know anything about." He sighed, took off his glasses, and rubbed the bridge of his nose between finger and thumb. "You're going to have to try to talk to her, Shirley."

"Why me? Why not you?"

"We're both going to have to try. I'll take care of the

algebra bit, and you work on the rest. And good luck to us."

As they spoke, the object of their discussion was leaning against her locker, groping through her books to be sure she had her social-studies text for first period, hoping she wouldn't be called upon to discuss the assignment on Gender Roles in Society. Allison had read neither the chapter nor any of the suggested outside readings. Allison could hardly keep her eyes open. She had had only three hours' sleep the night before, and no more than three for several nights before that.

"Hi, Ally," purred a voice in her ear. She glanced sideways. Dawn French, in all her tawny perfection. And her fluffy friend, Breeze Watkins.

"Hi," she said, sotto voce, unable to find more voice than that.

"Have you thought about it, Ally? We'd sure like you to join our group."

"Oh, really," breathed Breeze, with a sidelong glance at her friend. "You'd be such an asset, Allison."

"I'm considering it," Allison said. "I said I would. I'm just not sure about your . . . membership rules."

Dawn shrugged disarmingly. "Oh, don't worry about that part of it. I can help you out; so nothing happens, you know. It's just a kind of test, so we know we can trust you." She smiled sweetly, then leaned forward to press her cheek against Allison's. "I do hope you will."

Then they strolled away, smiling at one another, leaving Allison as confused and empty feeling as she'd been since Dawn had first invited her—if you could call it an invitation—to join their group. They called themselves the Bunch. And they happened to include the best-looking and the most popular kids in school. Probably

9

the richest kids, too. They shouldn't even be going to public school. They should be in a prep school somewhere. Dawn had been in a prep school somewhere, but she said she'd quit because it had been too . . . rigid.

Or maybe, Allison told herself, Dawn had had a Bunch there, too, and had had to quit because someone in authority had found out what the rules of membership were.

Half a mile east and around the corner from Rancho del Valle, Shadow Dancer, née Bridget McCree, was readying her hogan for a healing ceremony, stooping almost double to sweep the earthen floor with a turkey wing, the feathers making a soft *swoop shush* over the packed clay. A broom would be a lot easier, but the hogan roof was too low for her to stand up straight. The hogan hadn't turned out the way she'd planned it at all. It was supposed to be a four-legged hogan, over six feet high inside, and she'd ordered seven-foot poles for the frame, but then it turned out the bottom ends had to be sunk way down into the ground, and she didn't have the money right then to buy longer poles. The hogan ended up just a little more than five feet high inside, except right in the middle. Still, the turkey-wing brush was authentic, and so was the natural clay of the walls, well mudded over a foundation of saplings and brush. The clay floor was authentic. She stamped down the place where she hadn't gotten the floor quite level last time, scraping off a little damp soil with the edge of her shoe to make it flatter.

When it was as clean and flat as she could make it, she got her brush and jar of white paint and touched up the pentacle on the floor. She'd originally planned on doing sand paintings, real Navajo ones copied from a book she had, but they turned out to be much more difficult than they'd looked. She'd even bought a video of a Navajo medicine man creating a sand painting, and she'd recorded a PBS show about Tibetans doing a sand mandala. It looked so easy. All those fine little lines, straight as a ruler. When she'd tried it, hers had wobbled all over the place, and the colors all mixed together, so you couldn't tell what it was. Besides, it was so much work! You had to find the different-colored earths and pollen and corn, and you had to grind them. It could take days!

So, she'd settled for the pentacle and using some of her crystals. She didn't think crystals were really Indian, not Pueblo Indian, though she'd heard the Navajos had crystal gazers. Anyhow, the entities didn't seem to mind. They spoke to her, even when she didn't do anything special. And she would use three colors of cornmeal in her summoning ritual. That was Indian, at least.

Getting everything in place and purified with smoke took about half an hour. She put a cushion in the middle for the client and another one at the north side for her. Vigil lights were set at the points of the star, each one a different color. When she was finished, she lit some piñon incense to perfume the hogan while she went in the house to put on her leather dress and moccasins and have a cup of herbal tea—ginseng and bergamot—to purify her mind. She'd already braided her hair this morning, with leather thongs and feathers, so there was no hurry. She had plenty of time to relax and get into the proper frame of mind before the man arrived. His appointment was at ten.

The client had been referred, so he said, by another

client of hers. Millie someone? Shadow Dancer shook her head regretfully. She couldn't remember any Millie. But then, sometimes people didn't use their real names. They were ashamed of coming to a psychic healer. Maybe they figured if she was really psychic, she'd know what their names were. Silly. That wasn't the way it worked at all. She couldn't tell anything about a patient, name or address or any of that stuff, all she could do was feel the aura and convey the aura to the entities. It was the entities who did the healing, sometimes telling her what the person should do to be healed. If the person followed instructions, they got healed.

"How do you know?" her brother, Brian, had asked her. "How do you know it's healing them, Bridgy?"

Poor Brian. He'd always been like that, since they were little kids, always being the older sibling, talking sense to little sis. If he'd just let her show him! Or show Phyl! They could both have experienced it for themselves. And Brian might have, too, if it hadn't been for Phyllis, pooh-poohing everything, crying and carrying on. It made Bridget sorry she'd told them so much about herself. Not that she'd told them everything, but she had shared some private things, and then Brian and Phyl had to go and act that way!

She'd told them how she knew about healing, from personal experience; how something terrible had happened to her, how she'd been so anxious she couldn't eat or sleep or get over it. How she thought she'd commit suicide until she found Buffalo Man's ad in the freebie paper. She'd gone to him, three or four times; he'd told her what to do; and she'd done it, and here she was, living properly, in purity, all healed.

And when Buffalo Man got killed in that tragic accident, she knew it was up to her to pick up his work and go on, no matter what it took! Over a year now. And she was getting more and more clients all the time. It was meant to be, that's all.

She started to wash her paintbrush, but then a car drove into the driveway. Shadow Dancer put the paint and brush into the nearest nicho, then went out onto the porch, hand shielding her eyes against the morning sun. Not her client. Not a man at all. It was that Shirley woman from down the road, leaning out of the window of her car. Shadow Dancer went out smiling, offering her hand.

Shirley took the hand and gave it a brief squeeze. "I brought you some eggs, along with our thanks for referring the Williamses." Ordinarily, Shirley would have called her Bridget, but she couldn't quite bring herself to say "Shadow Dancer."

Shadow Dancer looked skeptically at the six large white eggs Shirley proffered. "That's very sweet of you, Shirley. They aren't fertile, are they? The eggs?"

"Nope," Shirley lied, without flickering an eyelash. The eggs had been laid this morning by hardworking Black Minorca hens, some might be fertile, but if this crystal gazer could tell the difference between fertile and nonfertile at that stage, Shirley would be a brass monkey.

"I don't eat live things," Shadow Dancer explained with a little laugh. "My brother and sister-in-law made such fun of me when they were here, but I think each of us has to find our own way, right? So I don't eat live things."

"Of course not. Only vegetables," Shirley agreed. "And grain, and maybe cheese?"

13

Shadow Dancer nodded, accepting the eggs while explaining fervently, "Nothing with the fire of life in it. Eating life is an impurity—not a sin, you understand, just an impurity—and I have to be pure to help my clients."

"Right." Shirley nodded, clamping her mouth shut so she couldn't ask why vegetables and cheese were less alive than a fertile egg. Grain would grow, if you planted it. You could take vegetable tissue and clone it. You could take a culture from cheese and make more cheese, but never mind. So far as some people were concerned, life seemed to be more of a religio-philosophical reset button than a continuous process.

"Did you see the morning paper?" Shadow Dancer asked breathlessly. "The article about the cattle mutilations? This time they're not going to be able to cover it up!"

"Cover up what?" Shirley asked, unthinkingly, regretting the words even as they left her tongue.

"The fact that we're actually In Contact," Shadow Dancer whispered. "The government knows, Shirley. Like in that *X-Files* show on TV. That's not just a story, you know. The government knows. They just don't want us to know."

"Why is that?" Shirley asked, giving up all semblance of being above it all. "Now, why do you suppose that is?"

"Power," she whispered. "The aliens have powers. Like that gravity ray that pulled those cows into the woods! Just think! A gravity ray! The government wants to keep that all to themselves. They don't want us ordinary people learning about it, or any foreign country getting it."

Shirley cleared her throat to keep from giggling help-lessly. "I missed the part about the gravity ray, I guess. I'll have to read it again when I get home. So. I'm going into Santa Fe, can I pick up anything for you?"

It was a knee-jerk, neighborly offer, a habit left over from her girlhood. People who live some distance from a town sometimes need to rely on one another.

"Oh, that's sweet of you. Yes. Could you stop at El Horno and get me a dozen whole-wheat tortillas, the big burrito size. Wait a minute and I'll get some money."

"Never mind," Shirley said. "Pay me when I deliver them. I'll be back around one or two o'clock, okay?"

"That's kind of you. Thank you."

"No thanks necessary. Looks like you've got a busy morning." Shirley smiled a leavetaking smile, putting herself and the car in gear.

"I've had a busy week!" Bridget cried, becoming animated and kittenish. "An old friend, all at once, out of nowhere! Someone I thought I'd never see again! And a new client! On the phone, he sounded really nice; troubled, but nice. He was referred by a former client, Millie somebody, but I can't remember any Millie. Maybe he meant Billie, Billie Ostrow. I'll have to look it up in my journal."

"You keep a journal?" Shirley wouldn't have thought she was the writing type. More the burble type, everything bubbling up, like a spring.

"Oh, yes. I set it all down. I keep a journal, under the stars." She laughed. "That's a family joke."

Shirley forbore responding to this patent invitation for further conversation and merely waved. Bridget, with a slightly disappointed moue, stepped back and

15

made a baby wave, fingers only, while Shirley drove away.

Once Shirley was out of sight, Shadow Dancer took the eggs into the kitchen and put them down the garbage disposal, one by one, letting the disposal run until it hummed only quietly. Shirley did let her chickens run loose, so these were free-range eggs, Shadow Dancer would give her that, but heaven knew what she fed them on the side! When she had visited Rancho del Valle to ask about borrowing chickens, she'd seen big blocks of chemicals set out for the sheep—mineral blocks, Shirley had called them, but minerals were chemicals, weren't they?—and if Shirley fed chemicals to the sheep, she probably fed chemicals to the hens, too! For her own diet she'd stick to the brown eggs she bought at the organic grocers in Santa Fe: The OG said brown was more natural than white, anyone could see that.

She had just finished disposing of the last egg when she heard a car drive in, then a sound on the porch, a knock on the door. She dropped the egg container on the counter, hurrying. From the nicho nearest the door, Shadow Dancer seized up a thumb-sized crystal of amethyst plus a couple of quartz chunks and some matrix emerald, and with these tools of the trade in her pocket, she went out to meet her ten o'clock appointment.

In Santa Fe, Shirley shopped for groceries. Marketplace for coffee, bulk olive oil, and honey. Albertson's for meat and veggies. She bought eggplant and zucchini, onions and garlic. A big kettle of ratatouille would be nice. She bought green beans and chayotes. Chayotes were interesting, now that she'd learned how to cook them. Neither she nor J.Q. had ever seen the

16

silly things until they came to New Mexico; they looked like hard green pears someone had sat on. The first time she'd tried them, she'd peeled them raw, and her hands had been smeared with a sticky substance that quickly dried to an impermeable and nonsoluble varnish that took half a day to peel off! Boiled first, however, then peeled, sliced, sautéed gently in a tiny bit of olive oil—for a rather long time, to dry them out a little—then sprinkled with toasted sesame seeds, they were a decidedly different vegetable.

She took the outgoing mail to the post office. She made a bank deposit and ordered new checks. She went to the Southwestern Seeds place off Agua Fria and bought some sheep fescue seed to sow in a bare spot outside the Ditch House, on the cool side. If she put it in now, it would come up in March or so. Finally, she drove home, zipping along the highway, going right past El Horno, the tortillería, before she remembered.

Cursing mildly, she turned the car around and went back. While she was at it, she bought two dozen tortillas to take home. J.Q. liked them with beans. Now that they'd moved to New Mexico, he was always cooking beans, though Shirley couldn't remember his having been a frijole-phile in Colorado. Allison liked tortillas rolled around cheese and bologna, with or without green chilies, then heated in the microwave. Shirley liked them as ingredients in any one of half a dozen enchilada recipes that were quick to make and nice to reheat for lunches and snacks. It was almost two when she turned north into the dead-end road that led to Bridget McCree's. Shadow Dancer's.

From the turnoff, the road ran level for a quarter of a mile, two houses on the right, two on the left, mostly

17

hidden by trees or walls or high coyote fence. Bridget's house was not visible at all until the road dipped over the edge of the ancient arroyo, onto a wide shelf lower down, then across the three big culverts to the corresponding shelf on the far side, where Shirley turned left into Bridget's drive. She parked behind Bridget's car, which stood in the open-doored, detached garage. When she approached the front door, she saw it was open also, but nobody answered her knock or her call. She thrust at the screen door and stepped inside, intending to leave the package, but she took only one step into the living room before she stopped, frozen in place.

The room was a shambles! Books and ornaments pulled off shelves, papers out of drawers, magazines tumbled, lamps fallen, the edges of the rug turned back. The short hallway leading to the kitchen had nothing in it to disturb, but the kitchen was a mess. Outside, on the back porch, nothing. The path led to the small round structure Bridget had called a hogan, though Shirley thought it looked more like a *horno*, the beehive-shaped, adobe ovens the Indians had adopted from the colonial Spanish.

"Bridget!" Shirley called. "Bridget McCree! Shadow Dancer?"

Not a sound, but the buzzing of flies. No, not flies. It was too late in the season for flies, really. Still, it was an insistent buzz. Like those little striped bees, those little flesh-eating bees . . .

Without any instruction from her brain, Shirley's feet took her down the path to the hogan. The buzzing got louder. The three-foot-high doorway faced her, covered with a blanket. Shirley leaned down from her six-foot-three and pushed the blanket aside.

Light fell through the smoke hole in the center of the roof, disclosing a body lying naked on its back. It had no breasts, only dry, raw circles swarming with bees, their eager noise amplified by the structure itself. The corpse's mouth was open, and there seemed to be no tongue. The legs were spread. Shirley glanced, only glanced at the groin, enough to see that whatever was usually there wasn't there now. She stepped back outside and took several deep breaths, looking stupidly at her hand, which held the plastic-wrapped package of a dozen whole-wheat tortillas. Setting the package on the hogan roof, she swallowed deeply to keep from gagging, then leaned over and put her head inside once more.

Around the bee-swarmed body, painted on the clay floor, was a star. Shirley leaned down and touched it. It felt damp. The clay floor itself felt damp. Well, damp in that one place. A foot away it was dry. Bridget's arms were spread wide. In one open hand lay a chunk of purple crystal, in the other a chunk of green. Two more pieces of clear crystal weighed down the eyes. Painted on the belly, in white, were odd-looking symbols. Not letters. Not words. The signs looked familiar, but Shirley couldn't remember where she'd seen anything similar. In a sand-filled pot to one side were the stubs of incense sticks. Two cushions and a clutter of candles had been thrust against the far wall. There was nothing else in the structure, no sign of clothing.

She went out again, picked up the tortillas, walked slowly around the hogan, peering at the ground. Behind the hogan, on the west, there were three circles burned into the herbage, each over a foot in diameter, the three making a triangle about eight feet on the side. The clay and wattle wall of the hogan bore a sign similar to the one painted on Bridget's body, and Shirley recognized the shapes. Circles joined by straight lines. Like crop circles.

Shirley turned, slowly examining the surroundings in all directions. The house sat on the wide east–west shelf that ran along the north side of Arroyo Largo—so called because its jagged length extended through the desert for several miles. Long ago a series of monstrous storms had washed a wide but shallow bed into the fabric of the desert, a vertical-walled slash some six or eight feet deep. Later, smaller storms had deepened the cut, but only at the center, leaving these terraces at either side to grow up in cottonwood and Russian olive and tamarisk. Some of the trees were now a foot and a half through the trunks.

The house faced the road. Across the road was a tall blind wall, laid up in mud brick and capped with red tiles laid in concrete. It hid everything of the house behind it except the chimneys. The hogan was directly behind the house, west of it and south of the garage. Farther south, the shelf fell off four or five feet into the sandy sixty-foot expanse of the present watercourse, now, at summer's end, dry except for a wandering rivulet a few inches wide. The shelf on the south was also grown up in trees and sloped up to the arroyo's rim. Downstream, past the hogan and the shed that had once held chickens and the ubiquitous New Mexico woodpile, the arroyo turned northwest and slid down into the wooded river bottom. Upstream were the huge concrete culverts, always a surprise in this arid land until the rains came and one saw them spewing muddy water to their tops. The culverts were topped with a wire fence.

Nothing overlooked the hogan. The view was blocked in every direction by structures or trees or terrain. A week from now these trees might be bare, but the fall had been mild, and they still made a leafy hedge against spying eyes. Someone might have peered from the edge of the trees north or south, from around the corner of the arroyo to the west, but it was improbable they had. No one had seen what had happened here. Little green men could have landed, taken their samples, and departed without anyone being the wiser. Or, some more pedestrian agent could have done an even more evil thing.

Now what? Call from here? Call from home? She was still holding the stupid tortillas.

She went back into the house, used a paper towel to hold the phone, and punched in the number of the Rio Grande County Sheriff's Office, recently memorized as an exercise in preparedness, though not with this particular need in mind. There was an empty egg container on the counter. She looked in the refrigerator. No eggs. She checked the sink, finding a bit of eggshell. So. She clenched her teeth ruefully. Bridget hadn't believed her about the eggs.

Liar, liar, pants on fire.

She should know better.

Someone answered the phone.

"I'd like to report a murder," she said in level tones, falling immediately into an informational quagmire. She didn't know the address. The phone number was on the phone, but nothing lying about in the kitchen had the address on it.

"It's a box number," she said at last. "Hold on, I'll go out in front and look on her mailbox."

21

"We need a street address," said the voice on the other end.

"I don't know what the street calls itself," she snarled. "It may be a private road, for all I know. It comes off County 92, which is parallel to State 503!"

Another voice took over. "Ma'am, where does it come off County 92? Who's the closest neighbor on 92?"

"I suppose I'm as close as anyone," Shirley admitted, giving her address and directions for reaching Rancho del Valle.

"Wait where you are, ma'am."

"Sure," she said dispiritedly, hanging up, picking up again to call J.Q.

"My God," he said. "You want me to come over?"

"If you wouldn't mind, J.Q. I'm kind of set back."

"I should think!" He hung up.

She put the phone onto the small table where it sat, beneath a nicho in the adobe wall. Carved and painted wooden santos or retablos were the usual occupants of nichos, with or without vigil lights. Here in Santa Fe de San Francisco, St. Francis was a favorite nicho tenant, as was the Virgin of Guadelupe. Non-Catholic residents used nichos for other things: kachinas, books, Indian pottery. Shadow Dancer had used hers to hold an assortment of crystals and a pint jar half-full of white fluid topped with a dry paintbrush. Shirley touched the brush, then sniffed it. She opened the jar and sniffed. The brush was caked with paint, almost completely dry. The paint looked like the paint on the hogan floor, and it had probably been used to make the signs painted on the dead woman's body as well.

She got out onto the front porch just about the time

J.Q.'s pickup rumbled across the culverts. He parked against the high adobe wall of the house opposite and got out waving a thermos at her.

"Coffee?"

Coffee was the remedy for all ailments, according to J.Q., and pretty much according to Shirley, too. "Lord, yes." She took the plastic cup with a hand that trembled only slightly, and they sat side by side on what the locals called the portal and Shirley usually thought of as the front porch.

"Can I?" He gestured with his head toward the back of the house.

"Be my guest," she said, shuddering.

He was back shortly, his face drawn. "Somebody did a job on her!"

"Little green men," said Shirley.

"What?"

"Did you look out behind the hogan? Three circles, neat as pie plates, burned in the grass back there."

"A UFO?"

"I'm sure that's what it's meant to look like. She was a real believer, J.Q. Just this morning, when I stopped here to thank her, she was going on about cattle mutilations and gravity rays."

"Gravity rays?"

"I missed that bit in this morning's newspaper account. She says now the government has to admit that we're In Contact. Capital letters right there in her voice, very firm: In Contact."

They both looked up at the sound of a siren, and in a moment the blue-and-white sheriff's car swooped over the arroyo rim and skidded to a stop on the gravel behind Shirley's car. The deputy got out, hand on his weapon.

"We're peaceful," said Shirley. "The body's out back."

Without acknowledging her presence or her comment, and without taking his eyes from her and J.Q., the deputy got on his radio and started muttering police jargon, words that had to do with securing crime scenes and awaiting backup. Shirley had another sip of coffee, sharing the cup with J.Q.

"Why?" J.Q. muttered. "She was harmless."

"She had an appointment with someone. One of her clients, Millie somebody, had referred this man to her. Her only appointment this morning, she said."

"Why did you come back?"

She gestured at the tortillas, now somewhat the worse for being repeatedly squeezed, still in their sealed plastic wrapper. "I offered to pick up anything she needed. She said pick her up a dozen tortillas."

"You got any frozen stuff in there?" He nodded toward the car.

"No, nothing frozen. Fruit. Veggies. I got us some chayote. There's meat in there, but if we're not kept too long, it'll be all right."

"So who is it dead?" asked the deputy, hand still on his gun.

"Her name was Bridget McCree," said Shirley.

"So, what're you doing here?" The question was a challenge.

Her eyebrows went up. "I stopped by this morning to thank her for sending us some guests, and she asked me to pick up some tortillas for her on my way back from

24

town. The door was unlocked; I started to go in to leave them inside, and I saw the mess."

"Mess?"

"Somebody's ransacked the place."

"Vandalized it?"

"I didn't say that. I said somebody ransacked it, looking for something, maybe."

"Like what?"

"I haven't any idea."

"She a good friend of yours?"

"No. She was a neighbor. Sometimes she mentioned our place to people who needed somewhere to stay."

"You rent rooms or something?"

"Yes," she said. The five houses rented to tourists at Rancho del Valle probably qualified as renting rooms or something. She heard another siren, far to the east, getting louder, then louder still as it made the turn from the paved road. Another Rio Grande sheriff's car pulled up behind J.Q.'s truck, this one with two men in it. The first man mumbled something to the other two, then he stayed where he was while the others went to the back. Voices were raised, someone cursed. Shirley took another swallow of coffee.

One of the second two came running back, went across the road to his car, and got on the radio. After a few moments his partner also returned, spoke briefly to the man first on the scene, then turned toward J.Q. and Shirley.

"Okay," he said heavily. "Tell me about it."

Shirley told him about it.

"What's he doing here?" The deputy nodded in J.Q.'s direction.

"I didn't like being here alone. We live just down the

25

road. I called him and asked him to come keep me company."

The deputy went to Shirley's car, opened it, checked through the brown paper sacks inside. "What's this?" he called, waving a small bag that had been stapled shut.

"Grass seed," said Shirley. "You can open it. Just don't spill it."

He did open it, then rolled it shut and put it back in the car.

J.Q. said, "You didn't give him permission to search your car."

She grinned without humor. "So he'll find a lot of inadmissible olive oil. And some nonrelevant lettuce."

The deputy opened the plastic olive-oil jug and smelled it. His partner returned from across the road. "Sheriff wants you to stay here," he said to Shirley.

She sighed.

The next arrival took more time. Shirley got up and wandered around, finally dragging two folding chairs from the garage into the shade of a tree beside the house. "More comfortable than the step," she told J.Q., dropping herself into one of them.

"But not much," he said grumpily, shifting from hip to hip.

The next arrivals were from the state, technical people, laden with cameras and bags of equipment, along with a bulgy, red-nosed man of about fifty who seemed to be in charge. He went back with the others and returned about fifteen minutes later, notebook open.

"What time did you get here?" he asked Shirley in a pompous tone.

"The first time, about ten. The second time, about two."

"Can you get any closer than that?" His sneer said he doubted it.

"You left the house at nine forty-five," said J.Q. "I looked at my watch."

She shrugged. "It's what? Three minutes? So I was here at nine forty-eight, more or less."

"Then what?"

"So I thanked her for the business she'd sent our way, then she asked me to pick her up some tortillas; then I went grocery shopping, and to the bank, and to the seed place. Oh, and to the post office."

"Can you prove that?"

"Well, the sales slips will be in the grocery sacks. I don't know if they have the time on them, but they should have the date. The sales slip for the grass seed is in my purse. I made a deposit at the bank; there's a stamped deposit slip in there, too."

She went with him to the car, where she dug into purse and sacks and furnished him with receipts and deposit slip after asking for and supervising the writing out of a receipt: documents dated and timed such and such, originating in the following establishments. This procedure seemed to surprise the sheriff.

"What about you?" he barked at J.Q. "What were you doing this morning?"

"I saw Shirley leave, then I did my laundry. Then I went over to the vet's and picked up a bottle of Ivomec-F and some disposable syringes, came back to the house, went down to the barn, and injected all the ewe sheep."

"What is that stuff? Ivar what?"

"Worm medicine. The acequias around here have liver fluke in them, and our sheep got exposed before

27

we knew about it. So, we have to deworm them. We'll have to do the goats, too, but I'd planned on doing that this afternoon."

"And then?"

"And then . . . let's see. I walked out to the road and picked up the mail, came back in the house, made myself a sandwich, ate it, read the mail, paid a few bills, and addressed some brochures to people who'd written asking for them."

"Nobody else was there?"

"Nope. Sorry. Just the livestock. Oh, and a few guests, but they were in their own houses."

"And then this woman called you?" *This woman* became an indictment in his mouth.

"That's right. She caught me just as I was heading out to do the goats, a few minutes after two. I poured some coffee in a thermos and came right over."

"Can you prove any of this?"

J.Q. thought about it. "Well, if you come on home with me, you'll see the envelopes with the paid bills in them, and the brochures, and the mail that arrived. And Shirley can tell you, she took all the outgoing mail there was this morning, so the new stuff was done while she was gone. And the vet can tell you I was there. That's about the best I can do."

"And you claim you didn't know this dead woman?"

"She was a neighbor. I knew her to say good morning to. We weren't friends."

The man shifted gears and went back to Shirley. "What was she wearing when you saw her?"

Shirley flushed. "A fringed buckskin dress and beaded moccasins, and her hair was braided, with feathers in it."

"I thought it might be somebody like that. That's the kind they seem to go for." He made a face.

"Kind who seems to go for?"

"The aliens. I've talked to six or eight of 'em. The ones who were abducted. They all seem to be a little ... strange, you know? I think the aliens are looking for a certain type."

"A certain type," Shirley repeated, astonished.

"What was that place out back supposed to be? A playhouse?"

"It was the place she did her ... ceremonies," said Shirley.

"Ceremonies?" His eyebrows went up.

"Ah. Yes. She was a ... psychic healer."

"Now see, that's just what I was saying. And there's the star painted on the floor. I'll bet she was In Contact. What did these ceremonies involve?"

"I haven't any idea. I never took part in one. She invited me once, but I never took her up on it."

"You?" he barked at J.Q.

J.Q. shook his head, mouth slightly quirked. "No. I've not been getting any psychic healing either. You'd have to ask one of her patients. Clients? Whatever they're called."

"Do you know any of them?"

"No," said Shirley. "Well, sort of. Some of her patients have stayed with us. We could look them up, I suppose, but if they stayed with us, they were probably from out of state. She told me she was expecting one this morning, but she didn't mention his name."

"Well, I'm gonna keep it in mind it may be aliens, but you don't need to say anything to the other guys."

Shirley swallowed deeply to keep from howling with

29

laughter. "They can find me down the road." She gave him the address. "Okay if we go on home?"

He nodded, as though unwillingly. J.Q. went back across the road and pulled the truck away, turning it in the driveway. One of the deputies moved the first police car so Shirley could get out. She got out, taking the tortillas with her, getting herself straightened out on the road just as two cars arrived bearing the logos of TV channels on the side doors and complicated antennae on the roofs. Another car pulled along the roadside to emit two men, one carrying a still camera.

The media had arrived. Shirley departed, posthaste. Now, how the hell had they gotten here so fast? She checked her watch. Almost four-thirty. There were no TV broadcasters in Santa Fe. The trucks had to have come from Albuquerque. It was two hours to Albuquerque. No way. No way at all. Unless they'd already been in the neighborhood.

Or unless they'd found out about it before Shirley did.

J.Q. was waiting in the driveway. He took a grocery sack in each arm and led the way toward the kitchen.

"Did you hear that?" she asked, in disbelief.

"Are you surprised?"

"Well, yes. A little," she said from behind him.

"You were saying just this morning—"

"I know what I was saying this morning, but I'm still surprised. How does the sheriff get away with that?"

"Shirley, you know as well as I do that a sheriff from a small rural county is a law unto himself. He's responsible only to the electorate and the county commissioners, and no sheriff gets elected unless he sees pretty much eye to eye with the county commissioners. If you go poll the commissioners, you'll probably find one businessman who thinks the government is lying to him about the UFO at Roswell and two ranchers who believe that cattle mutilations are done by ETs."

"Well, aliens or not. Whoever did it, I'm not getting involved."

"If you hadn't stopped there, you wouldn't have been involved." He pushed the gate open, let her go through, then let it swing shut behind them. "Now I think you are involved, willy-nilly."

"Somebody's nasty," she growled, surprising herself with the venom in her own voice. "Somebody was really beastly."

"You don't think it was aliens?" he asked blandly.

"J.Q.!"

"She was dead first, don't you think?" He set the sacks on the kitchen counter and began removing the contents.

"Of course she was. There'd have been more blood if she'd been alive. Some blood, that is."

"I've been trying to figure that."

"Nothing much to figure," she said, shuddering again. "It's just like the cattle. Kill her bloodlessly somehow, maybe by a knock on the head. Undress her and lay her down flat so the blood pools along the back. Maybe even leave her awhile, while you paint some symbols and fake a UFO landing site. Then take a sharp skinning knife, amputate whatever parts will confuse the issue, blot with paper towels if necessary, put the resultant towels in a sack along with the body parts. Thing I couldn't figure, the floor had a wet spot on it. Damp."

"Her clothes have to be somewhere."

"We didn't look in her closet."

"You think?" He looked doubtful.

"If they weren't bloodstained, that's where I'd have put them. Strip them off her and hang them in her closet. Same with her moccasins and the rest of her clothes, if she was wearing any." She rubbed her forehead fretfully. "Just nasty, J.Q."

"How was she killed?"

"Your guess is as good as mine. Not strangled, I'd have noticed that." Her eyes were wet, and she dabbed at them. "I think a whack on the head is the most likely. I feel awful about it!"

"Shirley, you didn't do it. For heaven's sake, you've encountered bodies before!"

"Oh, I sure have. Trouble is with this one, she was so . . . brutalized. Even if she was dead first. Somebody . . . somebody wasn't content just to kill her. They had to do all this other stuff. It's rotten. And I was there! Just this morning. I keep thinking maybe I should have done something, said something. . . ."

"Like what?"

"I don't know. Like it was dangerous to take male clients when she was all alone that way. Like maybe it wasn't really smart to advertise herself the way she did. She was young, J.Q. Young enough to attract the kooks."

"If you'd said something, you think she'd have paid any attention?"

"No."

"Then forget it."

They put the groceries away in silence. One of the guests came to the door to ask what was going on.

"I saw the ambulance go by," the guest said. "And the police cars. They end up over there, somewhere, but the trees block the view."

"I'm sure the police will take care of it," Shirley said

in a neutral voice. "I heard there'd been an accident. I'm afraid we don't know the people who live over there. Not well, at least."

"I guess the police don't know that," said the guest, with an avid expression. "Here comes a police car in here."

"Deputy," said Shirley, inviting the law in and pointedly shutting the door. The guest had shown no signs of leaving, but at least eavesdropping could be made as difficult as possible.

"Ms. McClintock," the deputy began. "Mr. Quentin. My name's Eddy Martinez. I need to find out anything I can about that woman over there. Nobody seems to know much about her. Would you know how long she's lived there, where she came from, anything?"

"She moved here a little over a year ago," said J.Q. "She'd been renting a house in Madrid, south of Santa Fe. Then she won some money at one of the Indian casinos and bought the place down the road. So she said."

"How did you know that?" Shirley asked, amazed.

"She came over here one day when you were gone. She said she'd heard our roosters crowing, and she wanted to borrow some chickens to eat her grasshoppers. I explained how you can't just borrow chickens. She thought they were like geese, or sheep, you could sort of herd them. I explained that chickens have this habit of flying off in all directions and getting eaten by coyotes. She got to talking about herself. That's how I know."

"Would you say she was a city person?" the deputy asked.

"I got that impression," Shirley agreed. "But if she was living in a town as small as Madrid, you ought to be able to find her neighbors, or whoever rented her the

33

place where she was living. Can't be more than a few hundred people there."

"She was into a rather different lifestyle over there, too," J.Q. confirmed. "She said the people weren't all sympathetic to her."

The deputy made some notes. "Now, can you tell me exactly what she said about this appointment she had?"

Shirley tried to remember. "She said a former client of hers named Millie somebody had referred the client she was seeing today. She said she couldn't remember who Millie was, she'd have to look it up in her journal. Or maybe it had been Billie somebody. She referred to the client as *he* and *him*, so the client was a man. She said he'd sounded troubled but nice when she talked to him on the phone. She was out on the porch the minute I drove in, so she must have been expecting him right then."

"We can't find a journal. You're sure she said journal."

"That's what she said. She might have meant a diary."

"No diary. No personal papers. No letters."

Shirley shook her head. "The place had been ripped apart. They, or he, had to be looking for something."

"Seems risky to me, hanging around to make a search."

"Not really," Shirley mused. "I've been thinking about that. You can't see down into the arroyo until you get right to the edge of it. On the other side, the road goes up onto a little rise and stops right there in the bosque, near the river. Since the road doesn't go anywhere, nobody much goes by there unless they're going to see her. This guy had made an appointment, so she wouldn't have told anyone else to come by at that time. The house across the way has that wall around it, and it doesn't

34

even have a gate facing Bridget's way. Also, she was odd enough to keep the locals at a distance. Most of the people around here are old originals. They've had enough experience with real Indians that they don't give the soul-sister wannabes a lot of attention."

"What did you think about that?" he asked.

"I thought it was sad," she replied. "A person who wants to be somebody else is always sad, don't you think?"

J.Q. added, "And when they don't even know enough about the thing they want to be to put on a good show, that's even sadder."

"She had some crystals in her hands, on her eyes. What do you think that was about?"

"She had crystals in the house. There were a bunch of them in a nicho by the back door. I saw them this afternoon. There was a jar of paint there, too, and a brush with paint dried on it. I figure that's what the murderer used to paint the symbols on her and on the wall."

"What are those symbols of, ma'am?"

"They looked like crop-circle diagrams to me. Isn't it part of the whole thing? Pyramids and crystals and channeling and the whole bit?" Shirley sighed. "I've read that one kind of Navajo diagnostician uses crystals. She may have been copying that."

"She wasn't into contacting extraterrestrials?"

Shirley started to say no, but was interrupted by J.Q.

"In a manner of speaking, she was. One of her clients told us that Bridget called up healing rays from outer space."

"Not exactly *outer*," objected Shirley. "From Jupiter, or one of its moons, maybe."

The deputy said, "Damn, that'll set them off." He

frowned, tapped his pencil a few times, then grimaced and wrote it down. "She didn't make jewelry or anything? The crystals wouldn't have been part of some hobby?"

"Not that I know of."

"I hate these kinds of cases," he said.

"What kind?" Shirley asked.

"Oh, these kind where it has something to do with religion or miracles or ETs or something. You never know where you are." He fished out a card, handed it to Shirley. "If either of you think of anything, please call me. Eddy Martinez."

Shirley stared at the card. "Is Cisso Pacheco still with your office?"

"I know Cisso, but he's Santa Fe County. How do you know Cisso?"

"We had a woman die about a year ago. He was one of the men who investigated it."

"Die, huh. Natural death?"

Shirley's mind did an agile sidestep, avoiding that precipice. "Just a rather mysterious death. Anyhow, thanks. We'll let you know if we come up with anything."

2

At three thirty-five, Allison lingered by the door of the high school as students poured around her, out and away, some on foot, some in cars, some in the buses lined up along the road. It was almost four road miles to Rancho del Valle, but it was less than two miles walking, and today Allison wanted to walk it, even though she was so sleepy it was hard to focus. Why couldn't she just whistle like the Lone Ranger and have her horse suddenly show up out of nowhere.

Which made her think of Beauregard with a cringe of guilty conscience. She hadn't even looked at him for days. She'd fed him and watered him and turned him out in the pasture, but she hadn't even seen him. Poor Beau. She was his only friend, and here she was, treating him this way. Rotten.

She raised her head, eyes suddenly brimming with tears, to see Tad getting onto the bus, turning at the top step, looking back at her, frowning the way he did sometimes when he wasn't pleased. Tad wanted her to make up her mind.

Allison pretended to be looking through her back-pack, capping off the fiction with a gesture of annoyance and a turn back through the doors into the almost vacant hall. She needed to think, and if she needed to think, the last thing she wanted was Tad Pole in the next seat, explaining things. He blew away her worries like they were nothing! "What's the real reason why not?" That was a favorite Tad question. "What's the real reason why not?" Why not smoke a little grass? Why not play around a little? Why not use your time to have fun while you're young enough to enjoy it, instead of spending it all on the books? You know you want to join the Bunch, so why not go to bed with me, Allison? What's the real reason why not?

Because Shirley and J.Q. would hate it. But she couldn't say that. The minute she said that, they'd all be on her trail. She could just hear Dawn French. "Allison's mommy and daddy won't let her. Allison is still a widdle kid. She listens to her mommy and her daddy."

"What it's called," said a voice from behind her, "is peer pressure."

She looked up, blinking. Mr. Patterson, Jeremy.

"What?" she blurted, still lost in her own private world.

"Whatever's going on between you and the in kids."

"In kids?"

"Whatever they call themselves. All groups like that are *in* kids by virtue of making everyone else *out* kids. That's how it works."

"They call themselves the Bunch."

"Innocuous sounding."

"They said I could belong."

"If?"

She shrugged, feeling her face go up in flames. "Just stuff, Mr. Patterson."

"Tad Pole's a member of the Bunch, is he?"

She shrugged again. "I'm not sure. Dawn is. And Breeze, and Summer."

"Dah-wun," he drawled. "And Bre-heeze. And Suhm-mer."

She giggled.

"Ever wondered what possesses people to name their kids Dawn, or Breeze, or Summer? Vaguely ecological, a little pretentious. Maybe it's Southwest chic. Like hanging chili peppers by your front door. I honest to God would find it difficult to worry much about anyone named Dawn or Breeze or Summer."

She smiled, with difficulty, and he nodded.

"I sought you out, Allison, to remind you about the pig."

She gasped, relieved. "Oh, right. The pig. I'll ask Shirley tonight."

"Hang in there, kid." He squeezed her shoulder and departed, out the door, toward the parking lot where his battered old Jeep anchored a far shady corner. The bus had gone, and Tad Pole with it. She buckled the straps on her backpack and went out again, this time heading across the parking lot toward two huge cottonwoods that overhung the arroyo. Between them was the start of a path that wound down Arroyo Largo for over a mile before intersecting with the Rancho del Valle road. A few other kids walked this way, but none of them were

39

in sight. The arroyo bottom was level and this time of the year it was dry, so it required no attention to follow, just put one foot in front of the other while figuring out whatever it was she was going to figure out.

Shirley always said specify the situation, then list the pros and the cons. Actually Shirley said to write the whole thing down, but maybe she'd do that when she got home. So. Situation. The Bunch, which meant Dawn French—whose family had money coming out of their ears—plus several other very popular girls and maybe boys, had told her she could join their group if she'd give up being so straight. The way she was, everybody in the Bunch would be worried she'd rat on them. And when she'd said, what did they mean straight? they'd said, you know, Allison. You're such a grind, Allison. You could enjoy a little grass or a little sex, you know. The Bunch doesn't have any virgins. If you want to be a member, you'll have to enjoy something partyish, otherwise nobody can relax when you're around.

Allison had told them she didn't have a boyfriend, thinking that would end the virginity hassle, but all it had done was get Tad sicced on her. Be glad to help, he said while she blushed red as a flowerpot.

The pros and cons. If she slept with Tad, she could join the Bunch and be in with these really popular girls, the ones who dated the really popular boys. If she slept with Tad, she risked what everyone risks having sex, what Shirley's factual lectures had covered more than once: pregnancy, disease, maybe AIDS, probably his spreading her name around. Both Shirley and J.Q. said boys did that. Counting coup in the locker room. If she slept with Tad, maybe he'd become . . . someone important to her. She wanted to have someone important, someone her own age, and all the people she'd thought about that way were back in Colorado. But then, it might just make her lonelier, because he could drop her. People said he'd dropped Lynn Redmond last year, and Lynn hadn't even come back to school. So, maybe he'd gotten her pregnant? Or given her a disease? Or, maybe, her family had just moved. Who knew?

The worst of it was, when she thought about sleeping with him, sometimes she thought she might want to. He was cute. He was . . . different. He had this way of raising his eyebrow, just one, so he looked sort of superior but interested. And he was smart and had a nice voice. And when he touched her, she . . . well, that was sex. Shirley said you just felt it, you couldn't do anything about feeling it, all you could do was learn to control it. So she had been controlling it. But now controlling it might not be as important as . . . just being like other people. Being like Dawn.

Shit. Did she care?

Dawn French could look at you like you were made out of horsehocky, but she could be interesting, too. She'd been a lot of places, done a lot of things. She'd said the Bunch was going to Aspen, skiing this year, and maybe Allison could come along. Allison had never been to Aspen, but she had taken skiing lessons, enough to get by. If she tried to make up her mind the way Shirley said, she could add skiing or subtract Tad, but it wasn't something she could figure out in her head, because all these feelings were mixed up in it.

She kicked a crumpled beer can that went flying into a clump of yellow chamisa, scattering a flight of equally yellow birds, like an explosion of sunlight. Her

41

mouth dropped open and she just stood for a moment, watching the sun sparkling on an almost invisible trickle of water in the arroyo bottom.

"Pretty, isn't it?" someone asked.

She turned, surprised, to see a boy from school standing above her on the arroyo rim. Ulti Consalves. He was a junior, and he was on the track team. Wordlessly, she nodded. He turned sideways and slid down the steep bank, landing on his feet in a cloud of dust, a wiry form in blue jeans and faded blue shirt with a new, brightly red bandanna knotted around his head. He wasn't much taller than Allison, and his long dark hair was tied in a tassel at the back of his neck. "They're headed south," he said. "The goldfinches. Sometimes they hang around for a day or two. If there's tamarisk blooming late, they stop to eat the blooms. Mostly they eat seeds, though."

"They looked like canaries," she said stupidly.

"Same family," he said. "Finches. They have a pretty song. Did you see the bluebirds when they came through in the spring? Mountain bluebirds, April and May, they come through the valley in flocks."

"Are you a birder?" she asked, continuing her walk as he fell in beside her. Xanthippe Minging was a birder, with a life list and everything. So far, Allison had managed to escape being indoctrinated in any major way, though her attention had been forcibly drawn to owls, woodpeckers, and kingfishers, as well as several kinds of hawks.

Ulti fell in beside her. "Sort of. The ones that come through here, I know pretty well. I guess I'm a snaker, too. My favorite is the coachwhip. They're red, did you know that?"

"A red snake?"

"Well, a real bright pink. Honest to God. And fast, you never saw anything move like that. Pink lightning. I know most of the animals around here, and a lot of the bugs."

"Bugs!" She shuddered dramatically.

"Butterflies are bugs," he said cheerfully. "And moths, and beetles and bees and ants. Crickets. Had one of those in my bedroom last night, all night, creaking his head off. I couldn't find him. He sounded like he was inside a drum or something, echoed like crazy."

"We have cats," Allison offered. "They catch the crickets."

They walked for a time in silence, quite comfortably, sometimes exchanging a word or two when Ulti pointed out a particular bird or bug or plant: snakeweed making bright yellow cushions along the arroyo rim, feathery blue asters and puffs of smaller, white ones, bright yellow daisies. "I really want to be a naturalist," he said. "Protect stuff like this. When I was a little kid, there was a lot more natural land around here; now it's getting eaten up."

"Shirley says there are too many people."

"She's right." He made a face. "I say that to my brothers, they tell me I'm crazy."

Half a mile on, they came to a split in the arroyo, one leg continuing the general northwesterly direction, the other turning toward the southwest, the two separated by a steeply prowed bank pocked with deep holes.

"Bet you don't know what that is," he challenged, pointing out a particular burrow.

"Kingfisher," she hazarded. "Don't they dig into the banks?" So Mingy had said.

43

He laughed. "One for you. That particular hole had three little ones in it this spring. I poked a flashlight in and looked." He lifted a hand and pointed down the northwest leg. "You live that way, don't you?"

"Rancho del Valle," she said. "It's a kind of guest farm. My guardians run it."

"I know where it is. I live on a real farm." He laughed. "A funny farm that grows apples and chilies. My grandpa and grandma, one uncle, one aunt, my mom and dad, and three sisters still at home. I have nine brothers and sisters. I'm the youngest. That's why mom named me Ultimo."

"Nine!"

"Ten, with me. Mom was a good Catholic. Until me. Then she decided enough was enough. She had her tubes tied. Now whenever she gets mad at one of us, she says she should have done it sooner." He laughed, unselfconsciously. "You don't have any brothers or sisters, right?"

"How'd you know?"

"Nobody else in school with your name. Unless you had one a lot older or a lot younger."

"No. I'm an only. My parents are dead."

"That's tough," he said sympathetically. "Are your guardians good people?"

"Very good people," she said emphatically.

"Well, hang on to that." He lifted a hand in casual farewell and strode off down the southwest way.

Allison stared after him, rather confusedly. She couldn't remember any other boy saying casually that his mother had had her tubes tied. Or anything like it! And why should he tell her to hang on to anybody?

44

He stopped at a turn in the path and called back to her: "Do you walk this way often?"

"I usually take the bus."

"If you walk in the morning ever, I'm usually here by eight." He waved again, went around a protruding bank corner, and was gone.

Well. That had been interesting. She hadn't thought about Tad or Dawn or any of them for a whole fifteen minutes.

Another half mile down the arroyo, then up onto the road for about a mile. She'd dawdled, but she'd still made it in less than an hour. She turned in at the mailboxes and was halfway down the drive when she heard a car coming out. A sheriff's car. He went by without a sideways glance.

When she went into the kitchen, Shirley looked up at her. "Was the bus late?"

"I walked," Allison replied, plunking down her backpack. "I met a boy."

"Walking?"

"He was on his way home, too. Ulti Consalves. Do you know him? I don't mean him, I mean do you know the family?"

Shirley frowned. "It doesn't ring a bell, Allison. Where does he live?"

"South of us somewhere. Down the other branch of Arroyo Largo. It's the one that runs all the way from in front of the school down across our road to the river? I was walking along there, and he cut off the branch that goes south of us."

"There's about a million square miles south of us." Shirley frowned, aware of the strain in her voice.

Allison looked at her sharply. "What's wrong?"

45

Shirley grimaced, feeling her lips stretch and curl painfully. "Damn."

"Shirley! The sheriff's car was here! What happened?"

"I'm going to tell you. I'm just reaching for words. One of our neighbors has been murdered, I guess that's all I can say. I found her body this afternoon. . . ."

"Well, you usually do," Allison said in a remote voice, as though totally unimpressed. "Don't you? You're always saying you find more than your share."

Shirley stepped back, appalled. "Allison! You sound like I'd commented on the weather!"

Allison took a deep breath. "I . . . I'm sorry. I shouldn't have sounded like that. I'm . . . I'm shocked, I guess. I really am, if I think about it. Really, Shirley, I didn't mean to sound like it was nothing, but just for a minute it was sort of soap opera, TV, not real. Who? Who got killed?"

"You were talking about Arroyo Largo. You know where it bottoms out, down at the river?"

"Where we go riding sometimes?"

"Right. The woman who lives up the arroyo from there."

"The one who goes around in leather clothes. The one with the Indian name."

"It's not an Indian name. It's a wannabe name. Like Moonlight, or Little Owl. She called herself Shadow Dancer, but her real name was Bridget McCree." She got up and ran water into a glass. "Somebody, whoever killed her, isn't satisfied to just be a murderer, he also has to be a smart-ass." She drank the water, poured out what was left, slammed down the glass, and went outside to fetch something from the car.

"She's in a temper," said J.Q., coming in from the pantry with a package of frozen steaks in his hands, closely followed by Tabasco, the kitchen goat, tap-tapping along, making butting motions at J.Q.'s legs.

"Why?" Allison asked, putting her book bag where Tabasco couldn't get at it. "She sounds really angry."

"Whoever killed the woman tried to make it look like something . . . supernatural or extraterrestrial. Like the so-called cattle mutilations."

"They cut on her?"

"They cut on her, yes."

Allison shuddered. "That's nasty."

"It was nasty. Here, unwrap this package, and I'll do the other two." When the steaks were unwrapped, he put them in the microwave and punched buttons, stepping over Dog in the process.

Dog looked up, puzzled.

"That's a good dog," murmured Allison. "J.Q. didn't mean to ignore you."

Dog thumped her tail half a dozen times, which attracted Tabasco's attention. He came over and butted Dog several times while Dog at first pretended not to notice and then, finally, growled a warning. Tabasco danced off sideways, curvetting, caroming off Allison's legs. He was brown all over except for a black shawl and black markings on his face.

"Isn't he big enough to go down to the pasture yet?" Allison asked.

"Who? Tabasco?"

"Who else?"

"He was there most of today. I just fetched him a few minutes ago to give him his bottle."

"He ate my homework last night. I had to copy it all over. And he poops all over everything."

J.Q. went to the refrigerator and took out a bottle of lamb formula for Tabasco. Shirley brought in a bulging paper sack, set it beside two others on the counter, and started putting away the groceries, still muttering to herself.

"Relax," said J.Q., unwisely, removing the steaks from the microwave and replacing them with Tabasco's bottle.

"Dammit, J.Q. I won't relax. That poor woman. Nutty as a fruitcake, no doubt, but harmless. That is, I suppose she was harmless. Even if not, you know what's going to happen. Firstly, the good people of Rio Grande County will, by and large, suppose exactly what the murderer wanted them to suppose, exactly what that stupid man believed, that she was killed by little green men who arrived in a UFO. If, and it's a big if, the law manages to find out who killed her, which I doubt, no jury will convict him—"

"Or her."

"Or her, I suppose, though mostly it's men who cut people up like that. No jury will convict, because the defense attorney will spin them a tale. You can't convict a murderer here in Rio Grande County, or anywhere in the surrounding area. Anybody can get away with anything. If the killer isn't related to half the county, then his verdict is in the hands of some of the most credulous people in the nation. Half the people who move here to Santa Fe do it because it's a comfortable environment for people who know nothing but will believe anything."

"Come on, Shirley. With Los Alamos right up the

hill, you've got more PhDs to the square mile than most places." The microwave beeped. He removed the bottle and knelt on the floor, to be assaulted by Tabasco.

"None of whom serve on juries. They're too important to serve on juries. Who serves on juries are bored housewives who were weaned on Geraldo or Sally or whoever that other one is. Who serves on juries are the nutcases who believe they're in touch with departed spirits. Spin them a tale, they'll believe it, the more illogical the better. See the poor defendant, he couldn't have beaten or raped or murdered that woman. No, he just broke her window by accident, then while they were having consensual intercourse in her own bedroom in the middle of the night, she attacked him and he had to kill her in self-defense. This other guy? He couldn't have shot that policeman, the policeman took out his gun and dropped it, shooting himself. And the drunk driver? He didn't commit vehicular homicide, he just drank all that liquor to get rid of his headaches, it wasn't his fault. And if all else fails, it wasn't the guy's fault, it was little green men."

She paused for breath.

"Are you finished?" asked J.Q., looking up from feeding the baby goat, who was now merely standing, eyes closed, mouth holding the nipple, a blissful expression on his narrow little face.

"Yes," she snapped. "Totally."

"Allison," said J.Q. "You finish putting those groceries away while I pour Shirley a small scotch. I think she's been overstressed today." He took the bottle away from the goat and put it in the sink. Tabasco went under the desk and lay down on his mat, slowly, having some difficulty remembering how his legs folded. Front legs first, down on his knees, then back legs down, then neck stretched out with one, last, almost inaudible baa.

"Sorry," Shirley muttered. "I am sorry, people. Really. I have no business carrying on like this. It was just so very . . . unpleasant."

"It was calculated," offered J.Q.

"That's it. It was so very calculated." She sat, accepted the glass J.Q. handed her, and took a sizable swallow. "Allison says she's met someone, J.Q. What was his name, Allison?"

"Consalves," Allison said. "He lives somewhere down the other fork of the arroyo. I was walking in it, you know. And it leads right down past that woman's house. Maybe right then, while I was walking there, someone was—"

"While you were walking home, the only someones were police," Shirley said. "It was done this morning, I'd judge. Around ten o'clock or so. Very shortly after I left her. How come you were walking, anyhow?"

"I needed to . . . I needed the exercise. And speaking of that, I've been neglecting Beauregard, so I've got to go tell him he's beautiful." She put away the last of the milk, folded the sacks, put them in the cupboard, and made for the door, stopping to remark, "I almost forgot again. Mr. Patterson wonders if you'd take a pig for him."

"A what?" J.Q. asked, pulling his head out of the refrigerator.

"Mr. Patterson works with the animal rescue people, as a volunteer. And they've got this pig. He was supposed to be a pet pig, and this lady had him in her house, and she went away for the weekend, and when she came back the whole house was torn up."

"A woman left a pig alone in her house?" Shirley looked up, totally detoured from contemplation of murder. "Any woman who does that deserves to come home to a pigpen."

Allison sighed with dramatic patience. "Some people have goats in their kitchens, some people have pigs in their houses. Anyhow, she got mad and gave the pig to the shelter, and they passed it on to these other people, but the new people had a little boy, and the little boy was eating candy and wouldn't give the pig any, so the pig bit him."

"As would any pig," said J.Q. "Is this one of those potbellied pigs?"

"Right. It's a black one, with white feet. So now it's at the shelter being tested for rabies, which it doesn't have, and when it gets out of quarantine, it needs a home."

"We just got rid of pigs," said Shirley.

"They were big pigs, this is a little one."

"How little?"

"Jeremy says—"

"Mr. Patterson says . . ."

Allison flushed. "Right. Mr. Patterson says he'll weigh sixty or eighty pounds. His name is Hamlet. And he's already fixed. Neutered. You know."

"Idiocy," said Shirley. "We are mired in idiocy."

"I thought it would be fun to have a little pig. He could live in the pen the other pigs lived in, only he wouldn't frighten the guests."

The former pigs, two, the total one half ton of them, had followed one hysterical guest all the way across the pasture, through the gate (which the guest was too terrorized to close), and back to her guest house, expecting

51

a handout. After sorting out insulted pigs and hysterical guest, Shirley had sold the pigs, albeit reluctantly.

"We have plenty of kitchen garbage," offered J.Q.

"Whatever," Shirley said. "I'll think about it."

Allison returned from the door, hugged Shirley, murmured a quick thank-you, and was gone.

"Interesting," said J.Q. "This's the first time in recent memory she's had anything on her mind but whatever it is she has had on her mind."

"Not a gem of clarity, J.Q."

"You know what I mean."

"I know what's been on her mind. It's a boy."

"Why are you so sure?"

"Homeopathy. What cures you is a little bit of what ails you. She met a boy and she asked questions about him, did we know the family? Did we know where he lived? Now, speaking as a woman who was once, long ago, a girl, I can attest to the fact that only a boy is an antidote for a boy. And vice versa."

"That was hardly a gem of clarity either, Shirley."

"If you treat the disease with a boy and it works, then the disease was probably another boy."

"Not was, is," he replied soberly. "I don't think one chance meeting in an arroyo will cure whatever's been bothering Allison. I think I'm going to make a few inquiries about Theodore Pole."

"It's not Theodore, it's Taddeus."

"Whatever."

Taddeus Pole, the young man in question, was leaning on an open gate outside the brick-paved portal of a long, adobe building that served the Dexter French establishment as a stable. Just emerging from one of the stalls was Dawn French's new gelding, His Honor, led by the lean, impassive young groom who had recently been hired to help James Bight, the older man who'd been, so Dawn said, with the family for years. Moving across the paddock toward horse and man was Dawn herself, her light brown hair floating abundantly about her shoulders, her heavily lashed bright hazel eyes glistening, and her pink lips curled in a mocking kiss. The tall gelding, polished to a high gloss and nervous as a Siamese cat, danced at the end of the reins, eager to be off, somewhere, anywhere.

Dawn took the reins from the groom, letting her hand linger on his, speaking to him softly, words Tad couldn't hear but could imagine. Dawn liked doing that. Turning people on. Especially people she wouldn't think of going out with. One of these days she was going to get herself into trouble, if she hadn't already. The groom said something short, she replied with a smile, he said something else, then turned on his heel and headed back into the stable while Dawn stood there looking after him. If Tad had had to identify Dawn's expression, he'd have said it was halfway between amused and angry.

Tad strolled over to her, trying to look casual about it.

"What are you doing here?" Dawn asked, tightening the cinch with a muscular and well-practiced jerk. "I thought today was the day for pinning Allison down. You must be losing it, Taddeus. You aren't irresistible anymore."

"Allison missed the bus, Dawn. She forgot a book or something. I saw her hunting for it. If I'd had the car today, I could have waited for her. Don't worry. I've got her so stirred up she can't keep her head straight."

Dawn stroked the glossy column of neck, not looking at him. "You thought you'd get her in bed right off the bat, Tadsy. Here it is almost two weeks later, and you haven't made it yet. One week more. Or you lose your chance with me." She turned toward him, smiled flirtatiously, licked her lower lip, and pouted at him.

Tad swallowed deeply and chose to change the subject. "Why've you got it in for her, anyhow?"

Dawn thought about this for a moment, one nostril slightly raised. "I may have to go to this stupid school. I may have to associate with the people at this stupid school. But I don't have to take her kind of attitude." She mounted the horse in one fluid motion and looked down at him, flicking her whip suggestively. "I don't like her."

"Because she's as good-looking as you are?" He heard his words and cringed. Wrong thing to say! "Almost . . ."

Dawn frowned. "Because she's a female nerd, Tadsy. Because she sucks up to people like . . ." She laughed, a little tinkling laugh. "Like Jeremy Patterson, who she definitely ought not to be sucking up to." She laughed again, tossing her head. "And because she doesn't know what or who's important and who isn't. I'm important, Taddeus. Very, very important. My mother is very important, and she tells me so. So does my grandfather, and he's even more important than my mother. We're part of the Pelton family, of the Dallas–Fort Worth Peltons. We have lots and lots of money. Allison, on the other hand, is not important. She's an orphan, she's a nothing, but she gets all A's, which she has no business doing because it's show-offy. It's time something disturbs her concentration, that's all."

She dug her heels into His Honor's flanks; horse and rider sprang away through the open gate, leaving Tad hanging like an old towel, or so he told himself. He'd first seen Dawn French a year ago last September when she'd entered the local school. "*Pub*lic school." That's how Dawn said it, with a sneer. "*Pub*lic school." Her mother had her in *pub*lic school because she'd been kicked out of several private schools since she was thirteen. Over a year now, and he'd been madly in love with her all that time.

The closest he'd ever come to getting her attention, however, was two weeks ago when she invited him to go riding with her, put him up on an old mare so fat she could hardly waddle, and then told him he could make love to her if he did Allison first. She said she'd told Allison some story about a girls' club that Allison couldn't join if she was a virgin, and Dawn felt Allison would want to join very badly. So Tad was supposed to take care of the virginity matter. Then when Allison said she'd lost it, Dawn was going to say the club was only open to virgins, she'd just been testing Allison's principles, which Summer and Breeze would back up. It was a lie all the way around, because there wasn't any club, and if there had been a virgins' club, Dawn wouldn't be in it because everyone knew she was getting it on with some guy from UNM.

It was a dirty trick on Allison, but Tad rather enjoyed dirty tricks. He wouldn't mind doing it even though Allison wasn't the kind of girl who appealed to him. She was too serious and too smart, but she was great looking and she had a body that didn't quit.

"Good afternoon," said someone from behind him.

Tad turned, meeting the quizzical gaze of Dawn's

55

stepfather: middling tall, darkly tanned, wearing slacks and a V-neck cashmere sweater, his bare feet thrust into espadrilles. According to Dawn, he dabbled at writing. Dabbled was Dawn's word. He didn't have to make a living at it, said Dawn, because Dawn's mother supported him. Dawn's mother, said Dawn, was New Money. The Frenches, on the other hand, were very Old Money. And Dexter French, said Dawn, had been a Good Catch.

Well-drilled politeness took over. "Good afternoon, Mr. French. Taddeus Pole, sir."

French smiled with blindingly white teeth. "Did I just see Dawn making off at a great rate?"

"Yes, sir."

"Not a polite way to treat a guest." One eyebrow up, charming expression.

Tad was, momentarily, charmed. "Oh, I'm not a guest, sir. I just stopped by to . . . to ask Dawn a question about some schoolwork."

"A case of the blind leading the blind, is that it?"

Tad flushed. Dawn got C's, nothing more and nothing less. Those in Dawn's clique did no better, or else. Tad himself did a little better, but boys could be excused. Males would have to get into college so they could have a career so they could support someone like Dawn. Unless Dawn chose to support someone on Granddad's money.

Dawn's father leaned on the paddock next to Tad, frowning slightly. "Taddeus Pole. Pole. I think I've heard Dawn mention you."

Tad wasn't sure how to reply to this, but French saved his having to do so.

"Your parents are . . . ?"

"My dad is Jonathan Pole. He's an attorney."

"With what firm?"

"Marquart, Henson and Pole, sir."

"Ah." Long pause, pursed lips. "And your mother?"

"She's an engineer. She works with a wetlands company. Ah, wastewater disposal?"

"A female engineer?" French smiled, making Tad wish he hadn't mentioned it. "It takes all kinds, doesn't it?" He stretched luxuriously, the wind ruffling his graying hair, then fixed Tad with a slightly amused stare and asked, "Do you, by any chance, know the name of the young man Dawn is currently bedding down with?"

Tad gulped, his mind whirling. "I'm afraid I know very little about Dawn's . . . personal life, sir. All I can say is, it isn't me."

"No. I'm sure it wouldn't be you." He smiled again, a mocking smile. "But it's no one at school, no one that you know of?"

"At my school? No sir. I've been . . . told she's interested in someone at UNM, but I haven't any idea who."

"Her mother and I would prefer that she stay out of trouble. Just between us men, you don't need to tell her I asked."

"Of course not, sir."

"If you do find out, at any point, we'd be most interested and most . . . grateful."

French turned and walked up the hill toward the house, and Tad was surprised to find himself sweating. Why did he feel like he'd been running from somebody? Dawn was underage, but hell, they were all underage. Why did French think it couldn't be Tad? What had that meant? And what had that crack about female engineers meant? Had he been insulted, or had his mother been insulted, or both of them? Or, had Mr. French just been teasing?

Whichever, Tad decided he didn't want to stick around until Dawn got back. Also, he didn't want to be in the shoes of the guy, whoever he was, from UNM.

Friday supper was a tradition at Rancho del Valle, at Shirley's insistence. She had had traditions in Colorado, customs to mark certain times and seasons, some of them dating from her parents' time. Except for matters relating to the sheep and goats and poultry, breeding and birthing, laying and hatching, this place had no real markers. Winters moved seamlessly into spring, into summer, into fall, most days mild, most nights starlit, with only the occasional blizzard or thunderstorm to mark the season. This was the first place Shirley had ever lived where the word *thunder-snow* was in use. So, to mark the passage of time, Shirley had instituted Friday-night supper as an obligatory event, during which time she and Allison and J.Q., and Xanthippe, if she was there, looked through the Friday Pasatiempo supplement to the daily paper, an overview of the week's offerings in the arts, and decided on at least one family outing for the following week: picnic, hike, art gallery, movie, concert, something to keep them, so Shirley said, from ossifying completely.

"Though I can't ossify completely," Shirley had commented, rubbing her new knee. "Being partly stainless steel. Still, we need stimulation."

"Oh, by all means," J.Q. had replied. "We must keep in touch with the creative world."

Friday supper was also supposed to be a low-labor meal. Beans and corn bread. Pizza. Chinese takeout, if anyone went to Santa Fe. Tonight, feeling totally unimaginative, Shirley had acquiesced to J.Q.'s suggestion that they have charcoal-broiled steaks and a green salad. Around five-fifteen, however, a misty fog began to gather, not quite rain but definitely more than mere dampness, so she gave up on the charcoal broil. "If this is the rain they forecast, it doesn't amount to much," she grouched at J.Q., as though he had forgotten to schedule the weather.

"The paper said rain. The woman with the stick and the map said rain. Maybe it will loosen up and start falling." He put on his jacket and hat, took a feed bucket from a cupboard, and went out, muttering to himself.

Shirley glanced outside the window. This would only moisten the surface. It would aggravate the fauna without doing the flora any good. She turned her attention back to the food and began cutting the meat off the steaks in narrow strips. When she'd finished that, she sliced onions and mushrooms into a frying pan.

"Goody," said Allison, returning from her trip to the stables. "Shostakovich. Want me to cook the noodles?"

Shirley nodded, and Allison filled a pot with water. "Why do you call it that?" she asked.

Shirley looked up, her expression softening. "When my son was little, he could never remember the word Stroganoff, but he was very fond of music, and the name Shostakovich stuck with him. He began calling it that. It sort of stuck."

"You've never really told me about him, Shirley."

Shirley leaned against the stove, pushing the onions and mushrooms about as they sizzled moistly, sorting out what to tell. "Marty was a nice kid, a smart kid. Not really good-looking, but he had a clever, attractive face

59

and lots of friends. He got his energy from me, but he got his nice way with people from Martin. Martin, my husband, was Jewish, so Marty was raised Jewish. . . ."

"I thought Jewish people didn't name their kids after living relatives," said Allison. "One of the boys at school says . . ."

"True," Shirley admitted. "Martin said I couldn't name him Martin, so I named him after my brother, Engmar Titus, and just called him Marty. Martin called him Titus." She blinked rapidly, refusing to cry.

"Anyhow, Martin always took him to temple; I never really converted, but I went with them most of the time. Marty had a bar mitzvah, all the usual rituals. He went to college, majored in anthropology, graduated, got picked as part of a team to do some university-sponsored research in Brazil. He was so excited, all lit up, full of wonder at himself and the world. They left from New York, flew to Florida, took a ship from there, then some kind of riverboat up the Amazon. The boat's engines broke down; some part needed replacing. They were tied up at the shore, waiting for the part to arrive, some of the younger people went exploring, four of them, I think. Two of them came back, two didn't. Marty was one of the ones who didn't."

"You don't know that he's dead."

Everything stopped. Shirley leaned her forehead against the stove hood and stared into the frying pan without seeing it. Oh, the number of times she'd thought that. The number of times she'd told Martin that. We don't know he's dead, Martin. He could be lost. He's a smart kid, he can survive. Saying it to him, then saying it to herself, until too much time had gone by, too much water down the river, too many years. "I'd have known by now, Allison."

"I guess." She came over and gave Shirley a hug. "I'm sorry."

"Yeah, honey, I'm sorry, too."

"How long ago was it?"

Shirley laid down the spatula and ran her fingers through her short, mostly gray hair. "Well, let's see. I'm fifty-nine, almost sixty. I married Martin when I was twenty-five and he was forty-three. Marty graduated in June of eighty-one and went away that summer. Fifteen years ago."

"And then your husband died."

"Two years later. A year later I married Bill, and we lived together for five years. He died in eighty-nine, about the same time my father died. That's when I came back to Colorado."

"And met J.Q."

"No. I knew J.Q. when I was in college. We were friends then. I ran into him in Denver and told him I was hunting for someone to help on the ranch. He was retired, as I was, so he volunteered."

"You had a little girl, too."

"Sal. Killed by a drunk driver. Turned out he'd been arrested four times before. I heard later he was arrested for the same thing at least two more times before he killed himself, and I confess I was delighted to hear he had done so. Sal was two years younger than Marty. She died when she was twelve."

"Now you've got me," said Allison, in a rather bleak voice.

Shirley turned to see a sad and thoughtful face. "I have. And I'm thoroughly pleased with you, Allison.

You couldn't be a better daughter if you'd been born to me."

Allison flushed. She'd been thinking of talking to Shirley about Tad and Dawn and the Bunch. Now, after Shirley had said that, how could she admit she was . . . tempted? Even though Shirley understood all about lust and sex and all that, would she understand about wanting to be one of Dawn's friends?

Shirley wouldn't think much of Dawn. Sometimes even Allison didn't think much of Dawn. Which all made it just that much more confusing. She leaned casually on the counter, peering at the newspaper left there since breakfast. "This man, Dexter French, the one who wrote this article . . ."

"The cattle-mutilations reporter?" asked Shirley, grimacing.

"Yes. His daughter is in my class."

"Is she really?" Shirley turned from the stove. "What's she like?"

Allison shrugged. "Her mother's got lots and lots of money. Her father writes for magazines and papers and he does what Dawn calls—"

"Dawn is your school friend?"

"Yeah. She says her father dabbles at stuff. He finds stuff for people, maids or houses or interior decorators. Different stuff. But Dawn's mother, she's the daughter of some oilman who lives in Dallas, and I suppose you'd say Dawn is rich. Or her mother is."

"Rich. In what way, rich?"

"Well, they live in this huge house with about six servants. And Dawn and her mother have a whole string of horses plus a stableman and a trainer to look after them.

And next year, when Dawn is sixteen, she'll get her own Mercedes. That kind of rich."

"That's rich," Shirley agreed, spooning sour cream over the onions and mushrooms. "There's some tomato sauce in the refrigerator, can you get it for me?"

Allison proffered the sauce; Shirley added several spoonfuls to the mixture, dashed it with Worcestershire sauce, then turned down the heat. In a separate pan she quickly browned the steak slices and set them aside.

"What do you want for salad?" she asked. "How about endive and tomatoes. I actually found a couple that don't feel like they're made of plastic. They even smell like tomatoes, instead of cardboard."

"That sounds all right." Allison began to accumulate the ingredients.

"So, this Dawn French is rich," Shirley said, as though there had been no interruption. "Something about that bothers you."

Allison started to deny it, then flushed. "I guess maybe."

"She's popular?"

"Yes." Then, being honest: "With a certain group, at least."

"Pretty?"

"Yes."

"You'd like to be part of her circle?"

"I don't know. She's going to Aspen, skiing. She said maybe she'd invite me."

"Maybe." Shirley turned from the stove, her eyes wary. "Maybe isn't friendship talking, Allison. Maybe is a tease word. Friends don't tease."

Without intending to, Allison found herself rising to Dawn's defense. "She didn't mean it like that; she meant, maybe she could take someone else, that's all. She's already taking Summer Smythe and Breeze Watkins, and she doesn't know if there's room for another one."

"I see." Shirley turned back to the stove, a worried wrinkle between her eyebrows. "Summer. Breeze. And Dawn. My, oh, my."

Allison giggled. "That's what Mr. Patterson says. He calls it Southwestern Chic."

"I'll bet you all three of them came from somewhere else. Chic, yes, but not necessarily Southwestern. I'll tell you something you might think about, Allison, and that is whether you really like her or just resent being excluded. Exclusivity is an old, old tactic, you know. That's how all those country clubs and private social organizations get their membership, making the members feel better than the common herd."

Allison shrugged, suddenly wary. "I don't know which it is. Aspen was just something to talk about. If she really invites me, I'll figure it out then."

The door opened, admitting J.Q., Tabasco, and a gust of cold air. "Blowing up a little storm out there. I was going to leave this critter down in the barn, but he objects to the temperature."

"He had no business being born in September," said Shirley.

"His siblings were also born in September," J.Q. pointed out.

"His mama is providing for the siblings, and they've all got nice thick outdoor coats of hair. Keep this one mostly outside for a few days, he'll get used to the chill."

64

"Have any of the goats ever had quadruplets before?" Allison asked, grateful for the change of subject.

Shirley put her hands on her hips and glared at the baby goat. "Triplets, lots of times, but no quads, not in my memory. Get him off the table, J.Q.!"

The kid had jumped from floor to chair to table, and was now onstage, dancing, pretending to butt an imaginary contender for this high ground.

J.Q. removed him from the table, then pushed the chairs tightly under it so the kid couldn't use them as takeoff points again.

"Chilly or not—"

"He's just a baby."

"I really think he must become a barn goat, J.Q. I do not mind kitchen goats, or kitchen lambs, for that matter, not when they're tiny, but when they start jumping onto the table, enough is enough. Chilly or not, he has to go down to the barn, no later than tomorrow."

J.Q. frowned and pursed his lips. He had a special fondness for goats, and Tabasco was his particular pet.

"We could rig him a light in a warm corner somewhere," Allison offered, very quickly. "Like we did for the baby-chick brooder. I know right where the one is that we used."

"Good idea." J.Q. nodded, his face clearing. "I've got a new infrared bulb. We'll do that, first thing tomorrow."

The phone rang and Allison went to answer it while J.Q. and Shirley bustled a bit, getting the table set, putting the meat in the sauce and both over the noodles, dressing the salad, and pouring the wine.

Allison finished murmuring into the phone and hung up.

"Who was it, Ally?"

It had been Tad, asking to see her tomorrow. "Just one of my friends . . . asking about an assignment," she said, hearing her voice squeak on his name.

Neither J.Q. nor Shirley seemed to notice the squeak as they seated themselves in a warm glow of lamplight. Shirley sighed deeply, setting aside the day's tragedy, for the moment contented to be where she was, among her own. J.Q. smiled expectantly at his wineglass. Tonight's bottle had been ranked in the midnineties by the *Wine Spectator*, and he was looking forward to it. After the very normal recent interchanges, neither of them paid particular attention to Allison's distracted face or her unaccustomed silence. Tad had said he would meet her tomorrow morning, at eleven. He had asked her to say where. She had told him at the fork in Arroyo Largo. So, now she was committed to it. At least she supposed she was. He said he was bringing a blanket.

On Saturday morning, Shirley was sweeping up the cottonwood leaves outside the kitchen door, somewhat handicapped by Tabasco, who thought she was sweeping them into mountains for his particular benefit. Last night's fog had not turned into rain. The morning sun had dried the leaves into a mass that rustled so loudly she didn't hear the car until it drove to the wall, gunned the engine, and stopped.

Shirley went to the gate and opened it, stepping outside while firmly preventing Tabasco from doing likewise. "Are you looking for someone?"

A pleasantly round-faced fortyish man got out of the car and approached her. "Would you be Mrs. McClintock?"

"Ms. McClintock," she said firmly. "I am."

"Brian McCree," he said, holding out a hand that trembled slightly. "Bridget's brother."

Shirley nodded, opened the gate, seized up the kid, which was determined to escape, and beckoned him in. "I'm so very sorry for your loss, Mr. McCree. Did the sheriff's office send you over here?"

He shook his head in slight bewilderment. "Nobody sent me. I mean, they told me you'd found . . . found Bridgy. I'm just trying to . . . I guess I can't make sense of it."

"Coffee?" Shirley suggested. "In the kitchen, where it's warm and where this beast won't be jumping into our laps."

She led Brain McCree inside, pushed Tabasco outside with one foot and shut the door in his face, divested McCree of his coat, and sat him down at the kitchen table while she poured coffee and fussed with the sugar bowl and cream pitcher.

When they were seated across from one another, she said, "I didn't know Bridget well. She sent us customers from time to time."

"No one seems to have known her well," he complained. "The people across the road, the neighbors down the road. It's as though she'd been invisible!"

Shirley reached across to pat his hand. "Don't read more into that than was there. She actually was mostly invisible. Her house was hidden, for one thing. Her way of life was difficult to understand, for another. The people up and down that road are Roybals and Martinezes and Luceros. Their families have been here, most of them, for two or three hundred years. They simply avert their gaze from us Anglo interlopers who've only been here a generation or less."

67

"Someone looked at her!" he cried, then dropped his head, letting tears drop onto the table. "Who would have wanted to do something like that to Bridgy? Pretty Bridgy. She was so . . . so naive about things. She trusted everyone."

"Tell me about her," Shirley asked, looking over his head at J.Q., who had just edged through the hall door. She shook her head slightly and he oozed out again.

"She was five years younger than me," he said. "I always took care of her, baby-sat her, you know, when Mom went out. We didn't have a father; he was killed when she was just a baby. She was so pretty, always, but sort of a scatterbrain. Music, art, things like that, she got high grades in school, but languages or history, she just got by. She was good at math, though. Always surprised me. She was married for a while, in her twenties, but he divorced her when they found out she couldn't have children. She never got over that; it hurt her. She said she'd never trust anyone again, after that, but she couldn't help trusting people. It was just how she was made."

"I don't care what they say. It wasn't aliens that did it."

"Who said it was aliens?" Shirley asked, afraid that she already knew.

"One of the sheriff's men said his boss is sort of leaning toward extraterrestrials. If they've learned all they can about cattle, maybe now they're taking parts of people. I don't believe that!"

Shirley sipped, swallowed, thought deeply. "If you don't believe it, we should do what we can to assure that no one believes it."

"Here?" He laughed shortly, without humor. "Phyllis—that's my wife—she says people down here believe anything. She was all the time trying to get Bridget to move up home with us, back to Denver. But since she fell for that man, Bridget's been immovable. Before that, maybe we'd have had a chance, but not since then."

"Since she fell for . . . ?"

"Four years ago Bridget had her own secretarial printing business, in Santa Fe. Desktop publishing, you know? She did all kinds of specialized work for people, putting together brochures or reports, preparing manuscripts, all kinds of stuff. She was good at it. I was surprised how artistic she was, and how efficient she was. She made good money. If she'd stuck with it, she'd have built a substantial business. What happened was, she fell in love with this man." He stopped, his mouth worked, he shook his head. "I shouldn't be telling her secrets."

"If we talk about her, we may come up with something to help find who killed her," Shirley suggested.

He sighed. "She fell in love with this man. I don't know who he was. She wouldn't tell me. She let slip to Phyllis that he was married. Anyhow, Phyllis told her, Bridget, you can't throw your life away on a married man who has no intention of doing anything for you beyond crawling into your bed now and then. That's Phyllis, not exactly tactful. Anyhow, there was a blowup of some kind, something happened between her and the man, and Bridget gave up the business and moved to this little town down south."

"Madrid?"

"That's right. I don't know what she lived on. She had some savings, so she must have used that, or what she got for the business. Anyhow, she was still in love with this same guy. Things went along, we saw her a few times, not many, and then about two years ago, in the fall, finally, something happened that made Bridget just come apart! She wouldn't come to us, but she wouldn't leave us alone, either. She was on the phone to Phyllis two and three times a day, she couldn't eat, she couldn't sleep. We didn't know what to do. And then she went to this healer, this Buffalo Man. Part Indian, I think. Part Indian and all phony, I thought, but Bridget swore he healed her. Maybe he did. He settled her down, I know that much.

"Then about a year and a half ago he was killed in an accident, and here was Bridget, sorrowful all over again. Next thing we knew, Bridget wrote and told us she'd won big at one of the Indian casinos, and she was moving back to Santa Fe and buying a house. I thought she'd go back to her old business, build it up again, but she didn't. She decided she'd be a healer, too, and she did it in that house, the one she was killed in."

"But you never knew who she was in love with?"

"I didn't. Phyllis didn't. Bridget never talked about him after she moved from Madrid and started her own healing business."

"She made enough to live on with her psychic-healing business?"

"I guess she must have. She didn't have anything else that I knew of. I tried to talk her into starting up again, but she said she had all she needed. I don't know what she had, except the house and some land in Montana Mom inherited from our grandfather. We were all *B*s. Grandpa was Barney, then Beatrice, then Brian and Bridget. There's nothing on the land but wind and grass and prairie dogs. It's miles from anywhere. When mother died, they said it was only worth about twenty dollars an acre, but we said, you know, we'd hang on to it, see if it ever got to be worth anything. Now Phyl's got lupus, she's in the hospital, and the bills are starting to get bigger than I can pay, and the insurance is about to run out, and I need to raise money any way I can. I told Bridgy I need to sell my share of the Montana land, she needs to sign off on it, splitting the property, half and half. It's been a month since I asked her. And she's been . . . she was giving me the runaround. How she'd lost the papers, how she knew where they were, she just had to find them, stuff like that."

"And you can't find them. You've searched her house?"

"Only . . . only looked around. I thought I'd look today. I have a key."

"Would you like someone with you? Would you like my help?"

He stared into his coffee cup. "I . . . I guess. I'm sort of . . . like frozen. I can't seem to get started."

"You wait here," she told him, getting up and going out into the hall and then throughout the house, looking for J.Q. She found him in the laundry, sorting out his socks.

"You want me to go with you?" he asked, when she had told him her tale.

"I'd really like you to hold the fort, J.Q. If you don't mind."

"I don't mind. I can hear the phone from in here."

"Where's Ally?"

"Not up yet. I peeked into her room and she's all curled up with the pillow over her head."

Shirley frowned. That wasn't like Allison, not on a lovely Saturday morning. Still, everyone had an off day now and then.

71

"What Bridget's brother told you?" J.Q. remarked. "It's in the morning paper. I was going to show it to you when I came over to the kitchen. All that bit about UFOs? The sheriff isn't the only one who's considering extraterrestrials."

"J.Q., don't tell me they're swallowing this ET bit."

"Honest to God. I told you the sheriff's opinion isn't that far out around here."

"Poor man. Poor Bridget."

She went back to the kitchen, collected Brian McCree, and the two of them, in Brian's car, went down the road to Bridget's house.

"Why don't you start with her desk?" Shirley suggested, when Brian had unlocked the front door. "Pick up all the papers on the floor and sort them out. I'll go through her closets."

"The deputy told me not to remove anything from the place."

"You don't need to remove it. Just find it. You can worry about getting possession later."

"I suppose," he said, shaking his head. He went to the desk, sat down before it, and opened the top drawer.

Shirley went into the front bedroom, obviously the one Bridget had used. The other one was full of boxes. In here, the bed was neatly made, the tile floor recently polished, no cobwebs or dust to speak of. In the closet hung the beaded buckskin dress, fringed at the shoulder and sleeves. It was the one Bridget had been wearing the day before. The moccasins were on the floor, neatly set side by side. Several dusty boxes on the closet shelf yielded stashes of sexy underwear, bustiers, crotchless panties. Shirley blinked and put them back where she'd found them. Bridget hadn't really seemed the type, but then . . .

The dresser held stacks of cotton underwear and T-shirts, cotton socks, a box of letters, most of them from Brian and/or Phyllis. Here, also, was another buckskin dress, neatly folded, and a few big T-shirts for sleeping in.

Shirley stepped out into the hall to ask Brian how he was doing, only to see him sitting as he had been, staring into the open drawer, not moving. She went over to him, shook him by the shoulder. He looked up at her with swimming eyes.

"You don't feel like doing this today," she said. "You're not up to this."

"I have to be," he whispered. "I can't leave Phyl to come back down. Anything I have to do, I have to do it this weekend."

Shirley went to the phone and called home. When J.Q. answered, she asked him to get Allison up and the two of them come on over, prepared to help Mr. McCree.

"I can't," Allison told J.Q., her face still blurred with sleep.

"We must," said J.Q. "The poor guy needs help. She was a neighbor, and neighbors help neighbors."

Allison got dressed in a state of confused half rebellion, drank a glass of milk at J.Q.'s direction, was handed a piece of toast, and got into the Jeep with no further demurral. Tad would be looking for her at eleven, up the arroyo. With a blanket, he said. Nothing like love-making out in the wilderness, he said. Well, maybe she could sneak off in an hour, meet him, and then . . . come back. How long did it take? Maybe she could . . . she lifted her wrist to see how much time she had. She had forgotten her watch. Oh, well, J.Q. had one. She felt all awash inside, sloshy, as though her balance was off. "Why are we going?" she blurted, almost angrily.

"Bridget McCree's brother is here. He needs to find some papers that Bridget had, and the whole house is messed up. Shirley needs us to help her search."

How long could that take? It wasn't a big house. Allison relaxed against the seatback. They'd just find the things and come home and . . . she'd take it from there.

When they arrived at Bridget's, Shirley put Allison to work at the desk, sorting the papers into piles. Anything that looked like a deed or a legal document was to be piled separately. Yawning, Allison began, gradually falling into the fever of the hunt, scanning documents, letters, the words flowing by like water. Bridget wasn't very neat. All her things were any which way, unless maybe whoever messed up the house had left them that way. There was a box of grocery receipts, and a box of other receipts, from the gas company and the electric company, and the water association. There was a prescription for glasses, and lots of old checkbooks and bank statements. Allison found another box to put them in, arranging them by year.

"Any luck?" Shirley asked.

"Not yet," she grunted. "Wait, here's one. . . ."

Shirley took it. "The deed to this house," she said. "Brian, we've found the deed to this house."

He shook his head sadly. "If she left it to me, it'll help, I suppose, but doesn't it take a long time to get things probated?"

"Are you her closest relative?"

"Her only one, really."

"Then whether there's a will or not, you'll probably inherit it. And yes, sometimes it does take a long time to get a will probated, but things can be speeded up if there's need."

Allison turned away from the desk, which she now had sorted into neat stacks, only to confront a messy pile of papers on the couch. Sighing ever so slightly, she began sorting them. This bunch was harder. She had to read them to figure out what they were. Copies of bills? Bills Bridget had sent to people for healing that she'd done? No. Receipts. Received of so and so, so much money. She started a new stack.

They all looked up at the sound of steps on the porch. Allison went to the door to see a tanned, lean, impeccably dressed man standing there, knuckles poised for a knock. "I am sorry to interrupt you at such a time," he said. "However, I thought someone might be thinking of disposing of this property, and I thought I'd leave my card."

"Brian," Allison called. "Would you like to talk to a realtor about this house?"

Brian shambled to the door. "I'm sorry," he murmured. "I don't know what I'm going to do at this point. My sister's not even buried yet."

"Your sister?"

"Bridget McCree. She owned this house. I'm Brian McCree. I suppose I'll inherit it, but until there's something certain ..."

"I understand. Do you live here in Santa Fe, Mr. McCree?"

Brian shook his head. "Denver. I've got to get back. If you'll leave me your card, Mister ... Mister ..."

"Crabbe." He fished in his pocket, looked dismayed. "Gerald Crabbe. That's silly. I've run out of cards. Never mind. I'll drop one by later. Sorry to have intruded." He nodded and was gone.

Brian trudged back to his position at the desk.

Allison, now that she'd been interrupted, asked, "What time is it, J.Q.?"

He stopped going through the bookcase and looked at his watch. "A little after noon. You getting hungry?"

"Noon! How can it be noon?"

"It was almost eleven when I woke you."

She simply stood there, staring at the paper piles, her face flaming. Damn. Maybe she hadn't wanted to go at all. Maybe she'd overslept just to avoid going. And what was Tad thinking? Oh, damn, damn, damn, she whispered to herself. Oh, shit, shit, shit.

An hour later the job was done. Brian McCree had even managed to bestir himself enough to help. So far as any of them could find, there was no deed to Montana land, no reference to it in any correspondence, and no safety-deposit key or receipt.

Shirley invited Brian to come home with them, for lunch. He shook his head, tears in his eyes. "I'm not hungry. Thank you, but I'm just . . . I don't know what to do next. See a lawyer, I guess. The deed is recorded in Mom's name, after all, and I guess I'm the only heir left."

"If I were you, I'd get some sleep."

"I think I will. I'm already checked out of the motel. I guess there's no reason not to stay here."

He turned away, and with a sympathetic look at his back, Shirley got into the Jeep next to Allison and J.Q. and was driven home.

"Lunch?" she asked, when they arrived.

"Not for me, thanks," said Allison. "I'd really like to take Beauregard for a little ride if you don't mind."

Shirley looked at her curiously. She didn't sound like herself. On the other hand, Beauregard could certainly use some exercise. "No problem," she said. "How about you, J.Q.?"

"Sandwich," he said laconically. "After which, you can come help me string wire."

They went into the kitchen, and Allison, after a quick stop to wash the dust from her face and comb her hair, went down to saddle Beauregard. Though no doubt Tad was long gone, she ought to go out there, so she could say she had come as soon as she could. Or, maybe, he'd waited for her. Or, maybe, he hadn't been able to find the right place.

She clucked Beau into a collected canter and went out the driveway to the road, then turned left, past the crossroad that led to Bridget McCree's, past houses on the left, houses on the right, then, about a mile from the house, oblique right, down the bank, and into the arroyo, headed southeast. Half a mile down the way, this arroyo would connect with the other one, coming in from the southwest.

She took a sudden breath, remembering the last time she'd been there. What if she had been there on time and she and Tad had ... and Ulti had come along? Gross! He'd have seen her!

Beauregard slowed to a walk and shook his head disapprovingly. Allison wasn't paying attention. He nodded, then did a naughty little sidestep, recalling her to herself. "Sorry, Beau," she said. "Good old Beau."

The sandy arroyo bottom was crisscrossed with hoof marks, people prints, and at least one set of pristine tire tracks, a four-wheel drive of some kind. The tracks went on beside them until the bank was just ahead of her, the one with the kingfisher holes in it, where she had seen Ulti last. There was no sign of Tad. He'd gotten tired of waiting and gone. Suddenly she was flooded with relief.

"Pay attention to how you feel," Shirley often said to her. "Sometimes your innards will tell you things your mind won't." So, evidently her innards were glad. Come to think of it, so was the rest of her.

She rode on, past the intersection of the gullies, eastward, toward school, almost a mile. No Tad. So, all right. She wheeled Beau around and headed back the way she had come, up the other branch of the arroyo for several hundred yards. The only thing in the arroyo that hadn't grown there was a pile of rusty junk, car parts and five-gallon buckets and a scatter of crumpled beer cans. No Tad. So, all right. She looked for a place Beau could get up the bank, a side gully that sloped, finally finding one that went up the left hand side. Up there she'd be on Indian land, but generally the Pueblo didn't mind if people didn't litter or make a nuisance of themselves. She put Beau to the bank, leaning forward while he thrust with powerful back legs, making it in two or three lunges.

They stood on open prairie, surrounded by little hummocks of blooming snakeweed and tall, gray-feathery fronds of chamisa. Junipers were spotted here and there, widely separated, so each could collect enough rain for itself from its network of shallow, wiry roots. Something whipped across the rosy sand in front of Beau's feet, so fast it was like a red blur. Beau reared, snorting, and she was almost unseated.

"Coachwhip," she found herself muttering. "Remember what Ulti said, it's a coachwhip." It had moved like pink lightning. Trembling a little, she patted Beau until he quieted, seeming almost ashamed of himself. "Come on, Beauregard. Enough of this stuff. We'll go along the top here until we come to the road, okay?"

Beau put his head down, as though sniffing the ground, then nodded again, agitated but not jittery, and proceeded at a slow walk along the arroyo rim. Ahead of them, near the intersection of the arroyos, a huge puff of chamisa overhung the bank, with something colorful in it, blue and red. Beau pricked his ears forward, making a troubled sound in his nose. As they came closer Allison could see that it was a person, lying half-hidden by the chamisa, peering over the edge of the arroyo. Tad? If it was Tad, why hadn't he called out when she rode by before?

"Tad?" she called.

The person didn't move. For some reason, Allison did not want to dismount. She felt safer where she was. "Tad," she called again, more loudly.

Still no movement. Gritting her teeth, Allison slid from Beau's back and led him by the reins as she went toward the still form. A small person. Dressed in blue jeans and a blue shirt, with a red baseball cap and a ponytail of long, dark hair. Ulti? Too little for Ulti.

She reached into the chamisa, grasped an upper arm in one hand and pulled. The figure turned slightly, then fell back, and Allison was on Beau's back almost before the movement ceased, urging him down the precipitous bank of the arroyo, and then at a full run down the arroyo, toward home, needing to get to Shirley, to J.Q., to somebody, to tell them Dawn French was lying dead with a hole in her forehead, near the place Allison had agreed to meet Tad Pole.

3

SHIRLEY CALLED THE Rio Grande County Sheriff's
Office and asked to speak to Eddy Martinez, who was,
the dispatcher said, available by radio and would be
right over. When the car arrived, J.Q. got in the Jeep
and drove out as a guide while Allison remained in the
kitchen, building a case of hysterics.

"I thought it was Tad," she said. "Then I thought it
might be Ulti. I never thought of Dawn, never. . . ."

"Allison . . ."

Her voice rose to a shriek. "She was dead. I'm sure
she was dead. She had to be dead. Should I have done
something? To make sure . . ."

"Allison . . ."

"Beauregard knew, he just knew, his ears were way
up, and he was jittery, but maybe that was the snake, I
just don't—"

"Allison, hush. I mean it. Just hush. Just sit there and

breathe, one breath after another. Don't talk. Don't go on and on."

"Sorry," Allison gasped, wiping at her wet cheeks with the backs of both hands.

"You have nothing to be sorry for." Shirley fetched a dampened paper towel and washed Allison's face with judicious swabs. "Now, when the sheriff's people come back over here, which they will, what are you going to tell them?"

"Tell . . . ?"

"Look at me, Allison. Concentrate. Why did you go riding out there, to that particular place?"

"I do ride there. Every now and then."

"You had no other reason today?"

Allison's face went up in flame.

"Allison, were you meeting someone?" Shirley kept her voice carefully neutral. What had the child been up to? Now wasn't the time to press, but she'd really like to know.

Allison swallowed deeply and found her voice down somewhere near her knees. She hauled it up by pure willpower and said, "I was supposed to meet Tad, at eleven o'clock. But I lost track of time. I didn't think he'd still be there, but I thought I'd check."

"Fine. That's what you should say. You were going to meet a friend from school and what? Go riding?"

"Tad doesn't ride. I mean, he doesn't have a horse of his own."

"You were just meeting to walk and talk, casually? As friends."

Allison looked at her shoes and scowled.

"Allison?"

"Yes."

"When was this meeting arranged?"

"Last night. When he called, at dinnertime."

"Fine. Now, when you got to the place . . . which was where, by the way?"

"At the place the arroyo forks, where the one cuts off that runs through the pueblo land."

"When you got there, Tad wasn't there."

"Nobody was there. I rode down the arroyo east, toward school, quite a long way, then I turned around and went back up the other way. He wasn't there. So Beau and I found a gully we could use to get up on top, and we started for home, cross-country. We were headed toward the road."

"And when you came to the place the two arroyos meet, you saw Dawn."

"I saw colors first, red and blue, then a shape, a person, blue jeans and something red on the head. And I thought at first it might be Tad, that he'd . . . I don't know, waited for me until he'd fallen asleep or something. Then I thought of Ulti, because he wears a bandanna, a red one, so I got down and reached in and pulled, and it was Dawn. I never thought of its being Dawn."

"Why do you suppose she was there?"

The question evoked an answer. Allison knew exactly why she was there. Dawn French had gone there to observe. To see what happened. To verify Allison's capitulation. Gross. Sickening! She made a face and muttered, "Maybe she was following Tad, I don't know. Maybe he told her he'd be there." As he had, of course. What had he said to her? That he was going to . . . to make love to Allison down in the bottom of the arroyo? He'd probably used another word than that. God!

"Are she and Tad a couple?"

Allison pulled herself back to attention. "No! Dawn was going with some guy from UNM, so Tad said. Nobody knows who he is. Dawn wouldn't tell. She and Tad were just friends." The falsity of this also came to her as a revelation. "I guess not really friends. He was more . . . like her puppy dog, I guess."

"A willing slave."

"Like that. She was always sending him on errands."

"So we have no idea why she was there, and we really don't know that he was ever there. When you turned her over, was she cold?"

Allison began to shudder, all over, tears pouring.

"Allison! Was she cold?"

"I don't know. I guess. I didn't touch her skin, just her jacket, I'm not . . . I'm not a policeman, a detective, I don't . . ."

"I know that, sweetheart. Nobody thinks you should be. What I am interested in is being sure you were a long way from there when she died."

"Oh!" Allison's eyes went wide, and she put a hand across her open mouth. "Would they think I did it?"

Shirley applied the paper towel once more. "They're almost required to presume you might have. Body discoverers sometimes are the killers, so they're often suspected, as I've learned to my dismay. If they didn't suspect you, they wouldn't be doing their duty. And if you want to stay out of trouble, you will tell them the truth, having carefully thought through what the truth is. We got back here after one. You were with J.Q. and me all morning. You went out riding as soon as we got back, and you discovered the body . . . how much later?"

Allison frowned, trying to estimate. "I don't know,

Shirley. I didn't have my watch on. I'd have to ride Beau the same route to figure it out."

"What did you have for breakfast?"

Allison's face went blank as she tried to remember. "Toast, I think."

"Sit right there. You had little breakfast and no lunch. I want you to have a bowl of soup."

"Soup?"

"As my first husband would have said, it couldn't hurt. You look as though you'd been dragged through a knothole."

Shirley fetched jellied chicken stock from the refrigerator, spooned a generous helping of it into a saucepan, brought it to a boil, threw in a handful of dried angelhair pasta, some chopped onion, and then, while it simmered, cubed the meat from a leftover chicken leg and thigh, which she added to the soup just before she poured it into a bowl.

"Is this Jewish chicken soup?" Allison asked, around her spoon.

"No Jewish mother would give table room to this soup, no. Jewish chicken soup starts with a whole chicken and has all kinds of vegetables in the stock. This is leftover soup. What David used to call, clean-the-refrigerator soup. It's warm, it's wet, and it's generally comforting. That's the best we can say for it."

"Have we got any crackers left?"

"No, but we've got some corn chips, try those." Shirley put the package on the table at the same moment as they heard the knock at the door.

The deputies. Eddy Martinez and someone named Romero. After muted greetings, Deputy Martinez said, "We called the state people. They're working the site over there. We'd like to talk to the girl who found the body."

Shirley invited them in, suggested they have some coffee, then provided same, taking her time about it. This gave Allison time to finish her soup, and she looked better by the time they started with the questions, less distraught and a bit less pale. She told her story hesitantly, answering all the questions except the one about what time she found the body.

"I don't know," she said, as she had said to Shirley. "I'd have to ride Beau out there again, to see how long it took."

"She left here about one-thirty, she got back here about three," said Shirley. "And Beau was lathered. He'd run most of the way."

"You thought the body was this kid you were meeting? The Pole kid?" asked Deputy Martinez. "Is he built small, like the deceased?"

"Tad isn't very big. He's heavier than Dawn, but he's short, not much taller than me. And I couldn't really see her, because she was hidden in the bush."

"And you don't know what she was doing there?"

Allison shook her head. She guessed a reason, but she didn't know for sure, so it wasn't a lie. Suddenly she gasped. "How did she get there?"

"What do you mean?"

"I mean, it's a long way from the road, and a really long way from her house. Dawn rides a lot. Maybe she rode out there, but if she did, where's her horse?"

Martinez scribbled. "Can you describe her horse?"

"Horses," Allison corrected. "She's got a whole stable full. I mean, most of them belong to her mother, but

Dawn rides them all. Geldings, mostly. Big horses. Thoroughbreds and jumpers."

"I guess we'll go break the news to her mother and see if there's a horse missing," said Eddy Martinez, with a resigned expression. Breaking the news of a death in the family was not something he looked forward to, especially not to some *rica gringa, con muchos caballos.* Ricos weren't like real people. They were more like rattlesnakes, only they didn't always warn you before they struck at you.

"Did it happen on Indian land?" asked Shirley.

"You mean, does the pueblo have jurisdiction?" Martinez asked. "I don't think so. She was definitely in Rio Grande County; Santa Fe County line is a quarter mile from there. And I think she was outside the pueblo boundary, on private land, by a few hundred yards. And of course she was Anglo. It could be an FBI matter, but I'm really pretty sure she was over the line."

Shirley nodded. She had encountered the question of jurisdiction before, an interesting one when law enforcement of pueblos, counties, the state, and the FBI overlapped. "Was she shot?"

Martinez simply stared at her for a long moment. Shirley stared back, uncowed. "I'm wondering where the shooter was."

"You mean the shooter might have been on Indian land?"

"Well?" She shrugged. "Couldn't he, she, or it?"

"We don't know yet. Yes, she was shot. From a distance. The way we figure it, she heard something, raised up her head, turned to look, and caught the bullet in the right temple. No exit wound that we can see."

"So the killer could have been on that side of the arroyo, or on the other side, but not down in the arroyo?"

He grinned at her, rather fiercely. "Ma'am, we've got deputy jobs open if you'd like to apply."

"Sorry. I don't think I'd like working for your boss."

"I can understand that," he said in a kindly voice that set Shirley's teeth on edge. It was the voice of someone saying, *Gee, Grandma, thanks for the hand-knitted socks*. Martinez didn't notice, he was busy addressing Allison.

"If you remember anything else, you please call me. Here's my card. I left one the other day, so you've got a couple of them now. Eddy Martinez, okay."

He shook Shirley's hand, and she saw them out. J.Q. came in from the driveway, where he'd parked the Jeep.

"Are you going to leave your horse saddled all afternoon?" he asked Allison. "He's out there tied to the hitching post wondering what the hell."

"Oh. I forgot. Poor Beau!" And she was out, still pale but moving, not crying.

"Well?" asked Shirley.

"I don't think you could call it *well*, no. Clean shot, though. Her face wasn't messed up. If that's any comfort to anyone."

"You didn't find a horse, by any chance?"

"Her horse?"

"One she might have been riding."

"No horse. No."

"According to Allison, Dawn French lives in Tesuque. That's a good six or seven miles from where she was found. How did she get there?"

J.Q. frowned. "There were four-wheel drive tracks in the arroyo, a clean, new set. I didn't follow them, not to the end."

"Where did they start?"

"I saw them at the road. East of us."

"South side of the culvert, or both sides?"

"I didn't look at the north side."

"The north-side arroyo ends up down by Bridget's place. When you say a clean, new set of tracks, you mean today? This morning?"

"Or yesterday. The weather forecast was wrong. We haven't had any wind or rain for a couple of days."

"Let's go look."

"By Lucy's left tit, Shirley! You said you didn't want to get involved. Are you all set to play detective now?"

"I just want to know. Allison's involved, sort of, and I just want to know."

"All right. We haven't been riding for some little time, so let's do it. I'll saddle the horses."

"Let's just take the Jeep, J.Q. It's getting late, and we still have to feed *los animales* before supper."

Grumpily, he agreed. They left a note for Allison on the kitchen table, then retraced the route Allison had ridden earlier that afternoon. Down the paved road to the east, all the way to the arroyo. They parked the Jeep by the side of the road and got out to examine the arroyo north of the culvert.

"Right there," J.Q. said, pointing at tracks that might have been left by a giant waffle iron. "Whoever it was came from down there"—gesturing northward—"and came up the bank to cross the road here, and then down into the arroyo again."

"Or vice versa," she murmured.

"Possibly."

They got back into the Jeep and went down into the arroyo, driving slowly southeastward in the tracks J.Q.

had made on his previous trip, keeping the other tracks to their right. At the forking of the arroyo, the tracks went both ways, southeast and southwest. Above them, on the bank, yellow strips of crime-scene tape flickered in a light wind, and when they stopped, they could hear men talking up there, then a car moving.

"That bush is where the body was." J.Q. pointed at a thick clump of chamisa, overhanging the arroyo.

"And the tracks go both ways."

"It's impossible to tell which way he went," J.Q. muttered. "He—"

"Or she."

"Or it, went east toward the road and back up the arroyo into Indian country."

"Let's try that way first. We better walk, though. If we drive, they'll get on us for messing the place up."

Mumbling to himself, J.Q. turned off the engine and together they moved around the steep, pointed bank to walk up the gully on the far side. The tracks proceeded ahead of them, past assorted clumps of vegetation, past a pile of rusty cans and old car parts. There they stopped.

"He, she, or it backed up," said Shirley, crouching down to peer down the tracks more closely. "There's no turn, just a backup set."

"As we are about to do." J.Q. began retracing his steps. "You want to follow them down the other way?"

"I want to look at it from up top, first."

They found a side ravine and climbed onto the level. Near the crime scene three vehicles were parked—lab truck, sheriff's car, and another one, a big car. Two people stood next to it, Anglos. Bouncing around them like a playful puppy was the rotund shape of the sheriff himself. Almost one might expect to hear the man say, *Fetch it, boy. Go fetch it.*

"Dawn's parents. The sheriff couldn't wait to go tell them," said J.Q. "He brought them back here, but the body had already been taken."

"Does he think this is extraterrestrials?"

J.Q. shrugged. "You ready to go down the other way?"

"Please. We can drive there, the arroyo's wide enough."

They followed the tracks eastward, along the arroyo bottom, up a shallow bank near the paved road, and away toward the blacktop.

"Okay," muttered J.Q. "It looks like we've got someone who started here and drove toward Bridget's place, then came back, turned the wrong way at the fork, realized it was the wrong way, then backed up and came the right way and out."

"We don't know the tracks go all the way to Bridget's. Let's go look at the arroyo down there."

"You are a glutton for punishment." He turned the vehicle left, onto the paved county road, and followed it north to the intersection with the Rancho del Valle road, where he turned left again, then right onto the road that led past Bridget's place. They parked at the culvert outside Bridget's house, went down on the upstream side into the arroyo—shallower at this point than it had been farther up—and found the same tracks.

"But only on the upstream side," murmured Shirley, who had crossed the road to peer downward at the sandy bottom from across the fence. "He, she, or it couldn't get on the river side without cutting the fence."

90

"Not even if the fence was cut. There's a three-foot drop-off," remarked J.Q. "So, what do you think?"

"I think someone ought to call Deputy Martinez's attention to the tracks. Is there any way to tell which way they're headed?"

"They didn't start and finish here. There are no tracks on the bank. They had to start at the other end." J.Q. stared moodily at the tracks, tracing them with a stick he'd picked up. "They're not directional. They're the same coming as going. But that's the only way they could have come to leave these tracks."

Shirley cast a quick look at the rapidly darkening sky. "Home, James. We've got suppering to do."

They climbed back into the Jeep and returned to the ranch, encountering a pair of guests in the driveway who wanted to display the marvelous finds they'd made at the Rio Grande Trading Post. Shirley took on this social duty, oohing appreciatively at a Hopi silver bracelet and a stone-polished Tewa pot while J.Q. recruited Allison's help and went off to tend animals. When they returned, half an hour later, Shirley had supper on the table, and was single-mindedly trying to prevent Tabasco from joining it.

"This *animal*," she snarled, "must go to the pasture, as I thought we had agreed!"

"We sort of got distracted today," said J.Q., in a tone of mild reproof. "We can't put him in there until we can keep him in there, because we are his mama and daddy and he will find a hole to get through so he can return to us, unlike his siblings and cousins who are perfectly content to stay with their mamas, right where they are! And, we can't keep him in there until we string some wire. Which, you will recall, we started to do this afternoon before Allison inherited your tendency to discover bodies."

"Right," Shirley murmured, chastened. "Sure. Okay. Tomorrow."

"I didn't!" cried Allison. "J.Q., I didn't inherit it. I don't want to inherit it."

Shirley, half laughing, exclaimed, "Allison, he was only teasing. Settle. Besides, your body was part of the same case as my body, or so J.Q. and I believe. Think of it as a sort of ancillary body. The tracks we found seemed to indicate that, at least."

"What . . . who . . . ?"

"Never mind. I'll tell you later. We are not going to spoil our supper talking about it at the table. Instead, we are going to discuss . . . what?"

"Local fauna," said J.Q. "I saw a coachwhip snake today."

"So did I," said Allison. "He took off in front of Beau's nose and scared him. Red."

"Really red?" Shirley asked.

"Really," J.Q. affirmed. "One surprised me, too. Where did you see yours, Allison?"

"When I was riding back along the top of the arroyo, before I discovered the . . . the victim."

"Same place," J.Q. observed. "Must be a nest of them there or something."

"I never saw one of those in Colorado," Shirley remarked, not wanting to get back on the subject of victims. "Are they a local beast? What's their range?"

Allison fetched the Audubon reptile book from the kitchen reference shelf for mealtime use, and they spent the rest of suppertime discussing fauna, including finches, which led to a discussion of Ulti's family, and the reason for his name, which led to a discussion of large families, pros and cons thereof, which disintegrated into a general lassitude. Tomorrow was Sunday, a good day, Shirley suggested, for them to go to Madrid and have lunch. For the time being, Bridget and Dawn were allowed to become, if not forgotten, at least not foremost in their minds.

The Sunday paper had a front-page story about Dawn's murder, as well as a follow-up story about Bridget having been killed by ETs, with pictures of the burn marks and the strange symbols, plus another story about cattle mutilations. The latter mentioned the gravity ray one rancher had seen pulling his cattle into the woods. "It was invisible," he was quoted as saying, "and it was just pulling my cattle into the trees."

"One might ask how he perceived this invisible ray," said Shirley around a mouthful of bacon.

"ESP," said Allison. "He sensed it." Ever since she'd awakened this morning, she'd been waiting for the phone to ring, so positive that it would ring that extrasensory perception was already on her mind. Surely Tad would have heard about Dawn by now! The morning paper told about her being shot and her body being discovered. It even mentioned Allison by name. Shouldn't he call her to say something? Like, where were you?

"Maybe this particular rancher sees in the ultraviolet," said J.Q. "Or the infrared. Like dogs hear things we can't, maybe this guy sees things we can't."

"Or maybe the cows floated," Shirley mused. "Like those old cartoons where the smell of cheese wafts the mouse or the smell of fish wafts the cat. Maybe the cows were sort of wafted."

"I never saw a purple cow, I never saw one wafted," J.Q. muttered.

"Ha?" said Allison after a long pause. "Draft, raft, abaft . . ."

"But if I had, I would allow, that it had been witch-crafted," said Shirley, with a smirk.

"The winner and new champion." J.Q. grinned. "I thought we heard about this gravity-ray business days ago?"

"Day before yesterday is all, J.Q. Bridget mentioned it Friday, when I took over the eggs. I figured it was in the paper and I'd just missed it."

He shook his head. "I guess we both missed it. Or maybe one of Bridget's clients told her all about it. Speaking of which, I wish we knew who her clients were. Whoever went through her house must have removed all reference to the people she saw. No appointment book, no journal, no correspondence."

"We are not going to talk about Bridget at the table," said Shirley firmly. "We're going to call Xanthippe Minging this morning, to see how she's enjoying her East Coast visit, then we're going to Madrid for wandering and lunch."

"I miss Mingy," said Allison. "I wish she'd come home."

"We're going to Madrid for lunch?" J.Q. asked skeptically, remembering that Bridget had lived in Madrid.

"Lunch," Shirley said, all innocence. "Of course."

The drive to Madrid took them about an hour and a half, since they had to go through Santa Fe, which had twice the traffic a town its size should have. Every other car was a rental car or a tourist's car, which meant that not only were there more vehicles than the town could hold, but also that the drivers often did not know where they were going. Even on Sunday, the streets seemed anxious.

They went out of town, into the hilly country, past dikes of white and yellow and salmon stone. They passed Cerillos, on their right, the church tower standing bravely alert amid a clutter of detritus. From a distance, it looked like a junkyard, its fringes littered with deteriorating vehicles and collapsing fences.

Madrid itself was only a wide spot in the road, lined on each side by commercial buildings that were now galleries, or houses that were now shops, or anonymous structures that contained material of a similar nature. Madrid had at one time been a coal-mining town, had subsequently become almost a ghost town, and had been revived in recent decades to become a minor colony of a mercantile type, one far less self-conscious than Taos and consequently, in Shirley's opinion, more fun. It retained a definite flavor of the sixties, an informal, make-do quality, an ambiguous charm, like a child parading in outdated and tattered finery. Shirley found this endearing, so long as she didn't have to live with it.

It didn't take J.Q. or Allison long to find the method in the day's madness. They stopped to watch a potter who was dropping horsehair on pots taken hot from the kiln, the hair shriveling into coils of ash that left wormy trails on the creamy clay. They stopped to look at the hand-loomed clothing and triangular pillows with black appliquéd hair and embroidered features, made to look like Indian mamas with babies in their shawls. They stopped in several small shops-cum-galleries devoted to what Shirley and J.Q. called hoon-kay, "junque": the trite, the arid, the banal, all offered for sale with total sincerity. In each place, Shirley conversed, she chatted, she smiled and was pleasant, and of every conversee she asked the same question. Had they known Bridget McCree?

In the street's one large gallery, from behind a large wood-and-tin cupboard seat that, though beautifully crafted, most resembled a satanic outhouse, J.Q. muttered, "We should have known something was up. She was entirely too nice at breakfast."

Allison, who had been watching Shirley with ill-concealed disbelief, nodded in agreement and wonder. The Shirley she was observing was a different Shirley. "How does she do that? How does she get them talking like that?"

"J.Q.," Shirley called from the other side of the room. "This lady is Laura Lee Prentice, and she knew Bridget when she lived here in Madrid."

J.Q., trailed by Allison, went solemnly over to the counter, where a lanky woman presided over the credit-card machine with the observant and slightly timorous air of a maidenly jackrabbit.

"Knew Bridget, did she?" J.Q. asked, with spurious geniality. "Isn't it a small world."

"I was just telling her about Bridget's sad death," said Shirley, with downcast eyes. "About wanting to find anyone who might have known her when she was here, for her brother's sake."

Laura Lee Prentice folded her paws at chest level, enthralled by the drama of it all. Twitching her nose, she said, "I didn't know her very well. She moved out here about four years ago. She rented one of those old houses on the hillside, west of here. It was just a shack, really. I wouldn't have lived in it."

"Is it still there?"

"Her house burned, but the house nearest it is still there. The people who bought it are fixing it up."

"You didn't know Bridget well?"

"Well, I didn't and I did." The paws came down to make little patting gestures at the countertop. "It's a tiny little town. Once the tourists leave, there's hardly enough of us to lose anybody. We all see each other, at the post office, at the grocery. People gossip. You know."

"They gossiped about Bridget?" Shirley asked, guilelessly.

"She had a lover," said Laura Lee. "Well, I mean, people do, don't they? One kind or another, spiritual or corporeal. Hers was corporeal, and he skulked, sneaked, slithered around. In Madrid, people don't bother sneaking much, so he sort of stood out. Or didn't, I guess you'd say."

"He drew attention to himself by his absence, as it were?" Shirley asked. "He was covertly conspicuous?"

"How was it he sneaked?" asked J.Q., alert to nuance.

"Never came until after dark, always parked behind her house, always left before sunup. I'd call that sneaky."

"Definitely sneaky," Shirley agreed.

"And then a couple of years ago, he stopped coming so often, and then he stopped altogether, and she took up with Buffalo Man, and everyone knew what *that* meant."

"What?" asked Allison, all eyes.

Laura Lee flushed. "Child, I forgot you were here."

"She's not really a child," Shirley advised. "She knows the facts of life. What did it mean?"

With a wary glance in Allison's direction, Laura Lee

97

went on: "Well, it had to mean she was sleeping with him, because the only women Buffalo Man ever bothered with were the ones he was healing or the ones he was sleeping with. He used to tell Myron—Myron was my partner who died last year—that if you were giving your life to the healing arts, you needed renewal more than most men."

"How did she keep them straight?" asked Allison, with disarming and unfeigned interest. "How did the sneaky one know when to stay away?"

"Oh, Buffalo Man never went to her. No. She came to him. He had a thing about territory. Women came to him, on his terms. At least, that's what Myron told me. Anyhow, she didn't really start with Buffalo Man until the other one had almost quit coming around."

"And where is Buffalo Man now?" Shirley asked, fascinated.

"North of town, six feet down. Poor man. Hit by a car, a year ago last summer. Bridget was all broken up over it. And then she moved. Couldn't stand the associations, I guess. Painful memories."

"Such a small place." Shirley nodded. "One would more or less have to remember the whole town. Not like a city, where you might only remember certain places. The park where you met. The first dinner together at such and such a restaurant. The wild passionate night spent in a certain hotel."

"This is a side of your life you hadn't told me about," said J.Q. gravely.

"I was being illustrative," Shirley confessed.

"I do think you're right," Laura Lee murmured. "I think the whole town reminded her too much. So she moved."

"Right near us," said Allison.

"I heard she moved north of Santa Fe, and that sort of surprised us, Myron and me. I mean, everyone knows that's very pricey territory up there. We thought maybe she'd come into money."

"It's not that posh where we are," Shirley confided. "But she would have had to have the money to buy her house. Her brother says she owns it outright, and the cheapest place along there is over two hundred thousand."

"The Bridget we knew thought she was lucky when she sold a story for a few hundred." Laura Lee shrugged.

"Wait a minute," Shirley begged, scenting an interesting bend in the trail. "Sold a story? She was a writer?"

"Well, she wanted to be. You know. She went to workshops and kept sending things to publishers and all that. She quit her job and moved here to Madrid so she could give it her full attention, or that's what she said, anyhow. She didn't sell very much."

"And then she took up with Buffalo Man, and then he was killed, and then she moved," J.Q. summarized, shifting from foot to foot. "After which she became a healer herself."

"That's what Lydia Wafferneusse said! But I didn't believe it!"

"Lydia Wafferneusse?"

"Buffalo Man's daughter. His name was Wafferneusse, too. Hiram Wafferneusse. I guess with a name like that, you'd just as soon become a bison, or even a warthog, maybe." She giggled, a bunny giggle. "Anyhow, if you want to know more, you might ask Joana Jones and Kip Ellis. They were Bridget's neighbors."

"Or we could ask Lydia Wafferneusse?"

"She might know. Lots of the time she and her father weren't speaking, but she might know."

"And where is she?"

"She inherited the hogan, on west, up behind all the other houses. You go out the highway, south, and then there's a road leading back on the other side of the gully. There's an old tailings pile up there, and that's where Buffalo Man had his house and did his healing. Now that he's gone, his daughter lives there. She says it's warmer and cheaper than her place in Santa Fe."

"Another hogan," Shirley grunted.

"Dirt floor and all," Laura Lee agreed. "Well, like Myron used to say, no accounting for what some people eat for fun."

They went back outside. J.Q. said musingly, "What some people eat for fun?"

"Oysters," Shirley muttered. "Sago worms; witchetty grubs; caviar; lambs' kidneys. Scrambled eggs with calves' brains."

"Yech," said Allison. "What's a witchetty grub?"

"Something the Australian aborigines eat. And of course many jungle folk eat partially burned monkey, or charred tarantulas." She looked up and down the one main street of Madrid, which was only a slowed-down stretch of two-lane highway. "She said an old tailings pile?"

"I can see it over there." J.Q. gestured to the west. "I guess we'll drive."

They did drive, as far as the road leading upward to the top of the tailings pile. When they arrived there, however, they saw that walking was probably the best way to get up it. The Jeep would do it, but why bother?

A burro would do it better. Shirley leaned into the hill and climbed, stopping every now and then to rub her knee, breathe deeply, and curse at people who made life difficult for her by living in inaccessible places.

The hogan, when they arrived there, was a far cry from the one in which Bridget's body had been found. This was a substantial house, its curved sides made of slabs of tree trunk, with the bark on, a rounded roof covered with roll roofing and pierced by a black smokestack, with a door that hung straight and true in its weathered frame. Hogan it might be; primitive it was not. It even had a window on the east, facing the town.

J.Q. knocked, and after a moment the door opened.

"Yes?" the woman asked. She was as unlike Bridget as it was possible to be, blond and statuesque, more like a Brunhild than Minnehaha, though somewhat past the first flush of youth.

"Lydia Wafferneusse?" Shirley asked.

"Yes," said the tall woman again. "I'm Lydia. You're the woman Laura Lee was talking to. She phoned."

"You have a phone?"

"Phone, bathtub, flush toilet, microwave, the whole civilized bit. What can I do for you?"

"I wonder if you'd mind telling me whether you knew Bridget McCree?"

The woman snorted. "Knew *of* her. Yes. She was one of my father's women, more's the pity. She's dead, you know. Saw it in the paper even before Laura mentioned it." She opened the door a bit wider and beckoned. "Come in."

They went in. The floor was spread with several layers of colorful rugs, Far and Middle Eastern. The ceiling was made of log octagons, the lowest one resting atop the walls, each of the recedingly smaller ones shifted forty-five degrees, the assemblage creating a shallow dome finished off at the top with sapling latillas. The mud walls had been whitewashed and were hung with blankets, leather goods, pots, pans, a coffee-pot, pillows in a clear plastic sack, quilts in another. A woodstove took up most of the back wall, while a door in the left-hand wall led into a bathroom, lit by a sky-light and neatly laid in tiles of so many colors, styles, and sizes that they could only have been the accumu-lated leftovers from a hundred other jobs. The only fur-niture was a table with two chairs plus one easy chair beside the window.

"When Dad was alive, he had the rugs and furniture in the shack out back," she said in a conversational tone. "This was where he did his ceremonies. It's at least twenty degrees warmer in here in the winter than out in the shack, or in the house I had in Santa Fe."

"Interesting bathroom," said J.Q.

"Dad started out as a tile layer, before he got the call to become a Native American animal. Actually, he hurt his back and couldn't stand up quite straight. Some guy called him a buffalo, said he had a hump, and that gave him the idea for the name. Dad always said he was part Apache; I never knew for sure. He had a mounted buf-falo head hanging on the wall there, by the stove, kind of moth-eaten, but in the firelight I guess it looked im-pressive. The stuffing was coming out, so I put it out in the shack until Dad's friend Pete Merwiczi collects it. Dad promised it to Pete."

"You're not a healer?" Shirley asked.

"Me? God forbid. I teach Sunday school at the Baptist church. I wouldn't give all that heathen stuff house room."

"We're really interested in anything you can tell us about Bridget McCree," Shirley said, shifting her weight off of her steel knee, which was aching from the climb.

"Sit down! Where are my manners. All of you, sit down, the carpet's clean, you can sit on it, mostly that's where people do sit." This to Allison, then to Shirley: "Take the big chair."

Shirley did, feeling the pain ease. She knew intellectually that steel could not ache, and yet it often gave that impression. She rubbed it through the fabric of her jeans, feeling the hard edges of the nonbone with ever-renewed amazement. "Bridget McCree?" she reminded.

"Bridget McCree I didn't know from Adam. All I knew was, a year ago Dad got hit by this car, or truck, or whatever, nobody saw it, so nobody knows. He was in the hospital two days, then he died, and I came on up here to clean up, clean out, see what needed doing. I found a will, he left the place to me, which was a surprise, considering the words we had from time to time. And I found an envelope with Bridget McCree's name on it, and Dad's writing, 'deliver this in case of my death.' So, I delivered it. Found out from Laura Lee where she lived, not far from here, as it turned out, knocked on her door, and handed it to her. And that is the sum total of everything I know about Bridget McCree."

"Thick envelope or thin? What size?"

"Thick. Nine by twelve or so. Stuff inside, loose, like maybe some little boxes, decks of cards. Sealed, need I say."

"You didn't open it?"

"I'm a Christian woman, and I try to live by it, which is more than I can say for some that call themselves by the name. I took the envelope, I knocked on her door, I said, 'My daddy left this with your name on it,' and I turned and left, and that was that."

"We hear she was supposed to be a writer."

"That's what Laura Lee told me. But then when Daddy died, she started doing what he'd been doing. Maybe he left her his gift in that envelope."

"His gift?"

"That's what he always blamed it on, his healing. He always said it was a gift, and he had to use it or be ungrateful."

"Did he really heal people?"

"From what I hear, he healed heartache real well. He was good at that. He didn't fool around with counseling or any of that stuff, he just laid it out that heartache was a burden, and it was the person's job to lay it down, not to blame anybody, not to get even, not to explain, even. Just get rid of it, and he told people how, and those that did it, they healed. From what I can figure out, it was a sort of Navajo way, coming back into line with nature. I don't think he was able to do anything much for people with real diseases, you know, depression or paranoia or any of those, but heartache he was good at."

"You said Bridget was one of your father's patients."

"Right. There was an appointment book in his papers. It had all the names in it, the people he worked with. She was one."

"But you have no idea what he healed her of?"

"Heartache, like I said. Sadness. He lit candles and made smoke and talked to the spirits, and then he gave her duties to perform and mantras to say to drive the thoughts away, and after a while she was healed. Of course, you know most sadness goes away in time anyhow. Likely most of the people he healed would have healed on their own."

"What kind of sadness?"

"Love affair, probably. Mostly that was it. Deaths or sickness or love affairs. It was about the time Bridget's visitor stopped coming."

"You knew about that?"

"Got told after I moved here. It's a small town. Actually, it's only a hamlet. You can't keep a secret in a hamlet."

"Laura Lee said she thought Bridget and your dad were having an affair."

"That's possible. She was nice looking, and with the nice-looking ones, he usually tried at least."

"But you don't know anything about it."

"Not a bit. Dad did what he did; I didn't approve and he didn't care whether I did or not. He got hit by a car, and that makes me mad because probably the driver was drunk, and I disapprove of that on principle."

"Probably was drunk?"

"Well, they never caught him. Or her. I'm supposing inebriety. Lot of it going around."

Shirley got to her feet and offered her hand. Allison removed herself from the carpet, and they made their good-byes. Once outside in the fresh air, Shirley stood musing for a few moments, then suggested they find lunch.

"Place we passed driving in?" J.Q. suggested.

"That'll do," she replied, leading the way down the tailings pile toward the car, then back to the town. Hamlet. Whatever.

They had hamburgers and home fries and very good cherry pie. Shirley inquired the way to the house of Ellis and Jones and was told it was the first blue house on the road past the one they had used to get to the hogan. When they had eaten, they went back westward, looking for a blue house.

They found a sapphire-blue house, with violet trim and deep green detailing, tightly girdled by a picket fence. A hundred feet away lay the charred bones of another house, evidently the one Bridget had occupied. A denim-clad couple of uncertain years were busy before the blue house, spading and raking the minuscule area inside the picket fence. A child's red wagon stood ready, laden with potted rosebushes.

"Jones or Ellis?" Shirley inquired.

"Yes," said both, looking up.

"Did Bridget McCree live there?" Shirley pointed at the remains.

"Up until a year or so ago," said the male half of the couple. Or, Shirley thought, the taller. Actually, each could have been either, and she was uncertain as to their actual sex.

"She did," said the other belligerently. "So what?"

"We're trying to find out anything that might help a murder investigation," Shirley said in her most pleasant voice.

"Who got killed?" the taller one demanded.

"And what's it to us?" said the other.

"Bridget was murdered."

"No shit!" remarked the taller. He or she put down the rake and came to the fence, offering a hand. "Kip Ellis. You think somebody from here?" Up close he was definitely a he.

"No particular reason to think that, no. My name's McClintock, Shirley McClintock. This is J.Q. and Allison. We're simply trying to find anyone who knew her, anyone who could give us some information about her friends, people she knew."

"She knew us," said the belligerent one. "I'm Jonah. My mother spelled it J-O-A-N-A, Mrs. McClintock—"

"Ms., not Mrs.," said Shirley, deciding that Joana was definitely female. "Neither of my husbands was named McClintock."

"Well, now we've got all that straight," said Kip, "come on in and sit."

Shirley, J.Q., and Allison went in and sat on the porch bench while the two gardeners sat on the steps.

"She had this guy used to come see her," said Joana. "He'd drive in at night, tennish or so, with his lights out. He'd park around behind her place and go in on the far-side door, so we never laid eyes. Big car, though. Black. Not a stretch, but biggish."

"Then," said Kip, with relish, "all hell would break loose. It was like a jungle film. All those howler monkeys."

"Fights?" Shirley asked, confused.

"Lust." Kip grinned. "Like a porn movie with the tube broke. All we got was the sound track."

Allison fixed her eyes on her shoes, told her face not to turn red, and tried to look uninterested. Shirley, with a sidelong glance at her, decided to plow ahead. "Did anybody use any names during these . . . set-tos?"

"Honeykins." Joana giggled. "Panther. Peach bottom."

"Peach bottom?" J.Q. asked, enthralled. "Which one, him or her?"

The couple broke up laughing. "Both!" he hooted, lost in raucous spasms.

Shirley grinned. Well. Nice to know Bridget had had a fun time sometime in her life. "You have no idea who he was?"

"Not a bit. Never asked. Made it a point of pride never to show any interest whatsoever." Kip nodded his satisfaction with this course. "So, one night I said to Joana, hey, Rolls-Royce isn't coming around so often anymore—that's what we called him, not that he drove one, he didn't, but his vehicle was big and black, that genre, you know. And then it wasn't but a few weeks until I said, hey, he's not coming around at all. And Joana said that's right. We never saw him after that."

"When did the visits stop?"

"Oh, was it a year ago? No. I'm a liar. Closer to two years. Rolls-Royce's visits got sort of sporadic through the winter; Bridget started keeping company with the bison; then the visits stopped altogether in the spring. Bridget and Buffalo became a thing, you know, then early summer, Buffalo got killed. Not long after, Bridget moved away. That was a little over a year ago."

"Buffalo Man wasn't her only visitor," said Joana. "There was that tycoon."

"Oh, right, the tycoon."

"Who was he?"

"Well, after she broke up with Rolls-Royce, this other person came to her house a few times. He had a white sports car, he came in the middle of the day. Tall, blond guy. We called him Tycoon because he carried a briefcase."

"Different guy from her lover?"

108

"We assume so. Different car, different behavior," said Kip.

Shirley said, "You say she and Buffalo Man became a thing? You mean more than just her going up to his place?"

"All over town. In the saloon. Having lunch together. Snuggly as a bunny."

"Was that typical for Buffalo?"

Joana replied, "He wasn't the sort of man you could call typical. Nothing typical about him."

"How about Bridget? What was she like?"

"I thought you knew her?" Kip said, suspicious.

"As a woman who lived down the road, sure. I knew her name, I knew she did healing ceremonies in a kind of hogan thing she built out back, I knew she dressed in fringed buckskin. That was about it."

The two of them looked at one another, eyebrows raised. Kip shrugged finally. "I guess we don't know much more than you did. She'd come over for coffee sometimes. We thought she was poor, like all the rest of us. Mostly she talked about her writing. That's what we mostly talk about here in Madrid. Our art. Whatever it is. If you live here, everybody supposes you've got an art. You may not be much good at it, but that's not the point.

"So, one day she said she was moving, she'd bought a house. She got the money from somewhere."

"She didn't say where?"

"She didn't say. Kip and me, we figured Buffalo left it to her."

Shirley shook her head. "He left all his property to his daughter."

"Maybe she inherited it," said Kip. "Maybe that's what Tycoon was there for, bringing her an inheritance."

"She got out just in time," Joana mused. "House burned the week after she moved. Wonder where Bridget got money?"

Shirley, disbelieving the casino story, also wondered. In her experience, unexplained money was often associated with unexplained death.

On the way back through town, they stopped at a place where Shirley had spotted a pig, a very tiptoed spotted pig, snout raised and ears erect, carved out of wood and standing about six inches tall.

"Where are you going to put it?" Allison wondered.

"In my room," Shirley replied. "On my desk. I like looking at it. To my mind, that's what a pig ought to look like."

"Um," said Allison. Jeremy's pig wouldn't look anything like that. He would be fat and short and saggy. Still, it was evidence that Shirley was thinking about pigs, so it was probably a good sign.

They returned home, with a side trip to the dairy to pick up milk, and one to the drugstore to get some antihistamines for Shirley. When they drove into the driveway, about five, Brian McCree was sitting in his car, head back, eyes closed. For one terrible moment Shirley thought he was dead, but he roused himself when they drove up.

"Ms. McClintock? I've got to go back to Denver tonight. I stopped by to thank you, and I wanted to ask a favor. . . ."

Shirley invited him in, sat him down at the table and offered him a cup of something warm. "Tea? Cocoa?"

"Cocoa," he murmured. "You know, that would taste

good. I haven't felt like eating, and I didn't sleep all night."

Shirley busied herself. Hot fresh milk, sugar, and Italian chocolate, frothed together with a whisk and flicked with cinnamon. She and Allison each had a cup also, though J.Q. preferred a small glass of Madeira.

"You stayed at Bridget's last night?"

He nodded. "I'd already checked out of the motel and I had my suitcase in the car. This morning I went for a walk, thought it might clear my head a little, but it didn't seem to."

"You wanted to ask a favor?" Shirley said.

"Yes. If you hear of anything to do with the deed on the Montana property, would you give me a call. I'll stay in touch with the sheriff's office, but I don't think they're going to find much. Did you see the papers this morning? The paper's playing up this extraterrestrial thing like crazy. I thought the sheriff was sort of off-the-wall, but evidently a lot of people down here really believe this stuff."

"Maybe we can get them off that track," Shirley said.

He thanked her, taking a card from his wallet and painstakingly writing his home address and phone number on it, blinking as though he found it difficult to focus.

"You're still tired out," Shirley commented. "Do you think it's wise to drive when you're this tired?"

"No," he admitted. "I don't. I'll probably stop the car at a rest stop and sleep for a few hours. I just couldn't get to sleep last night, and I can't stay any longer."

"You can sleep here, in a bed, more safely than at a rest stop." And more soundly, she thought, than in a room near that hogan where Bridget's body had been found.

"I don't want to impose. . . ." He sighed.

"It wouldn't be," said J.Q. "Bring that cup with you. You can stretch out on the bed in my quarters for a few hours." J.Q. occupied a small bedroom/sitting room combination near the apartment Xanthippe Minging usually occupied, giving him room, so he said, to flatten out if he liked.

When J.Q. returned, he was shaking his head sadly. "Poor guy. He's so worried about his wife he's at wit's end. They're not sure she's going to make it. Then to have this happen to Bridget. Sounds like he was pretty fond of her."

"Do you suppose someone stole his papers?" Allison asked.

"He said the land was worthless," Shirley mused. "So what motive would there be?"

"I guess mostly people steal things they can use," Allison commented. "Or sell."

"Or they steal out of altruism, to keep the economy alive," Shirley said, taking a sack of broccoli out of the refrigerator.

"What?" J.Q. asked, pulling his head out of the pantry, where he'd been looking for his pipe cleaners. "What about the economy?" J.Q. normally reserved to himself all matters pertaining to the economy, considering other members of the family insufficiently informed to have the right of comment.

Shirley turned, hands on hips. "I've been thinking lately, in this country, manufacturing is only managing to stay afloat because the market is multiplied through theft—"

"What do you mean?" asked Allison.

"You buy a TV or a car, somebody steals it, you col-

112

lect on your insurance and buy another one, the manufacturer has sold two for one. Meantime the thief sells the thing, whatever, supporting yet another economy. Multiply that by millions, all of us with insurance evening out the cost of extra everythings for everyone. The theft economy keeps the country running. If we actually stopped people stealing, the economy would collapse and so would the standard of living for poor people. They're mostly the ones that buy the stolen stuff, cheap."

"That's why poor people all have TVs?"

"Sure. Not telephones, or washers, but TVs. They're portable, they're stealable, so they get heavily doubled in the economy. If we really wanted to increase manufacturing and improve the standard of living, we'd start making useful things that are easier to steal. Portable washers and dryers, for instance. . . ."

"Microwave dryers," J.Q. said. "In the near future."

"Sure. And folding sonic washers you can tuck under your arm. Folding refrigerators and stoves. And we're already seeing heavy theft of cellular phones and car airbags. Well, you get the idea."

J.Q. snorted and went back to burrowing.

"What are we having for supper?" Allison asked.

"We are having ham and potatoes au gratin. I put that in the oven before we left this morning. And we're having broccoli, and tomato salad, and there's an ice-cream pie for dessert. We'll leave a little for Brian, when he wakes up. Poor man."

"Poor wife, too," said J.Q. "I still think it's strange the papers he needs should have disappeared."

"No doubt it was the same extraterrestrials that did away with Bridget," Shirley said, slicing tomatoes with great vigor. "They've done enough cattle mutilations and kidnappings to have figured out our culture. Now they're going to steal some property and settle down. Montana's their chosen place, because there aren't many people there to worry them."

"Are you going to share this theory with the Rio Grande Sheriff's Office?" asked J.Q., clearing the newspapers off the table.

"No, I can almost guarantee they'll come up with it all by themselves." She sprinkled parsley and chopped onion over the tomatoes, threw in a handful of ripe olives, and reached for the salad dressing. "Let's eat. And let's talk about something else."

About me, thought Allison, in a panic. She's going to want to talk about me.

Like a reprieve, the phone rang and she ran to answer it.

"Allison? It's Tad. Listen, did you go there, you know, yesterday. Before, I mean."

"What do you mean?" she gargled at him.

"I mean, I wasn't there. I couldn't get there. But the paper says Dawn was there, and you found her."

"Taddeus," she said, suddenly gaining ten years' wisdom in one fell stroke, "she was there because you told her to be."

Silence.

"She was there because . . . she wanted to watch."

Still silence.

"Right?"

A gurgle. "Oh, God, it's all such a mess. . . ."

She hung up on him.

"Watch what?" asked Shirley, suddenly looming.

Allison burst into tears.

4

"And then," said Shirley in an agitated voice, "Allison tells me all about this Bunch, this club, this . . . abomination."

"Which probably didn't actually exist," said J.Q. They were sitting by the fire in the library, a smaller and cozier room than the cavernous living room, which J.Q. persisted in calling the Salon Grand Central.

"Which probably didn't. It was a setup, designed to humiliate and embarrass. And this Tad person was part of it."

"You believe."

"Allison believes. The only way Dawn would have known to go to that particular place is if she and Tad had conspired. Why else was she there?"

"Are you going to call the sheriff's office and tell them about this?"

"I can't!" she exploded. "Not without explaining

what Allison was doing there, why Dawn came there. Not without telling the world that Allison was going to get herself tupped in the arroyo out of a desire to be one of the girls."

"Was she, really? Going to?"

"Well, we'll never know, will we?"

J.Q. frowned, distinctly uncomfortable. "What does she say?"

"She says she thinks not. She thinks she'd have gone partway there, then decided not to."

"Did she like him that much?"

"Oh, J.Q., it isn't always liking at that age. When I was fifteen, the boys I liked the most weren't the ones I was drawn to sexually, you know? The ones I was drawn to sexually were the bad ones, the wicked ones, the ones girls' mothers told them to stay away from. It was that taint of the forbidden that really pushed all the lust buttons. That and curiosity."

"How about Martin? Your first husband?"

Shirley gave him a strange look. J.Q. never, ever asked such a personal question. "Martin wasn't really sexy, no. He was just a lovely man. But by the time I married Martin, I'd had some experience with the sexy ones. Fireworks boys—all that transitory brilliance and bang. Bill was sexier than Martin. Very uncomplicatedly sensuous."

J.Q. found his discomfort substantially increased by this reply, so he pursued the subject no further. Besides, Allison was the immediate concern. "So you don't think she really has a passion for him."

"I think she hasn't. I think she's curious, adrift, that she feels all her hormones in a sort of unfocused way, and that she's susceptible to nasty little manipulators like Tad Pole."

"So, what do we do about it?"

She flung herself down, recoiling at once as her steel knee refused to accommodate itself to this vehement treatment. "What we do is fill in the gaps, I guess. Allison and I have had lots of talks about sex, but I've never had to talk with her before about handling her own feelings and instincts, because she's just now really beginning to have them. So I talked to her about that, in spades, likening her hormones to an untrained horse that may be very exciting and wonderful, but you don't ride it until you can get a bit in its mouth and it's had some training."

"Interesting analogy," he snorted.

"Well, it's one she understood! I also gave her a book I've been saving." She heaved a huge breath, trying to calm down. "I also suggested that intimacy, by its very nature, exposes one to the extremes of both pleasure and embarrassment, both reward and danger, and that the best protection against being injured by intimacy is a long and trusting relationship. We talked about how the media, particularly TV, has broken down the normal barriers, the reticence, the shyness that used to serve as protection for women. Once you hear all the words and see all the acts on TV, what's there to be shy about? I've suggested that if she gets tempted again, on the basis of any but a long and trusting relationship, she should recall how she felt when she realized Dawn had been there as a witness."

"She had a camera, you know?"

"Dawn did?"

"Um. It was under her body. I didn't think of it until just now."

"That little bitch!"

"Was that the sum total of your conversation?"

"I may have mentioned that Tad's coming from a so-called good family does not make him immune to AIDS."

J.Q.'s nostrils lifted slightly. "I'm *so* glad you waited until after supper to tell me all about this."

"Well, I'm probably angrier now than I was then. I tried to keep myself bridled when I was talking to Allison."

"How does she feel?"

"About the way I would have, under similar circumstances." She sighed, reaching for the glass of Glenfiddich J.Q. had thoughtfully provided. "Hideously self-conscious. I'm going to have to talk to Tad."

"Why?"

"Because I don't want to set the police on him, for reasons already mentioned. Someone has to find out what the little punk knows, if anything. He told Allison he couldn't get there. I'm betting he did get there."

"You think he saw something?"

"Saw, or heard."

"Saw Dawn get shot?"

"At least."

"Very well. How do we get at him to talk to?"

"At school tomorrow. We wait outside until he shows up and then we abduct him. We tie him up and beat him with heavy sticks."

He rose and patted her on the shoulder. "There, there," he said. "Calm down. I honestly don't think your committing a capital crime would be at all helpful."

118

"You sound like Numa," she said, sulking. Numa was her Colorado lawyer, one who had always counseled patience.

"Good. You need a stabilizing influence."

"Well, you come up with something."

"I suggest you involve that teacher Allison thinks so highly of. The one who wants you to adopt the pig."

"Jeremy Patterson."

"Himself. Explain to him that Tad and Dawn were involved in a prank—nature of prank unspecified—and that it is necessary for you to talk to Tad, quietly, privately, rather than go to the police."

She sighed. J.Q. was right. "He's probably in the phone book. You or me?"

"Me. Man-to-man."

"Thank you, J.Q."

"Not right now, however."

"Oh?"

"I just saw Brian go by the window."

They went out to join Brian in the driveway, where he was going through his pockets, looking for keys.

"Did you have a rest?" she asked.

He yawned. "I slept hard. Must have been two or three hours, at least."

"Closer to four." She opened the car door for him, then frowned and shut it again. "J.Q., look here."

He and Brian both came to look at the large dark stain coming from the car.

"Something's leaking," said J.Q. He got down on his knees, rolled onto his back, and peered up. "Brian, have you had any trouble with the brakes on this car?"

He shook his head in bewilderment. J.Q. got laboriously to his feet and brushed off his trousers. "It looks like to me your brake line has been cut. The fluid has all leaked out."

"Cut?" Brian's voice squeaked. "How could it have been cut?"

"By somebody with a pair of snips, I'd say. It's a clean cut, not a bash as though you'd hit something."

"Come in the kitchen," Shirley demanded. "We'll call the garage. There's a man we know who does emergency repairs."

"Oh, I'm sure I can get to a garage. Surely it's—"

"It's dangerous," said J.Q. firmly. "Maybe fatal. Phyllis wouldn't want you to risk your life, Brian. Now come on."

They went into the kitchen, and J.Q. busied himself with the phone, tracking down his friend who, on a Sunday night, was not eager to fix brake lines. He finally agreed to do so first thing in the morning.

"You'll stay here," said Shirley. "There's a guest room. J.Q. and you can see to the car in the morning, and you'll get home a few hours late."

"Late for work—"

"Call your boss."

"With Phyllis sick, I've had so much time off lately. . . ."

"Tell him there's been a death in the family and you'll be a day late getting back."

After a few more halfhearted demurrals, Brian consented to stay. J.Q. served him the food they'd set aside and, when he'd finished eating, took him to the guest room.

"Poor guy," he said, returning to the kitchen where Shirley still sat over her scotch.

"Did you really think the line was cut?" she asked. "First Bridget, then Dawn, now Brian?"

"A murder attempt? Surely not."

"If he'd left when he meant to, he'd have been up on La Veta Pass when his brakes gave out."

"Who?" J.Q. murmured.

"Wouldn't we like to know?" she replied, rubbing her forehead fretfully. "Also, why?"

On Monday, after Brian had been sorted out and sent on his way, J.Q. went to see Jeremy Patterson at the school, waiting around until he was free for a few moments between classes. Though Patterson was intrigued by J.Q.'s request, he repressed any sign of curiosity when he found Tad Pole in the cafeteria and asked him to come to his classroom that afternoon after school.

Tad arrived to confront not one but three people, including two he would just as soon not have seen under any circumstances.

"We've met," said Shirley. "Allison introduced us. You remember J.Q.?"

"Mr. Quentin. Ah . . . how are you, sir?"

"Not in a very good mood," J.Q. responded. "More to the point, how are you?"

"I'm . . . I'm all right."

Shirley settled herself. She and J.Q. had already agreed with Jeremy Patterson that he should be a witness to the conversation so they didn't get accused of abusing Tad psychologically, or beating on him, which Shirley rather wanted to do. She began without equivocation.

"What time did you get to the arroyo on Saturday, Tad?"

"I . . . I didn't, I mean I couldn't. . . ."

She adopted a pained expression. "Please. We know you were there. At this point, we don't want to involve the police, but we will, if necessary."

"Listen, you don't understand. If my father got to know about this, he'd . . . he'd kill me."

"That's helpful to know. If you refuse to talk to us, we'll call your father." She regarded him balefully. "Now. What time did you get there?"

He flushed, started to deny, caught Jeremy Patterson's skeptical eyes fixed on him, muttered, "A . . . a little before eleven."

"Was Dawn already there? Or did she arrive later?"

"She came with me. I picked her up outside her house; we parked up by the road and we walked down the arroyo from there."

"You remained down in the arroyo, and she went up on the rim to find a place to hide, right?"

He was sweating. "Actually, we both went up on top and found a place for her to hide first. Then I went back down."

"You knew she had a camera?"

"She did?" He flushed scarlet.

"She did. Did you talk back and forth?"

"Not much. We thought . . . someone might be coming."

"Allison."

"Right. I mean, Allison said—"

"Never mind what Allison said, Tad. She didn't get there, so she's out of it. You were there, so you're in it. Now, you're down in the arroyo, doing what?"

"Standing there, looking down the arroyo, waiting for . . . for Allison."

"Not talking?"

"Not really. It was quiet. I leaned up against the bank and just sort of waited. There was a bunch of crows down there, perched all over a pile of junk, pecking and squawking, making a racket. I watched them for a while. I looked at my watch a couple of times. The last time was two or three minutes to eleven. Right then I heard Dawn say something, and I turned around and looked up where she was. She'd been lying flat, and now she was reared back on her arms, looking over her shoulder, and she said something—what are you doing here, or why are you here, or something like that. Then I heard the shot and she . . . she fell forward. Her arm flopped over the edge and just sort of . . . dangled there."

"Where did the shot come from? What direction?" asked J.Q.

"I couldn't tell. It came from up there somewhere, but like from all over. No direction to it. I thought it must have come from behind her, because she was looking in that direction."

"What did you do?" Shirley demanded.

"The arroyo bank makes a sharp point where the arroyo splits. I went around the point, around the far side, away from whoever was up there, and I pushed right up tight to the bank, to hide. I figured whoever it was might come after me. The birds had gone quiet. The shot scared them, I guess. I could hear someone. . . ."

"Moving? Talking? What?"

"Moving. I thought the person might come down in the arroyo, after me, so I got away from there, right along the bank—"

Shirley interrupted. "The arroyo runs southeast–

northwest along there. Where it splits, one leg goes off southwest. You were in the northwest leg, moving away from the bank Dawn was on? In the direction you expected Allison to come from?"

He nodded. "I came to a cut in the bank with some stuff growing in it, and I went in there and hid for a long time. After a while the crows started making a racket again, and I figured whoever it was had gone, so I came out and walked back. She was still there, with her arm dangling. She wasn't moving."

Shirley scowled. "Did you go up top? Did you look at her?"

"I . . . no. I ran down the arroyo to the car."

"So you don't even know if she was dead?"

"I knew."

"How?"

"I don't know. I just knew." He rubbed at his face. "Maybe I figured whoever shot her checked to be sure she was dead."

"Then what? You got in your car and went home?"

He nodded miserably.

"No call to the sheriff's office? No nothing?"

"I didn't know where to call! I don't know where the county line is out there. Some of it's Rio Grande County and some of it's Santa Fe County, and some of it's San Pedro land. You don't understand. If my father—"

"What's to understand?" she exploded. "You're a cowardly little shit. What were you going to get out of all this little plan?"

He flushed brick red, shaking his head.

J.Q. said in a sarcastic tone, "No doubt Dawn offered

some inducement. More to the point, who could she have been speaking to?"

"I don't know."

"Someone she knew, obviously. If you've quoted her correctly, that is. 'What are you doing here?' You don't ask a stranger that question."

"Maybe her boyfriend," he mumbled, looking at his shoes.

"Who was he?" Shirley asked.

"I don't know. Nobody knew. She told Breeze he was from UNM."

"Did her parents know?"

Tad shrugged, then straightened. "Her father . . . her stepfather knew she had a boyfriend. Dawn was talking to Summer, on the phone, all about him, and she said, 'Damn, my father overheard me.' "

"Summer told you this?"

"Yeah."

"But her stepfather didn't know who it was?" asked Patterson.

Tad shook his head. "No. He didn't know. Last Friday he even asked me if I knew who Dawn's boyfriend was."

"Why would her boyfriend want to kill her?" Shirley asked.

"Maybe she . . . she was getting it on with the guy that takes care of her horses. Maybe her boyfriend was jealous."

"You know this?"

"I . . . maybe she was."

"Why?"

"The way she touched him, and talked to him. Like he . . ."

125

He'd been going to say, *like he was one of the horses,* but he decided that sounded silly. "They just looked like a couple who might be . . . you know."

J.Q. drawled, "This is based on how many observations."

"A few." He flushed. "Three or four. I used to go over there and sort of hang around. I'd see her, and him."

"Him being?"

"She called him Seed-row. He's . . . Hispanic, or maybe Indian, I don't know."

Shirley nodded. "That gives us two candidates for murderer, both motivated, presumably, by jealousy. Anyone else you can think of?"

He shook his head. "Ask Breeze and Summer. They were her friends."

"We shall," Shirley promised. "If Mr. Patterson will kindly consent to arrange it. Meantime I think you should go to the Rio Grande County Sheriff's Office and tell them what you have told me."

"My dad . . . he'll—"

"I think your father will find a good deal more fault with you if you don't. You picked up a friend and decided to walk down the arroyo to do some bird-watching. Your friend was watching from up on the bank, and you were down in the arroyo, both of you observing crows, when you heard the shot. Is there anything false in that?"

He shook his head angrily.

"You hid, you came out, you saw she was dead, you went on home. You were no doubt in a state of shock. The only thing anyone will hold against you is that you didn't tell anyone, or call the police. That does somewhat baffle me, as well."

"I'm just not as good at thinking up stories as you are," he exploded. "I didn't want to tell him."

Shirley drawled, "You didn't want to tell him your real reason for being there. I quite understand. It doesn't cast you or Dawn *or* Allison in a very flattering light. I'd prefer you don't talk about that little plot, not to anyone. That includes your friends, male or female, here at school. If I ever hear one word involving Allison, you may be sure I'll do everything in my power to make sure your parents and neighbors and every distant relative knows just what you were up to. Nonetheless, I do think you need to tell the sheriff's office you were there."

"They might think I—"

"Do you have a rifle?" asked J.Q.

"No. My mother doesn't like guns."

"Sensible woman. Have you ever fired a rifle?"

"No."

"Then their interest in you shouldn't last long. The victim was shot from a distance by a good marksman, and you don't qualify. We're not going to press the matter, Tad, but if someone asks us, we'll tell them."

Jeremy Patterson, who had been sitting silent throughout all this, leaned forward and asked, "Anything else?"

Shirley started to shake her head, then stopped. "Yes. When you were standing there, Tad, looking down the arroyo, did you see tire tracks? A four-wheel-drive vehicle, maybe. Waffle-iron-type tires."

He frowned, then nodded. "Yes. There were tracks

down both legs of the arroyo. We noticed them when we were walking, on the way there."

Shirley waved her dismissal. Patterson nodded at the door and, when Tad had taken himself off, asked, "Do I understand from all this that Dawn and Tad were going to embarrass Allison in some fashion?"

"Embarrass is a good word," Shirley confirmed. "I think they would have done that, at least."

"A sexual encounter in front of a witness?"

Shirley smiled grimly.

"Why?" the teacher asked, leaning back in his chair.

"I think Dawn put Tad up to it because she didn't like Allison."

"The presence of the camera made that clear," said J.Q. "It was under her body."

Jeremy nodded, bemused, slowly turning a pencil in his hands. "This was Dawn's second year with us. This isn't her type of school, as she has from time to time made abundantly clear. She was a shameless manipulator, especially of male teachers; I can attest to that. She disliked the female ones. She didn't mind grovelers and sycophants, but she wouldn't stand for competition. I witnessed a conversation between her and Summer once, during which Dawn managed to convince Summer that she'd look better in another hairstyle. Summer showed up looking like something off the rock stage; it's partly grown out, but it's still unflattering, and I know very well Dawn intended it to be.

"You think the other two girls were in on it? You really want me to arrange an interview?"

"I think we need—someone needs—to know what they know, but I really don't want to drag Allison's name into it if it's unnecessary."

"Would you leave it to me to find out what Summer Smythe and Breeze Watkins know?"

"Gladly." She got to her feet, offering J.Q. a hand. "If those three are the psychological measure of your student body, I don't know how you stand it."

"Oh, I let it run off me. I'm working on my doctorate at the university. I get down there a couple of evenings a week. That sort of keeps me sane."

Shirley started out, pausing at the door to say, "By the way, Jeremy, we'd be glad to solve your pig problem for you."

He grinned, rather ruefully. "Pig pro quo?"

"Something like that."

When Tad left the school building, he went through the parking lot on his way to his car, not his, precisely, but one he sometimes drove if his mother didn't need it that day. He had to pass the Jeep that said RANCHO DEL VALLE on its door, with Allison in the front seat. She wasn't looking at him, or at anything much. He could probably go on by and she'd never see him, which somehow seemed about as annoying as it seemed attractive. He went directly to the Jeep, therefore, where he stopped and rapped on the glass.

She looked up, without expression. He opened the door a crack.

"Allison, I . . . I'm sorry."

"Yeah," she replied. "I'm sure."

"I had this thing for her," he blurted. "She . . . she sort of led me on."

Allison couldn't help it. "Poor thing," she whispered. "Her led him on. Nasty her. Is that why you killed her?"

129

"Come *on*, Allison. You know I didn't kill her."

"I don't know that! You were ready to do ... do something awful to me!"

He attempted an unsuccessful leer. "It wouldn't have been that awful."

"Tad, get out of this car, and get away from me, and go away generally. I hate you." She pulled the door to, locked it, leaned across and locked the other side, then turned her back on him. Why had she ever thought he was interesting? Why had she ever thought he was sexy? He wasn't sexy. He was just ... gross.

He slouched away, angry at her. He'd apologized, hadn't he? What more did she expect? What did any of them expect?

The answer to that question was clear. They expected him to go to some sheriff's office and tell what he knew. Well, he wasn't going to do it. And if somebody dragged him into it, he'd just tell them he didn't know he was supposed to tell anyone. He fueled his usual sense of dissatisfaction with this annoyance, though it didn't last. Within a few moments he was merely vaguely sad—a vague sadness was the best he'd been able to summon up regarding Dawn, which, in itself, was a source of some dissatisfaction. He had thought he was in love with her.

Meantime, behind him in the lot, Allison was receiving another visitor.

"Ally, let me in," she said pleadingly.

"Go away, Summer."

"Pleeeease."

Allison rolled the window halfway down. "What do you want?"

"It's just so awful about Dawn."

"Yes. Getting killed is awful. Right."

"Do you think it was, you know, the man she knew?"

"What man was that?"

"The man she was dating. She was going with this man. He got her . . . things, you know."

"Things?"

"You know?"

"Stop saying I know when I don't. I don't know. What things?"

"Drugs. And, you know, sex things. I thought maybe, maybe he thought she'd get him in trouble or something. Maybe that's why he killed her."

Allison opened the door, somewhat unwillingly, and scooted over on the seat. Summer climbed in beside her, dragging her fingers through the tattered blond mop Dawn had suggested she wear, eyes very wide and plaintive.

"Tell me," Allison demanded.

"I don't know anything to tell, really."

"Whatever she said about this person, you tell me."

"Oh, Ally, I don't think—"

"When the sheriff's men came, one of them left me a card. Eddy Martinez, his name is. He told me to call him if I thought of anything, so I think I will call him and tell him you know something."

"You wouldn't!"

"The hell I wouldn't. You and your Bunch. I'd like nothing better than to get you and Breeze in it up to your necks. Now tell me or get."

Tears trembled. Of course, with Summer, tears always trembled. She could turn them on and off, like a shower.

"I mean it," Allison threatened. "You can cry a bucketful and I don't care." She felt suddenly very secure, very sure, warmed by anger and full of righteousness. She reminded herself of Shirley.

"Dawn said she was going with this older man. Breeze asked if he went to college, and Dawn said like maybe he did, maybe he went to UNM. She had this picture in her notebook, and she said it was him, he was to die for, you know? Like that guy in *Baywatch* only younger and better looking?"

"She actually had a picture of him?"

"He looked like about twenty-two or twenty-three. And she said he brought her stuff. She showed us some of the things, sex-shop things. And she had some cocaine. Breeze and me, we tried it."

"What was it? What kind?"

"Crack."

"Did Dawn use it?"

"I didn't see her. She gave it to us, though."

"You're really an idiot, you know, Summer."

"It was just a little bit. We didn't get hooked or anything."

Allison started to say something, then shut up. What business did she have telling Summer she was stupid. Look what she herself had almost done!

"Allison . . ."

"What!"

"It was all Dawn's idea, about the club, you know?"

"Is there a club?"

"Not really. She was just going to get you all . . . involved with Tad, then she was going to tell you it was a virgins' club."

"That's rotten."

"I know."

"Why did you and Breeze go along with that?"

"Why did you?"

Good question. Really good question. "I see Shirley and J.Q. coming, Summer. If you don't want them asking you questions, you'd better get out of here."

Which she did, sliding out the door and away before Shirley and J.Q. got to the car.

"Who was that?" Shirley asked.

"Summer Smythe. One of Dawn's friends."

"Ah."

"Came to apologize. I think. She admitted Dawn put Tad up to it."

"Well. Live and learn."

Allison burst into tears once more. It felt like she'd been doing nothing but cry since Saturday afternoon! "I feel like . . . I feel like an idiot! And I should have kept her here for you to talk to."

J.Q. put his arm around her shoulders. "Come on, kid. You're not dead or dying. You're alive, healthy, and in full possession of your faculties. Besides, your friend Mr. Patterson is going to do the inquisition bit with Summer and Breeze. He'll find out what they know, if anything. Right now we're most interested in who her boyfriend was. Tad thinks she was engaged in . . . ah, dalliance with the stable hand."

Allison shook her head angrily. "Then Tad doesn't know her very well. She wouldn't do that. Not Dawn. She'd tease him. She loved to tease men, she'd do it to anybody in trousers. But she'd never do anything much with some guy that works in a stable."

"Why is that?"

"She was too stuck-up. He wouldn't be good enough for her. She was careful about herself. She'd talk her

133

friends into things, but she didn't do them herself. Like, Summer just told me Dawn gave her and Breeze some crack, but she didn't use it herself."

"But she was a tease?" Shirley was going through her pockets, looking for the car keys.

"You said so yourself when we were talking about her. You said maybe was a tease word. She was that way with boys, too."

"Right. And in some cultures, teases get punished for it." Baffled in her search, she started over.

"You mean he might have been tired of it. Got mad at her and killed her."

"Might. Murders have happened with less reason."

"Summer says there's a picture of Dawn's boyfriend in her notebook."

Shirley's head came up, nostrils dilated, scenting the wind. "Well, now, that's interesting. Do you suppose you could catch Jeremy before he leaves, J.Q.?"

J.Q. went back the way they had come.

Shirley leaned on the car, thinking. "When you walked home from school on Friday, Allison, did you notice tire tracks in the arroyo?"

"Friday? They were there on Saturday, when I was riding Beau."

"I know. You said so. But what about the day before?"

"I think I'd have noticed them if they'd been there."

"The boy you met, Ulti? Do you think you could ask him?"

"I looked for him today, but he wasn't in school. At least I didn't see him."

"Tomorrow, then. If you don't see him, get his phone

number, if you can. Did Summer have anything else to say?"

"She said Dawn's boyfriend got crack cocaine for them, and that he bought a lot of sex toys for Dawn."

"Sex toys?"

"Oh, Shirley. You know."

She supposed she did. "Did they see them, or just hear about them?"

"She said Dawn showed them the sex things, and they tried the crack."

"Idiots."

They waited until J.Q. returned. "He'll get into her locker in the morning and call us. Also, don't you think that car-track information ought to be passed on to Eddy Martinez?"

Shirley nodded. "I'll drop in and tell him tomorrow, when I go to the newspaper office."

"Newspaper?" J.Q. asked, suddenly patting his pockets, taking the car keys from one of them and offering them to her.

"Oh, right," she said absently. "I couldn't find the keys because you had them. Well, yes, newspaper. They jumped on that ET business so fast, and the media got there so quickly. It would be interesting to know who tipped them off."

She got into the car, started the engine, listening to the hum of it for a moment before she put it in gear. "And there's the question of how the shooter got there."

J.Q. exclaimed, "I forgot to tell you! Martinez called this morning, while you were out. They found hoof tracks near a clump of piñons about fifty yards off the road. He thought they were left by Dawn's horse."

"Tad just told us they drove to the school, then walked."

"That's what I meant. If it wasn't her, it could have been the shooter's horse."

"Or someone else's horse, or a horse running loose, or tracks left there from three weeks ago, or—"

"Not much help, I agree," he said. "Are we going somewhere, or are we going to sit here thinking for a week or two?"

"We're going," she said, looking over her shoulder at the now empty lot. "If we're capable of any thought, we can do it somewhere else."

Tuesday morning, Shirley left J.Q. immersed in the month-end sorting of bills and balancing of the checkbook while she drove into Santa Fe. She dropped in on the Rio Grande Sheriff's Office to tell Eddy about the tracks, then she drove on into Santa Fe and visited the *Santa Fe Star*, where she was generally ignored until she accosted a slender midtwentyish creature with a harried air.

"You want to know what?" she asked, when she had separated herself from two other persons demanding this that or the other. "I'm sorry. We've got several people out, and everyone wants me at once."

"I wanted to know how and when your reporter learned about the death of Bridget McCree."

"I think Harold wrote that. Wait a minute." She scurried away to talk to a crouched gnome in blue, who shook his head violently and pointed over his shoulder. The inquirer made another stop and then came galloping back. "It was Wilson Brett. You want to talk to him?"

"If he will."

"He says sure." She pointed at the Santa Fe type in a Navajo-pattern sweater, and he raised one eyebrow in answer.

Shirley went over to his desk, waited while he dumped some papers onto the floor in a heap, then sat down. After mutual introductions, she said, "I'm a neighbor of Bridget McCree's. I was the one who discovered her body. The media arrived—that is, the TV truck did—just minutes after the police. Do you know, were they tipped off?"

He stroked his neat little beard and muttered, "Police radio. All the channels monitor the police radio for their damned insta-cams. Im-media-cams, I call'm. As in immoderate, im-moral, and im-material. Damned voyeurs!"

"They got here that fast, all the way from Albuquerque?"

He sat up a little straighter. "Maybe they were already in town."

"I wondered about that. It seemed fast, that's all. How was the paper informed about it?"

"We definitely picked it up from a police radio."

"Then, also, I wondered about the extraterrestrial emphasis. Who decided on that?"

He barked, a single humorless laugh. "I don't know where the TV got it, but you can blame my editor for it here on the paper. Somebody went to some trouble to make it look like ETs, and it fit right in with the cattle-mutilation story we'd been running."

"But if you don't believe it was ETs, why did you decide to play along with the killer?"

He frowned. "People were interested in the mutila-

137

tion story. Papers are about selling copies, you know. It was just natural to emphasize the weirdness."

"Nothing more than that? Just to sell copies."

"What other reason could there be? Everybody here at the paper had ETs on the brain already."

Shirley nodded. She'd had similar experiences, where coincidences seemed to take on a life of their own. "I was particularly interested because I knew French wrote about the mutilation and it was his daughter who was shot. Do you know about French's daughter?"

"Heard it on the news Sunday."

"There's an actual physical connection between the two deaths."

His eyes narrowed. "You're telling me what?"

"There were fresh tire tracks in the arroyo outside McCree's house, and they went all the way from there to the place Dawn French was shot, following the arroyo."

"Does the law know?"

"I told them just before coming here."

"Tracks that were there before the girl was shot?"

"Yes."

"When were they there?"

"Not immediately after the McCree killing. But by the next day."

He hummed to himself for a moment. "People ride horses in arroyos, or motorbikes or 4x4's. Around here, arroyos are sort of like roads. Just because a road runs past two places, that doesn't mean the two are connected in any other way."

She could accept that. "Possible. Maybe someone with an off-road vehicle might have heard about the

138

McCree killing and decided to go see the site via the arroyo."

"Still, it's interesting," he mused. "I'll keep it in mind. Might make a story for me, so I won't mention it to Dexter French. Or to Anne."

"You know them?"

"Well, yes. I was with a paper in Texas before I came here, and I covered those of Anne Pelton's activities that didn't show up on the society page. Horse shows, mostly. There were some things we knew we couldn't print. Like, she married some gangster when she was about eighteen, got pregnant, then he got himself killed over some drug deal. Not a word in any of the papers about that, not a word. There was a story going around how her dad, old man Pelton, sent her to Switzerland for a couple of years, then he picked Dexter French out of a catalog, and married her off to him."

"A catalog?"

"Like the horse-breeding book, you know?"

"A stud book?"

"I meant it metaphorically. Pelton wanted an Old Family, with Old Money." His intonation capitalized the words. "He wanted an Acceptable Son-in-Law, so he hired French for the job. The way Anne told it, her dad put Dexter on a salary, then he threw a huge Dallas wedding to make everybody forget she'd been married before. No child in evidence, either. Dawn got sneaked back into the family later, renamed French. I think Anne told me the truth, because even Dex calls himself a salaried employee, but I guess as a stud, he's a flop. They never had any other children."

"Do you know him well?"

"Well enough to call him Dex to his face. Well

139

enough to drink a beer with him now and again. That's about all. None of us common folk know him well. Salaried employee or not, he's a cut above the common herd."

"Moneyed dilettante?"

"No. I don't mean that. He's smart, and he's not afraid of work, and he's not a snob. He does a good job on whatever he writes about, but he's just not a working stiff. He writes what and when he chooses. He doesn't take orders from the editor or publisher. It's the Pelton family money that really supports him and Anne. When he works for money, it's for champagne money or for gambling money, maybe."

Shirley regarded him thoughtfully. "Why would you think that?"

"Because the word is he likes to gamble, and his allowance doesn't stretch that far. So he scratches a little. A writing job here, a commission there. He finds and sells houses for people. It comes easy, because of who he is, because of who he knows. He'll be here in the office, using the files, he gets a phone call, Dexter, honey, find me a nice place in Santa Fe, I'm bored with the Bahamas. Or somebody says, Dexter, sweetie, find me a buyer for this old place in Santa Fe, I'm going to try Palm Springs. He gets his commission whether they're going or coming."

"That must be nice."

"He just knows a lot of people. When Dex got into the Pelton clan, he got access to a lot more people who know people who know people, if you know what I mean. You pick up things in that kind of environment."

She frowned thoughtfully. "The Pelton clan being Mrs. French's people?"

"Right. The Frenches know the old money, and the Peltons know the new money. Between them, they pretty well blanket the investment field."

"But Dexter French doesn't have old money."

"He did have, he just went through it. The way I get the story, he came into the family fortune when he was about twenty-five, and by the time he was thirty, it was gone. That's when he married Anne Pelton. She was twenty-two, twenty-three."

"So Dawn was just a small child."

"Right. Since then Dex has made out all right. Lives on Anne's money, gets along with her, too. She dotes on him. And he makes enough of his own money to amuse himself with."

"One more question."

"Shoot."

"Why did you get picked to do the McCree story? Since it did have an ET angle, I'd have thought they'd put Dexter French on it."

"I told you. They don't *put* Dexter French on anything. He comes in, slaps the boss on the back, offers him a cigar, says he wants to do a story on Indian mysticism, will they buy it? Then they say yes or no."

She stood, offered her hand, and wandered out, lifting a hand to the harried female en route. "Thanks much."

"I heard you talking about Dexter French." She gave Shirley a wide-eyed look of complicity, dropping her voice. "It's so sad about his little girl."

"It is sad." Though perhaps inevitable, she thought to herself, emerging into the daylight once more.

When Shirley arrived at the ranch, she found a strange car parked there, a sleek, low, red vehicle she identified immediately as something pricey and foreign. A Porsche, perhaps. A Jaguar. A Mazzerwhoopee. There was nothing foreign, however, about the couple who got out of it. She was quintessential Santa Fe, from the designer cowboy boots to the swirling denim skirt, cashmere jacket, and felt hat with the silver-and-turquoise band. She was also a sullied beauty: pale, red-eyed, and pinch-lipped. He was lean and tanned, very slightly and becomingly graying, with lazy eyes.

Speak of the devils, Shirley told herself as the two approached. What do I want to bet—

"McClintock?" the woman asked while Shirley was unfolding herself from the driver's seat.

"Yes, ma'am," said Shirley, standing up straight and looking down at both of them. Even the man was a good deal shorter than she. "What can I do for you?"

"You can tell me what was going on between my daughter and your daughter," the woman grated, biting her words as though barely holding in a scream.

The tone set Shirley's teeth on edge. "Your daughter being?"

"Dawn! I'm Anne Pelton-French. I'm talking about Dawn!"

"Dear, now, now," said he, patting her shoulder in an accustomed gesture. He thrust out a hand. "Ms. McClintock, I'm Dexter French."

Shirley nodded. "I'm sorry for your loss. Please, come in."

The woman cried, "I don't want to come in. I want you to tell me—"

Shirley stiffened. "I'm going in. If you want to talk to me, you can come in. I'm not going to conduct a personal conversation out here in the driveway." She turned and went toward the kitchen door, paying no attention to the muttering behind her. At the door she stood aside and ushered them in. "Please sit down over there at the table," she said, then got out the kettle and filled it. When she had it on the stove, she sat down opposite them.

"I'm making us some tea. Now, what is this?"

The woman drew a deep, shuddering breath. "The sheriff's men said she was out there to meet your daughter!"

The man reached out once again, squeezing her shoulder.

Shirley shook her head slowly, deciding what to say. "That's not strictly true, no. Allison had planned to meet Taddeus Pole there at eleven Saturday morning, but we dragged her off to a neighbor's to help us with a job we were doing there, so she didn't get back here and get her horse saddled until after one. She rode out to see if Tad had by any chance waited for her. That's when she found your daughter's body."

"She wasn't supposed to leave the house. . . ." Anne French's voice trailed off, tears leaking from her eyes.

Dexter, on the other hand, seemed in full command of himself. He asked, "What was Dawn doing there?"

Shirley mused over this question, wondering what would be least false, least hurtful. "I assumed your daughter was out bird-watching with Tad. According to Tad, when the shooting happened, he was frightened, so he hid himself, then left the scene without reporting it. Actually, Allison wasn't there until later. Except for finding Dawn, Allison had nothing to do with it."

The kettle cleared its throat with a whistly gargle. Shirley removed it from the heat, rinsed out the pot,

143

measured tea, filled the pot, fetched cups, and set pot and cups on the table. During all this, Anne French merely sat, staring at her boots, tears trickling down her jaw in a slow, unconsidered rivulet while her husband patted her hand and watched her with total concentration. Shirley fetched a box of tissues from a drawer and put them on the table as well.

Seating herself, she asked gently, "Have you talked to the sheriff's people?" She poured tea, pushing cups toward her guests.

"Fools," said the woman, without thought or consideration, her voice a harsh, unthinking monotone. "Fools, my father says. All local enforcement. Hacks. Timeservers."

"Anne!" Dexter said. "Really."

She took a cup and sipped at it thirstily, seeming not to have heard him. "My father says they're good only for crowd control and shoot-outs."

"That hasn't been my experience," Shirley murmured. "I've met a good many intelligent, hardworking policemen, some clever, intuitive deputies. I've met two of the local men. They seem to know what they're doing."

"Not for us." She ignored her husband. "For ordinary people, maybe. Not for us."

"The police are all right for the simple folk?" Shirley breathed innocently.

"Yes. Not for us."

"Us, who?"

The woman looked up, eyes blazing, then suddenly realized where she was, who she was talking to. She flushed a deep, bruised red, lips pinching once more. "I'm sorry. I forgot myself."

144

Dexter French shook his head, said through gritted teeth, "She's very upset. She really did forget herself, Ms. McClintock. Sometimes she sounds more like her father than he himself does."

Shirley said dryly, "She might wish to remember herself when talking to the deputies, who are very probably among the simple folk, just as I am."

"I didn't mean . . ." Anne murmured.

"Yes. You did mean. I've heard that Dawn meant much the same kinds of things, and that attitude is what may have gotten her killed."

Anne French's face hardened. "Dawn knew what she was, who she was! That's all! Just as I know who I am!"

"Who are you?" Shirley asked.

"Anne Pelton-French! Daughter of Harry Pelton the Third. Of the Dallas–Fort Worth Peltons."

Eyebrows raised, Shirley glanced at Dexter French. He shrugged, with a rueful smile. "And who are they?" Shirley asked.

The hard face could not hold itself together. It dissolved, like sugar in a cup. The shoulders sagged, the head went down. She sobbed.

Shirley gritted her teeth. "I'm sorry, Mrs. French, truly. But an attitude of rather mindless superiority won't help find who killed her."

The woman went on crying, her husband went on patting, and Shirley cursed at herself. Why did she have to be so contentious? She had asked herself that one thousand times since New Year's, when she had made the resolution not to be obstreperous, only to break the resolution ten minutes later.

J.Q. came in through the kitchen door, peered at the

145

sobbing woman, and raised his eyebrows. Shirley shook her head and made an equivocal gesture. J.Q. went back out, and she heard him talking to someone outside the door. Too early for Allison to be home from school. Who?

"Will they find out who?" Dexter French asked. "I gathered the impression they had no clues at all."

Shirley started to tell him there were clues, of a sort, then swallowed the words. She didn't want to be involved with the Frenches, that much she was sure of. The woman set her hair on end.

Anne French murmured, wiping at her face with a tissue, "We just don't think they're getting anywhere."

"If you have no confidence in them, ask your father to hire investigators, or hire them yourself. But don't insult the sheriff's officers. They're doing what can be done."

"Would you ... would you investigate it?" the woman blurted.

"Me?" Shirley was dumbfounded. "Why would you ask me?"

"One of my acquaintances knows about you. He's an art dealer. Dennison McFee. He says you found out who killed a girl here, year before last. Someone who was shot?"

Shirley almost smiled. Dennison McFee. She hadn't seen him in too long a time. "That's true, but it hardly qualifies me as any kind of investigator."

"I'd pay you. A lot!"

Dexter French interrupted. "Now, Anne. Ms. McClintock is not an investigator. She'd have to be licensed to take money for doing something like that. Think, dearest. Please."

"Oh, Tigger, I'm so tired! Poor Dawn. And nobody's doing anything!"

She dissolved in tears, and he stood, bent over her, and wrapped her in his arms, murmuring sweet, meaningless words, in which "my little Pooh" figured frequently. Shirley kept her face impassive. Tigger and Pooh. Who would have thought it?

When Anne surfaced, her face had lost its hauteur. "I'm sorry. I'm being . . . unreasonable."

Shirley shook her head. "Look, if it will ease your mind, I'll go on asking the kinds of questions I've already been asking."

"What? What do you want to know?" Anne was all at once fervid, eager. "I'll help. Anything you want to know."

"Anything at all," agreed her husband. He handed his wife a tissue from the box on the table and sat forward, giving every appearance of rapt attention.

Shirley reached for the pot, filled their cups once more. "I'd like to know the name of the man Dawn was seeing."

Dexter French's eyes turned hard and cold. Anne French looked dumbfounded.

"Man? What man?" she asked.

"That's the question. She told her schoolmates she was dating an older man, a college boy, or a recent graduate. She mentioned UNM."

"Dawn wasn't. She wouldn't!"

"Wouldn't date?"

"Wouldn't associate with anyone without telling me!" Anger overcame grief for the moment. "We were very close! Besides, she hasn't been allowed to date."

"She could have been making up a story to impress

147

her friends," Shirley said, keeping the matter of crack cocaine and sex toys to herself. "The thought crossed my mind. But if she wasn't involved in some way with someone, it's rather hard to come up with a motive for anyone killing her."

Dexter French said, "We don't know anyone meant to kill *her*. Perhaps the person thought she was someone else."

Shirley shook her head. "No. Tad was some distance away, he didn't see anything, but he could hear Dawn speaking. When Dawn saw whoever it was, she asked the person what he or she was doing there, which would indicate she knew the person."

Anne French shuddered, wiped at her eyes once more. "I'm sure Dawn wasn't seeing anyone. I'd have known. She couldn't have been seeing anyone. We were keeping her . . . keeping her at home. Oh, God, I want to know about this, I want to know why. You don't want money, but if you find out why, I'll . . . I'll give money to a charity in your name or something."

She stood up, touched her cheeks and hair with her fingertips, putting herself in order. Dexter adjusted her crumpled collar and stroked her cheek.

Shirley murmured, "Let's just see how things turn out. They should have the . . . some forensic report soon, which may tell us something useful."

She led the way through the door, where Anne French proceeded toward the car, leaving her husband to turn to Shirley and say, "You mean the autopsy. That's really what you mean."

"I mean the autopsy," Shirley agreed.

He nodded and went to join his wife.

Shirley looked around. J.Q. was nowhere to be seen.

Allison was still at school, of course. Whoever J.Q. had been talking to had also departed. From the open window of one of the guest houses, where the new housekeeper, Jennie, was cleaning, came the sound of a vacuum. All very tranquil, nonthreatening, nonviolent, and two women dead in as many days. Shirley stood, watchful, as the couple got back into the car, as the car turned, then as it went, too quickly, with too much flung gravel. The spray of pebbles hit the adobe wall like a burst from an automatic weapon.

They had spoken of the autopsy. Shirley went into the kitchen, found the card Eddy Martinez had left for Allison, and called him.

"I may have something that will help," she said. "But I don't want to make unnecessary waves for the family. Did the autopsy report, by any chance, mention any evidence of sexual activity?"

Long silence at the other end. She could hear background noises, phones ringing, people talking. She sighed and remained patient.

"I shouldn't give you this information," Martinez said, very quietly.

"I won't spread it around," she said.

"She was three months pregnant."

"Well, well."

"What have you got?"

"Dawn told some of her school friends that she was having an affair with an older boy or man, a student at UNM. None of the kids know who, but according to one of them, this boyfriend supplied Dawn with crack cocaine."

"Ah." Silence again.

"I suppose you routinely take a tissue sample of the fetus, so you can rule out possible fathers."

"Yeah. We've got a sample."

"She was only fifteen. What she thought of as an older man could be someone as young as ... say eighteen."

"I'm just trying to figure where we go from here. We can't hardly canvas the entire student body of UNM. That'd be impossible."

"People tell me the French house is full of servants. If the boy, or man, ever came to the house to see her, a servant may have seen him. And Mrs. French said they'd been keeping her at home, which would suggest they'd been keeping an eye on her. Her teacher implied she'd been in trouble in other schools; you might want to find out about that. She might have been involved elsewhere, and the person followed her here to Santa Fe. Her parents tell me she was being kept at home, but perhaps she was allowed to visit a girlfriend, stay overnight? If so, was she actually with the girlfriend on those nights?"

"You really think there's something in this?"

Shirley shrugged, then realized he couldn't see this admission of uncertainty. "Somebody killed her. And it wasn't an accident."

J.Q. came in as she was hanging up the phone. "Young man was here, looking for you earlier," he said. "I told him you couldn't be interrupted right then. Who was it?"

"Dawn French's mother and stepfather. Who was looking for me?"

"Allison's acquaintance, Ulti Consalves. He said Allison spoke to him at school today, so he came over

150

to tell you what he'd seen. I suggested he come back in about an hour, if it wasn't inconvenient. What's that all about?"

"Ulti? Or the Frenches?"

"Both!"

"The Frenches are very upset and wanted to know if Allison or I knew anything. I wanted to ask Ulti about the tracks. Were they there when he and Allison were walking along the arroyo, Friday afternoon? Allison thought not. In which case, when were they there, and did they have anything to do with Bridget's death?"

"Did you see the paper this morning?"

She shook her head.

"Another of French's articles about extraterrestrials. Somebody named Denton, across the river from Bridget's, claims to have seen a UFO. Plus letters to the editors, some of them from her former clients, saying the murder was definitely aliens. She'd been summoning aliens with her ceremonies."

"Oh Lord, the nuts are loose. Do you want some tea, J.Q.? There's a cup or so left here."

"No. What I really want is a large bowl of menudo."

"We had some of your last batch frozen."

"I ate that weeks ago."

"I see. Do we have the makings?"

"No blanket tripe. No pigs' feet. I'll have to go to Santa Fe."

"Well, if you start with a trip to Santa Fe, we should have menudo by about midnight. Are you willing to wait that long?"

He shook his head, looking slightly grumpy.

"What's the matter?"

"I don't like this Allison business," he growled. "All

151

of a sudden I have this awareness of mortality. She's too young for us to be able to—"

"Careful, J.Q.!" she said crisply. "You're about to utter some very Victorian sentiment. Quite frankly, I think we'll live long enough to see her through college, by which time, if she has no sense, she never will, and our living forever wouldn't change it."

"I suppose. She just came so close. . . ."

"The burned child fears the fire."

"I hope!"

They were still sitting glumly across from one another when Allison came into the kitchen, trailed by Ulti. "Hi. I found Ulti outside. He wants to talk to you."

Ulti sat. J.Q. herded Allison out, ostensibly to look to her horse. Shirley offered milk and oatmeal cookies, aware of a slight incongruity. Ulti was young, true, but he was certainly no child. He sat straight and tall, very much the young man. Still, even J.Q. was fond of oatmeal cookies.

"These are good," he said forthrightly. "Mom makes good ones, too. Biscochitos, mostly. Lots of lard in biscochitos. I tell her they've got too much fat in them, we should eat less of that."

"These have hardly any," Shirley agreed. "I make up for it with the raisins and nuts."

"Allison said you wanted to know about the tracks?"

"Right. When were they there?"

"They weren't there when Allison and I walked along there on Friday. Saturday, I was up really early, just after light, because I was meeting some friends to go into Espanola and work on a car. We bought this car together, me and two other guys, to make a low rider out of, you know?"

"I've seen them," Shirley replied. "Very flashy."

"Okay, so I was up real early, and my one friend, he was picking up the other two of us at the school, so I was walking along the arroyo on my way there. The tracks were there then. I know, because there was all this racket from some crows down in the arroyo, and when I looked down, I saw the tracks. They started just about there."

"And went on . . ."

"And went on down the arroyo, past the fork, until they came to the paved road, where the banks are shallow. They came up and out there."

"Did you notice if they ran the other way, down the other fork? The one that runs northwest, to the river?"

He nodded. "They made a kind of Y, yeah. Two sets of tracks, some places beside each other, some places on top of each other, you know, one set going in, one set going out, like the driver came from the east, from the paved road, went down the main arroyo to the McCree place—Allison says they go the whole way— then back from there, turn right at the arroyo split, go a little way, maybe figure that's the wrong way, turn around, and go back down the main arroyo to the road."

"And it could have been a thrill seeker, just driving to get a look at the murder scene."

"Sure. Like my ma says, the world is fulla people with too much feeling and not enough thinking."

"I think I'd like your ma."

He grinned. "Since my dad got sick, she's got militant. You should hear her going on to Father Cisneros. He threatened to excommunicate her."

"Over what?" Shirley asked, shocked.

"Something about women being priests. Anyhow, if there's anything I can do to help . . ."

"I'll let you know. Mostly, just help us keep Allison from brooding."

"I like her," he said, fixing Shirley with intent brown eyes. "I really do."

Shirley nodded, not ready to reject this intelligence out of hand, but not ready to accept it willingly.

"That Tad, he's no good around girls," Ulti went on. "Any girl he goes out with, her name's spread all over by the next day. I wouldn't let my sisters go out with him."

Give him a beard, Shirley thought, and you'd have a patriarch. "You can control who your sisters go out with?"

"Well, you know. Sometimes you can't control the girls, so if he's really a t—if he's really rotten, you have to go to the guy and say stay away or I break your arm. If it's somebody I can't handle, my brother can. I'd tell him. Girls don't know what kind of person boys are, you know? They don't hear them talk when there aren't any girls around. They don't know the things they say. Way I figure it is, somebody ought to tape them saying the things they do, then play it to the girls. That way, they'd have better sense."

Shirley raised her brows in amazement. "Thanks, Ulti. I do appreciate the word, and I'll pass it on to Allison."

He lifted a hand in salute and went away, encountering J.Q. at the door. J.Q. bid him farewell, then came in with a questioning look.

"Knight errant," she said. "Breaking the limbs of malefactors in order to rescue maidens."

"From?"

"The likes of Tad Pole, who evidently memorializes his conquests in lewd talk among his peers, along with a little bathroom graffiti."

"Little bastard."

"So Ulti believes." She sighed.

Allison chose that moment to come in, noting their furtive expressions. "What?" she demanded.

Shirley made an equivocal gesture.

"Tell me! What did Ulti say?"

"Ulti said the tracks were there early Saturday morning, but not on Friday afternoon when you two walked home. Ulti said that whenever Tad goes out with anyone, he describes the encounter to his friends."

J.Q. snarled, "A word to the wise."

"Tad's disgusting," said Allison, without a tremor. "I already decided that. What's for supper? I'm starved."

"There's all kinds of sandwich stuff. There's the leftover soup from the other night. If you want a salad, there's lettuce and spinach and cucumbers."

"What I really want," she said, "is some of J.Q.'s menudo."

"He ate it all. We have to make more. That will take at least eight hours, including a trip to get the ingredients. How about a nice ham-and-cheese sandwich?"

"Car coming," said J.Q., who was wiping out the sink. "Who's coming today?"

"Lord." Shirley ran her fingers through her hair. "I completely forgot people." She went to the calendar and stared at it, trying to remember what day it was. Couldn't be Sunday. Allison had just come home from school. Couldn't be Monday. They'd interviewed Tad on Monday. Must be Tuesday. "The Swales," she said firmly. "Mama, son, daughter-in-law, two kids. They're coming to the Big House. I'll take them their key."

She took the key from the board and strolled out into the early evening, intercepting the rotund Mr. Swales in full trot.

"H'lo," he said, bubbling. "Such a nice place. I know we're going to enjoy this, oh yes, we really are. Such a nice place, I said to Mother when we drove in, this is one of the nicest places we've ever been, and she said right, Bobby, that's right it is. I'm Bobby Swales." He poked out his hand, rather in the manner of a man poking a reluctant fire, grasped Shirley's, and pumped it up and down in three measured strokes. "There now, we're getting Mama's chair out, and she's going to sit out there in the evening, just enjoying it, don't you know, and then later we'll all go in and have a bite. Becky made pigs in the blankets for all of us, to hold us until supper, and we'll just heat them up a bit, and then we'll be all set, won't we, is there charcoal for that there barbecue grill, or do we need to get some of that?"

Shirley, suddenly conscious of holding her breath, took a deep one and let it out slowly. "I think we have some charcoal, Mr. Swales."

"Well then, that's good, isn't it? There's Mama, in her chair, you come meet Mama, she'll want to meet you, I know she will." And he started across the parking lot, again at a trot, fetching up before a vast folding wicker contraption, on or in which lay a lightly blanketed bulk of pallid flesh staring with innocent eyes at the glory of the evening.

"Mama, this here's Missus McClintock, you know, the lady that wrote us, and this is her place, and here's where we're staying for the next few days, so you just settle in there, and we'll get us some charcoal started in this here barbecue."

"We stayed in this place had a barbecue," said Mama. "That was in Georgia, wasn't it, Bobby? How do, Miz McClintock."

"How do," echoed Mrs. Swales Jr., a spidery woman who seemed to be made up largely of elbows. "Say how do, Marilyn, say how do, Jesre."

How do, said they-all. Shirley located the charcoal and fled. J.Q. let her into the kitchen.

"Who is that?" He jerked a shoulder in the direction of the driveway, where Mama's bulk was parked like some large organic RV, awaiting hookup.

"That's Mama." Shirley gulped, desperately fighting laughter. "The girl's Marilyn, the boy's Jesre."

"Mary-Lynn? Jezz-rah?"

"That's what she said. Like Ezra, only with a *J*. They all said how do."

"How do," he repeated faintly. "Oh, my. Where are they from—I forget."

"We sure get some funny people," Allison remarked, from her position by the window.

"Don't stare," Shirley murmured.

"They can't see me. The lights aren't on. Where are they from?"

"West Virginia. Tennessee. The backwoods of Arkansas. The upper peninsula of Michigan. Somewhere where they say how do."

"There is no place where they say how do," said J.Q., who had burrowed into the file. "These people are from Chicago, Mr. and Mrs. R. K. Swales, from Chicago."

"Maybe they're character actors," Shirley remarked. "Boning up for a role." Mrs. Swales had just emerged from the Big House bearing a heavily laden plate, which she handed lovingly to the elder Mrs. Swales. Mr. Swales emerged from the house and trotted intently toward the gate once more.

Shirley went out to intercept him.

"That there house, you heat that house with the fireplace?" he asked.

"It has a furnace, Mr. Swales. And radiators."

"Radiators. We lived in a house with radiators once. Well, that's nice. Just wanted to be sure before Mama complained of the cold."

"Mr. Swales . . ."

"Um, you should call me Bobby. Everbody does."

"Perhaps, when I know you better. Until then, however, I think your mama would be more comfortable in the patio that goes with your house." Which was in back of the house. "Rather than in the parking lot." Which was right out front.

"Oh no, Mama loves parking lots. Loves to look at cars. Loves to talk to people. That's where people come and go, isn't it, through parking lots. She's fine." And he was away again.

"She's taking up at least two parking spaces," J.Q. murmured when Shirley reentered the kitchen. "And they're staying a full week."

"Maybe it will rain," Allison offered.

"If it does," Shirley predicted faintly, "I'm sure they have a tent to pitch over Mama."

5

SHIRLEY WAS DRINKING her first cup of the morning when Allison burst into the kitchen, crowing like a rooster.

"You'll never guess!"

"I won't even try," Shirley replied grumpily. She had not slept well. A chorus of coyotes had assembled under her window at about two in the morning to give a canine rendition of something Handelian—*Orlando Furioso* had come to mind—all in full, florid howl with trills, scales, and arpeggios pouring forth as from a whole choir of off-key castrati. Long after the dissonance was done, she had lain awake, listening to the quiet and thinking about Bridget McCree, Dawn French, and Brian's cut brake line.

Allison challenged: "Well, you wouldn't ever guess, even if you tried."

Shirley yawned. "So tell me? What can't I guess?"

"Why the Swaleses are here. I got to talking to Marilyn. Her father, Mr. Swales, is Bridget McCree's half brother. They came to see Bridget."

"They don't know she's dead?"

"I didn't tell them. Mr. Swales's mother, his real mother—not the fat lady out there, that's his grandmother—had him when she was just my age; illegitimate, you know? And then she ran off and left him with her mother, that's Mama. And Mr. Swales, Bobby, when he got to be forty, he started searching for his roots, Marilyn says, so he tracked her down—his mother, I mean—and he found out she was dead but she'd had two other children, Bridget and Brian. Marilyn says Mr. Swales came to reestablish family ties."

"And you didn't tell them she was dead."

Allison pursed her lips before uttering a Shirleyism. "I didn't think it was my place."

"Quite right," said J.Q., emerging from behind the Western edition of *The Wall Street Journal*. "Shirley will take care of it."

"Oh, I can't thank you enough," Shirley snarled, going to the coffeepot for a refill. "Did they pitch a tent over Mama last night?"

"She slept inside," J.Q. murmured.

"Amazing. Is she out in the parking lot yet?"

"Not yet," Allison responded. Her voice echoed from the inside of the refrigerator, in which her upper half was burrowed. "Don't we have some of that pizza left?"

"Not for breakfast," J.Q. said in a disapproving tone. "Have some cereal."

"I like cold pizza."

"Allison, quit shifting stuff about," Shirley grumped. "That pizza was dry as old boot leather, and I fed the

160

last of it to the dogs. Have some cereal or some of J.Q.'s grain, or some eggs, whatever, but stop pulling the place apart."

"I don't have time for anything. I've got to get to school."

Shirley looked at her watch. "You do have time. You have at least fifteen minutes. Eat something."

"Mr. Patterson said he'd give me a ride home today, and we'll bring the pig." She came out of the refrigerator, bumped the door closed with her bottom, and advanced on the stove, one egg in each hand.

J.Q. murmured, "Hasn't this pig been an indoor pig?"

"I think so."

"He'll get a bit chilly down there, then. I'll pick up some straw and we'll give him enough of it to bury himself in."

"He could share Tabasco's heat lamp."

"He could, but he won't. Pigs have this selfish quality. They don't share. They do, however, burrow."

J.Q. subsided behind the paper, Allison concentrated on scrambling and then gobbling her eggs, Shirley sipped her coffee, wishing she'd had at least two hours more sleep. Out in the parking lot a great flurry of shouted warnings and supplications announced the arrival of Mama, wobbling on tiny feet toward her chair, supported on either side by solicitous kinfolk. Dog barked sotto voce at this, nose down, tail motionless, as she always did when deploring though tolerating eccentric behavior on the part of guests. *I draw your attention,* her bark said, *to a situation which is out of the ordinary and therefore possibly improper. I do not threaten, I do not harass, I merely mention.* It was the same bark she used for the gas-meter man, whom she also deplored.

"It's too cold for Mama out there," Shirley remarked.

"Blubber," said J.Q. from behind his paper. "Like a seal. Or a whale. Arctic insulation."

Allison put her plate in the sink and almost ran for the door.

"What are you in such a rush for?"

"Ulti goes by about eight. If I hurry, I can walk to school with him."

"Oh." Shirley, watching her go, shook her head. Out of the frying pan and into what? Something even hotter? Sighing, she stood up to go do her duty in informing the Swaleses about Bridget's death.

Mrs. Swales the younger greeted her at the door of Big House with tired eyes and a cheerfulness that was clearly at least nine tenths sheer determination. "Goood morning, and how are we all this morning?"

"We all are fine, Ms. Swales."

"Missus. I'm Missus Swales. Mama doesn't hold with this new stuff, this Miz business. She says women should be proud to be married, proud to be missuses."

Shirley sighed, held up a hand to forestall a further spate of explanation, and said, "I'm afraid I have some bad news for you."

"Well," said Mrs. Swales, with a shocked expression, "you tell Bobby, then. Bobby, he does all the bad news. He's got more what you call sangfroid; he can take it easier than me or the children. With us, it's just fall apart, right now, and months to get put back together. We just got put together from Papa dying—like Humpty-Dumpty, took all the kings men and then some, and the glue's scarce dry yet. You wait right there, I'll get Bobby."

She went off like a praying mantis, all angles. Mama,

162

swathed about with blankets, roused herself to say in an approving tone, "The one good thing about bad news is, it's usually interesting. Trouble with good news is, it's dull. Just you look at TV. Where would that be without bad news? Now, I ask you."

Mr. Swales emerged. "What's this? Ms. McClintock, I hope you're just playing fun with us. What's this bad news?"

"My foster daughter, Allison, says Marilyn told her you'd come to see Bridget McCree."

"That's right. My half sister. Never met her. Didn't even know she existed until just recent, and I guess she still doesn't know about us. She lives right down the road from here, and we've come to meet her, and find out about my brother, didn't even know I had a brother—"

"She's dead," Shirley said, too loudly, shutting off the flow. "She was murdered." She immediately regretted the baldness of this announcement and started rewording it in her head, only to be defeated by silence.

Mr. Swales looked at Mrs. Swales, who looked at Mama. Mama stared at Marilyn, who looked broodingly in Jesre's direction. Jesre ignored all this in favor of throwing pebbles at a guinea hen who was perched uncertainly on the patio wall.

"We don't throw rocks at the poultry," Shirley murmured, raising her voice and repeating herself when the first admonition had no effect.

"Jesre," said his mother. "Quit that. Hear me?"

Jesre settled for juggling the pebbles, though he kept his eye on the hen.

"Gracious," said Mr. Swales. He smoothed his already sleek hair with both palms, a quick swipe down from the central part. "Oh, my." He brushed his mustache similarly, using two index fingers to smooth the fine, glossy hairs sideways.

"When?" asked Mama, her eyes meeting Shirley's with alert and unsentimental intelligence. "When was she killed?"

"Friday. Sometime around noon."

"Do they know who?"

"Not a clue at the moment. So far as I know."

"How about her family. Her brother?"

"Brian. He was here this weekend. He went through her things, looking for some papers that were missing."

A quick glance between Mama and grandson. "The deeds," breathed Mr. Swales. "Bet you anything somebody made off with the deeds."

"To the Montana property?" Shirley asked, surprised. "You knew about that?"

"It was my daughter's property," said Mrs. Swales the elder. "Bobby's Ma. She inherited it from my husband when he died. She was just fourteen years old."

"Didn't your daughter-in-law say Papa just died recently?"

Swales interrupted, shaking his head emphatically. "Not that Papa. Mama means her first husband, Barney Crowntree, Beatrice's papa. The Papa that just died was Papa Bubba, Bubba Swales, Mama's second husband, the one that raised me. Anyhow, Beatrice took the deeds with her when she run off."

"No reason she shouldn't take 'em," remarked Mama. "They was hers." Tears trickled down her face.

"Were the papers part of the roots you were looking for?" Shirley inquired.

Bobby Swales shook his head, smoothed his hair once more, then turned and fled into the Big House.

Mama, ignoring her tears, said in a mildly lecturing tone, "Mr. Crowntree, my first husband, we met on the rodeo circuit, where I was a trick rider and he rode the bulls. Barney died when our daughter Beatrice was fourteen, just like Bobby says. After he passed, I couldn't do a thing with Beatrice; she was just wild from the word *go*. This nothing much of a boy that was passin' through on his motorcycle got her pregnant, then after she had Bobby, she left him on my parlor couch and went out to get a Coke, and that was the last we saw of her, not countin' the postcards ever' now and then. I subsequent married Papa—that's Mr. Swales. And seein' as he raised Bobby from a pup, Bobby always called hisself Swales, even though on his birth certificate he's Bobby Crowntree."

"And it was Beatrice Crowntree who was mother to Bobby, Bridget, and Brian?"

"All those *Bs*." Mama shook her head wonderingly. "Like a hive. Knowin' Beatrice, it was just her way of keepin them straight, so's she'd know which was hers and which was somebody else's."

"She's dead, now? Beatrice?"

"Far's Bobby can find out. We had the postcards she'd sent, and Bobby hired a man to find her. Accordin' to him, Beatrice married this McCree man in Colorado, then he up and run off on her when her littlest was just about five, so she married this other man, name of Willard, and they was both killed in a car accident back about fifteen years ago. That's how come Bridget and her brother came by Beatrice's property up in Montana."

"Which has something to do with Bobby seeking his roots," Shirley asserted.

"Well ..." The woman thought it over, then nodded ponderously. "I suppose that's partly true. Musta been five years ago this man come to our place lookin' to buy the property. He didn't let on they'd found anything, but he was with some big mineral company, so we got the idea then it might have more on it than just rattlesnakes. Bobby was inter'sted, and so was I. Not wantin' it so much as just to know about it. Then later we got the notice about the copper up there. Here all of a sudden, after all these years—"

"Copper?"

"They found copper. Biggest strike ever. And we got the notice—"

"*You* received notice?"

"Sure. It's our address on the records up there. Barney Crowntree, my first husband, when he quit the rodeo, he was a roughneck, you know what that is?"

"Oilfield worker?"

"That's right. Anyhow, he was workin' up there in Montana, and he used to gamble. That man would gamble anything. Is that cloud goin' left or right; is that bird gonna go up or down; he'd bet the shirt off his back, his car, or his daughter. So one time he gambled for this big piece of Montana land, and he won. The man he won it from said it wasn't worth a thing, but Mr. Crowntree he got it recorded in his name, and our address was where the county sent the tax notices."

"You paid them?"

"Us? Not after he was dead and Beatrice went off. Why would we? Didn't belong to us. There was a few times I sent cards to places Beatrice sent me cards from, tellin' her about it, but she never wrote back."

"The land has probably been sold for back taxes."

"Nope. Bobby checked. Somebody's paid it up, just lately."

"And they've found copper on it."

"Biggest deposit in the world, they believe." She nodded to herself. "Bigger than that big hole they've got in Utah."

"How much land did Mr. Crowntree win?" Shirley asked.

"Oh, it was some square miles. Over three thousand acres. Nothing on it but antelope and prairie dogs and wind."

Shirley rapidly rearranged her thoughts to allow for several square miles' worth of land, shaking her head in wonderment. Wouldn't Brian be surprised? Wouldn't he be delighted! That is, if Bobby and he could reach an agreement. If they could find the papers.

"Why did your husband leave the land to Beatrice instead of to you?" Shirley asked curiously.

The huge woman shrugged. "He was always off here, there, and someplace, and I was home by myself. So me and Mr. Swales kind of kept company when he was gone. Mr. Crowntree, he found out about it, and he had a fit. Wrote him up a will leavin' everythin' to Beatrice. He'd write to Beatrice, he'd send stuff to Beatrice, pretendin' I wasn't even there, not that he'd paid that much attention before! I'd always had to have a job, take care of me and Beatrice. He never sent any money to take care of us. But then, when he died, Beatrice didn't pay any mind to who'd fed her and housed her and all. She blamed me, tole me I'd broke his heart. His heart!

Hell's bells, he'd dragged his heart all over the country givin' it to this one and that one. I didn't have his heart. I was only twenty-nine when he up and died, and I swear, he hadn't been around for more than about six months total durin' all those fourteen years, and that was mostly two, three days at a time."

"You were fifteen when you married?"

"It was legal. He was about thirty, and he was close with my daddy—Daddy was rodeo, too, you know—and Daddy sort of give me to him. Knowin' what kind of man Barney Crowntree was, maybe he won me in a poker game, I don't know."

"When you were fifteen," Shirley said faintly.

This woman had been Allison's age when she'd married and become a mother. She'd been barely thirty when she'd been a grandmother and taken on the care of a grandson. And how on earth had she managed? How was she managing now?

Mrs. Swales was staring at Shirley, her eyes seeming to probe so deeply that she grew slightly uncomfortable.

"Your name's Shirley, isn't it? You ever watch the soaps?"

"Seldom. Maybe a few times when I've had the flu and no energy to read."

"You ever notice how every time there's two or three people tellin' each other how they feel."

"That's what soaps are about."

"Did you get hooked on them? When you had the flu?"

Shirley cocked her head. "Some of them, I wanted to know what happened, if that's getting hooked."

"But you wasn't hooked hard enough to sit there and watch once you got over the flu?"

"No. They never got anywhere."

"That's it exactly. I figure the reason people watch the soaps is they're more comfortable not goin' anywheres, you know? Goin' someplace is hard work. Lots easier just feelin' things, not goin' anywheres at all. This woman loves this man, and so what? Last year she was lovin' some other man, and a hundred years ago, people was doin' the same, and a thousand years ago, the same thing. Go far enough back, you'd find some ape in the tree in love with some other ape. It don't change nothin', hate or love, now or a hundred years ago, it don't change nothin' at all. It just kind of occupies the time, like the soaps do.

"It's like men with their sports. Ever' weekend, back at the house, here's Bobby and two or three of his friends scrunched down in front a the TV, drinkin' beer and watchin' these men chasin' up and down after a ball. They chase it this year, and next year they chase it, and prob'ly a thousand years ago, they chased it then. And you know, it don't cure nobody of a sickness, it don't feed hungry people, it don't save the whales. What does all that chasin' matter, all that feelin' matter, when it don't go nowhere?"

Shirley's jaw dropped, and she stared in amazement.

When Mama spoke again, it was in answer to an unspoken question. "I got me a cancer, spread all around. Too far gone to operate. Can't take the chemo. Likely be gone this year, so they say. Set me to thinkin' about all those feelin's. Ever' one of us goes through life feelin' ever' day—good, bad, happy, mad, ever' day, and I can't honest say it matters how we feel, it don't change anything big. No matter how I feel, sun's still comin' up tomorrow. So you can't say it's important, but you still wonder, you know? Like you did with the soaps, you wonder what happened to this one, to that one? Like the guys with their sports, they want to know who won.

"So, I figure, may not be important, but here when things are comin' to an end, you want to feel like you tied up the loose ends. This is sort of a last chance to find out, last chance to finish things up right, last chance to tie up any loose ends. So I kind of thought it'd be nice to see Beatrice's children. It wasn't the property. Part of it was just . . . I've thought about her a lot."

"I'm sorry," Shirley said, feeling guilty.

"Don't be. We all gotta go. And Bobby's been sweet to me since the day she left him there, just a baby. And his wife, Ella, she's just as sweet, and usually the kids are, too. Jesre's going through one of those teenage things, but he'll come out of it. Haven't traveled much—me, I mean. This is kind of fun for me, you know?"

Shirley patted her hand and fled. From inside that incredible bulk, a girl child had looked out at her, wondering and unafraid, the same kind of look she intercepted from Allison every now and then. J.Q. found her bent over the kitchen sink, weeping silently.

"What?" he said, close to her, making a troubled sound in his throat.

She told him. "It just . . . it got to me."

"Because she's a huge old thing and you told yourself she was just an odd duck, right? As I suppose I did, too."

Shirley had been toting up the years. Fifteen when she was married and had Beatrice, thirty when Beatrice had Bobby, and Bobby looked to be near forty.

"She's only a few years older than we are, J.Q. And

she's ... reconciled. Something I've never managed. Never!"

He nodded, thinning his lips and mentally kicking himself. "Well, Shirley, we're not perfect, you and me. It's good something comes along every now and then and reminds us."

"I think I'd better call Brian. Tell him he's got a half brother and a grandmother and a nephew and niece." She dug out the number Brian McCree had given her and dialed it, then listened to it ringing endlessly. Nobody home. No answering machine. She taped the number to the wall above the phone. She would keep trying.

About noon, the phone rang. Shirley answered it, hoping it might be Brian.

"My name's Merwiczi," said a furry voice, more than a little drunken. "Pete Merwiczi. Lydia told me to call you."

"Lydia?"

"Hiram's daughter. Buffalo Man."

"Oh, right! What can I do for you, Mr. Merwiczi?"

"More the other way, acshully. Lydia gave me this buffalo head, used to belong to Hiram. And when I went to hang it up, this stuff fell out. And Lydia says I should call you, see if you want it."

"What kind of stuff?"

"There's some letters. And some tapes. And some videotapes, too. Lydia says you might give me a few bucks for it. Let you have the whole thing for fifty."

Shirley thought intently. It could be just junk, but on the other hand, there might be something. "I'll give you fifty, if you deliver it," she said.

171

He sounded willing though not energetic as he took directions to Rancho del Valle. She asked J.Q. to be on the lookout for him. "J.Q., don't give him the money until you get all three elements of the deal—letters, tapes, and videotapes. I'll be in the laundry if you need me."

By the time Merwiczi showed up, however, the laundry was long done, and Shirley observed the interchange from the kitchen window. Pete had evidently gone on drinking and had brought himself to the expansive stage. He took the proffered money without counting it, shoved it inside a breast pocket, then hoisted one foot onto the bumper of his car and engaged J.Q. in a lengthy conversation. Shirley strolled out to see what was what.

"I'm Shirley McClintock, Mr. Merwiczi," she said. "Thanks for coming all the way out here."

"That's okay. The stuff's all there. There's a videotape."

"Did you look at it?" Shirley asked.

His face grew shifty. "Well . . ."

"Doesn't matter if you did or didn't, I'd just like to know."

"Well, yeah. But it was just some guy and her, you know, the one Hiram took up with."

"Bridget? Bridget McCree?"

"Yeah. Her. I thought maybe it'd be somethin' else."

"Like what?" asked J.Q., lazily.

"Oh, he, Hiram, he said he got some hot stuff. Some stuff that'd make him a lot of money. He took it to this guy, and the guy told him he'd pay, every week, just to keep it quiet." Pete nodded blearily. "Hiram, he figured he had to keep her quiet, too."

"Keep who quiet?" Shirley asked.

"Her. The one you said."

"Bridget?"

"Yeah. Her. He kep her quiet, all right." He sniggered. "Kep her busy, too."

"Buffalo Man kept Bridget busy. You mean, he had an affair with her."

"Affair?" He puzzled over this. "He was fuckin' her regular. I guess that's what you'd call it. Then he got himself killed. He was greedy, Hiram. I told him, I said, don't be so greedy, you're settin' yourself up."

Shirley took a deep breath. "You think the person he was blackmailing killed him?"

"Somebody killed him. I dunno who else. Some big, heavy car, run him over twice. Went over him then turned around an' went over him again. Making sure. I told him. I said Hiram, you get too greedy, you'll regret it."

Though they went on talking, the visit yielded nothing else. When Shirley went inside, she opened the large envelope and dumped it on the counter. A bunch of letters. She spread the letters like a fan, then set one videotape and one audiocassette tape on them.

"Do we count Buffalo Man's death as another murder?" J.Q. inquired.

"Could be," she murmured. "Blackmail had crossed my mind." She opened one of the letters, started to read it, flushed brick red. "Oh, my," she murmured.

"Interesting?"

"If one were ... very prurient, I suppose, yes." She flipped through the pages, finding more of the same. "No salutation, no name signed, no idea from whom to whom. Are the others the same?"

The others were the same, all in the same hand.

"Man's handwriting?" asked J.Q.

"I don't know. It could be."

"No flourishes. No little circles dotting the *i*'s."

"I'll go back in the library and have a look at the tapes."

"Want company?"

"Actually no, J.Q. I find this sort of thing quite embarrassing. I was taught not to peek, you know. In my childhood, if one passed someone's window, an open curtain wasn't considered an invitation to invade their privacy. We were taught not to window-peek, not to listen at doors."

"And not to hover over an accident or encourage someone threatening suicide."

"Exactly. Now we learn that other people's pain is our amusement. We're like the Romans in the Colosseum, watching victims being killed or torn apart. We have afternoon shows to see which guest can be most vulgarly crude and least decent. And *Talk Soup*? Where the sophisticate raises an affronted nostril at the behavior of vulgarians while passing out vulgar tidbits for our delectation. I prefer the earlier way, honestly."

He nodded. "I'm not going to argue with you."

She went back to the library, let the VCR gulp down the videotape, and pressed Play. Static and a long, long leader, then dim images. At first she couldn't make them out. Then she could. Bridget McCree, quite naked and very active. Her partner's face was hidden from view. He had some kind of birthmark, bruise, or tattoo on his bottom, a round area darker than his skin. The room was not any room in Bridget's house down the road. The viewpoint was fixed, not moving about. All it showed was the bed, a table beside the bed, and over that a window, the bottom half of it curtained. Shirley concentrated on the top half, which disclosed a steeply pitched line of roof with a gable silhouetted against lighter, perhaps moonlit sky. The steep roofline was typical of the houses they'd seen in Madrid, including Kip and Joana's very blue house. The bedroom could have been in Bridget's house in Madrid.

The tape sputtered to a close, ran on black, then started another sequence. Same song, second verse, same players, only worse. Same location. Different costumes. Leather this time, with studs and chains. Shirley's attention wandered as this episode played itself out and two or three others went by, each one differently costumed. The last episode on the tape was different, though. Bridget had been replaced by another participant and the action had moved elsewhere. This was a much younger woman, highly made up, very pretty, wearing a fancy getup, black lace garter belt and stockings. This was a different room; the background was a solid wall with a set of low bookshelves and one long, narrow picture hanging above them, slightly tilted, a line of masked Indian dancers. The male half of the party was the same, the spot on the bottom was definitely a tattoo, letters over a small, compact design, but this time the viewpoint was from the side rather than the foot of the bed. When he half turned, Shirley saw that he wore a mask, a tiger mask. No, not a mask. Too closely fitted for a mask. A tiger face, painted on. Like something out of a Kabuki drama. The videotape ended.

She rewound it while playing the cassette, all the sounds of the jungle, as Kip and Joana had remarked. Voices in pairs, a him and her, then the same him but another her, whispering and shouting, urging one another on. The words were clear, but there was no voice she

175

recognized. When she had listened to all of it, she put the tapes and the letters into a large envelope and put the envelope onto a bookshelf, behind a row of books.

She went to the phone, punched for information, and asked for Lydia Wafferneusse's number in Madrid. A few laconic questions and answers later, she returned to the kitchen to find J.Q. still there, combing burs out of Dog's chest while Dog concentrated on being patient.

"Interesting?" he asked, searching her face.

She shook her head. "Vital, maybe; interesting, no. Bridget and an unknown partner, engaged in sex play. Repeatedly. Same unknown engaged in sex play with a young woman, eighteen to twenty-two or so. Sound effects on the cassette, just what the two neighbors in Madrid described. One male voice, one female voice, then same male voice, different female voice. I called Lydia."

"The buffalo's daughter?"

"Right. I asked her if Daddy would have been capable of blackmail. She said maybe, but she knew he sometimes took pics of himself and partners, for his own amusement. She knew he'd done that, more than once. When I asked her if he had a tattoo on his buttock, however, she said no."

"Would she necessarily know?"

"Said she identified his body, signed the forms, and there were no scars or tattoos listed on the forms except the ones she knew about, on his arms. He had an eagle on one arm and a snake on the other. The taped man has no tattoos on his arms. She gave me the name of the mortuary, in case I wanted to check with them."

J.Q. pondered. "So, since Buffalo Man sometimes took pictures of himself and partners, we can assume he had the requisite photographic equipment. Since the tapes in his possession were of Bridget with some other partner, however, the pictures were probably taken before he was sexually involved with Bridget."

"Which still allows for two possibilities. He took them, or he got them from someone else, perhaps Bridget herself."

"And if he took them, did Bridget know about the tapes? I think yes, because after he was killed, his daughter took something back to Bridget."

"The originals," said Shirley. "Lydia said the envelope she took to Bridget had a lot of loose stuff in it, and when I spoke to her just now, she described it as thick, as though it had half a dozen tapes in it. I just ran one tape with several sequences, which says to me that Buffalo Man copied them sequentially on one tape for himself."

"How about the letters? Were they written by this same man to Bridget? Did Bridget give Buffalo Man the letters?"

"Again, two possibilities. She either gave them, or he stole them. Nothing Lydia said about her father indicated he was lawless, not in that way. If he'd had a cache of letters from or to different people, we could figure he habitually stole letters, but these seem to have been the only ones. I think it's more likely she gave them to him."

"Why?"

"Drama, J.Q. She was into drama. Remember what Brian told us, and Kip. Bridget gave up a good business in Santa Fe and moved to Madrid. Why? So her lover could come and go as he liked. Think of the drama of that. She gave up her business, lived on her savings, spent everything for love! So, then the visits from the lover began to taper off, and Bridget, who gave up everything for love, was very upset over that. She went to a healer, someone who's supposedly good with heartache, and she said, see, he loves me, here are his letters, but his love is waning. I gave up my business for him, I gave up everything for him, now what do I do?"

"And the healer says . . . ?"

"The healer says, you're entitled to some recompense. We need some tapes, for proof, let's get some compromising pictures of the bastard, just in case. We know from Brian the guy was married."

"And Bridget goes along with that? The pictures aren't of him, they're of her. We can't identify him."

"Maybe he could be identified. Maybe if we could see that tattoo, it would identify him. In any case, Buffalo Man arranges to take pictures of Bridget and lover. I have no trouble imagining that at all. I do have trouble figuring out how he got pictures taken of that same lover in another location with another woman. Did Bridget know about those, too?" Shirley rubbed at the lines between her eyes, thinking. "Did she ever use the tapes?"

He thought about this. "There was that big win she talked about, the one she said paid for the house."

"At one of the Indian casinos. Who told us that?"

"Brian. He said she won big at one of the Indian casinos and bought the house."

She threw up her hands. "How would we find out about that?"

"I think in this case, we'd have to call Eddy Martinez. They've got the manpower and the authority to check the names of winners. We know the approximate date it must have happened, but we don't know which casino. Every tribe seems to have one. It could have been Tesuque or Pojoaque or San Juan or San Pedro. Or, considering she was living in Madrid, maybe one of the pueblos farther south."

She nodded, thinking it through. He was right. The chances of her finding out the names of big winners on her own was nil. Sighing, she turned to the phone once more. Eddy Martinez wasn't in, but he would call. She tried Brian again. Still no answer.

Dog barked purposefully. Shirley looked out the window to see a car approaching. Jeremy Patterson and Allison. "I think the pig has arrived," she called to J.Q.

They went out to meet Hamlet, a small, self-possessed pig with a harness and leash. His back was quite straight, and the potbelly was modest.

"Hamlet doesn't have rabies, which we were sure of even before quarantine," Jeremy told them. "You need to know that the only way the pigs can be kept very small is to keep them half-starved. Naturally, they are hungry all the time, and they tend to eat anything and everything—or try. Hamlet was hungry, so he bit the kid that was withholding food. If you let this one grow normally, he'll hit about eighty or a hundred pounds, possibly more. If he gets plenty of exercise, he'll be healthier."

Shirley regarded Hamlet with slightly jaundiced eye. "He'll need company," she said. "Pigs are family animals, not loners."

"We get a pig like this from time to time. People buy them at fifteen pounds and think they're darling. Then the owners feed them, and the pigs start to grow, and pretty soon they aren't darling anymore. If you're willing, I'll call you when we get another one."

"Keep it in mind," she agreed. "Allison, why don't

you walk the critter down to the barn. J.Q. put a straw bed in one of the pens, and when he gets used to us, we'll let him out in the pasture."

"He'll root," Jeremy offered in a slightly worried tone. "He'll dig up stuff."

"Can't hurt much down there," she said, watching Hamlet mosey off at the end of his leash, Allison leading and J.Q. herding him along. "Funny little guy. Not much personality."

"Phlegmatic," agreed Jeremy. "He's had a troubled pighood."

"Shoathood," she corrected. "So, what you find out from the girls?"

"The girls." He sighed, making a throwaway gesture. "Sometimes I despair."

"Little fruitcakes?" she suggested.

"Not that sweet, not even that nourishing. Summer and Breeze haven't a thought. Not one idea between them. Not even the idea that they should have ideas. They think whatever they are told to think. That's why Dawn did so well with them, she told them when to breathe! Dawn's murder was probably the best thing that could happen for them. Don't tell anyone I said that, I'll deny it."

"So?" she repeated.

"Summer says Dawn talked a lot about her lover. The older man. He was really terrific in bed, according to Summer's recollection of what Dawn said. He knew all kinds of techniques. He had all kinds of sex toys. They said this, mind you, as though hoping to shock me. Breeze asked Dawn once what her mother would do to her if she found out, and Dawn laughed first, then said her mother would kill her. In Breeze's opinion, Dawn was serious. Her mother really would kill her."

"I've said similar things," Shirley confessed. "I've said, Allison, you do that again, I'll do something or other. That didn't mean I meant to do it."

"According to Breeze, Dawn thought her mother would really mean it. Which may indicate only that the lover was someone of whom Mama would disapprove. Have you met Mama?"

Shirley nodded. "I've met both of them. Anne Pelton-French would disapprove of most people. She is one self-conscious *gringa rica*. Noblesse, but no oblige."

"I had the same impression."

"She came here, wanting to know what the connection was between her daughter and Allison. I told her Dawn had bragged about having an older boyfriend. Mama wouldn't believe it. She said she and daughter were too close for Dawn to have hidden it. Self-delusion, you suppose?"

He shrugged. "I'd say so. The reason Dawn was going to public school was that she'd been kicked out of several private ones. I'm assuming the cause was the behavior I myself witnessed: Dawn's attempts to compromise faculty members. She did it for fun, and she tried it on several of us, including me."

Shirley's eyebrows went up. "How?"

"My classroom has a storage closet at the back. One afternoon I returned to the classroom to see Summer slipping in there. It was the last period of the day, I had no class, so why was she there? I sat down at my desk to see what developed, and very shortly here came Dawn, with her 'Please Mr. Patterson, I've done something to my neck and I can't move it, will you massage it for me?' "

"Rather clumsy."

"No, actually, it was quite believable, or would have been if I hadn't known Summer was there as a witness."

"How did you handle it?"

"I leered at her and said, 'Not here, Dawn, come with me.' Then I led her out into the hall, into Susan Williams's classroom, and explained the situation. Susan responded by massaging Dawn's neck vigorously while I stayed as witness to prevent Dawn accusing her of making lesbian overtures. After which I checked with her previous school, and while they wouldn't come right out and say so, they didn't contradict what I told them. Then I inquired around and found out Dawn had tried some ploy or other with at least three of the teachers. It's simply what she did. She counted coup."

"There's a stable hand at the French place I'd like to talk to. I wonder if she counted coup on him."

"You'd probably get thrown out on your ear."

"Maybe not. Mama wanted me to investigate. No faith in the sheriff's people. She might let me wander around, ask a few questions."

"It's worth a try. Some days I think it's only my university classes that keep me sane." He climbed back in his car, started the engine, then got out with an exclamation. "I almost forgot. The notebook." He fetched it from the rear seat of the car. "Return, please, after scanning, in case the deputies go through her locker again."

"They've been through it?"

"Monday. They took everything out and put everything back, but they didn't read anything. They had a warrant to look for drugs. That's the currently understood motive for everything; if it isn't drug-related, they don't bother with it."

"As a matter of fact, it could have been drug-related." Shirley told him about Summer's confession to Allison. "Crack cocaine is drugs, even if they only used it once."

He climbed back in the car. "Then it's obvious Summer and Breeze didn't tell me everything they knew. Breeze particularly. She had an air about her, sort of an 'I've got a secret' manner. Let me know if I can help in any other way. And thanks for the pig rescue. Ask Allison to bring back the leash and harness whenever's convenient." He waved as he drove out.

Shirley put the notebook away in her room, then wandered down the hill, into the barn, to the pen at the far end where Hamlet was industriously piling straw.

"All the right instincts," J.Q. opined. "He tried digging into it and it wasn't quite deep enough, so he's been bulldozing more straw into the pile."

"Hog-dozing," offered Allison. "Will he be warm enough?"

"Plenty warm enough," Shirley said. "He's little, but he's got a nice layer of fat on him. He'll do fine."

Hamlet finished the dozing and burrowed into the pile, disappearing completely except for his snout, which emitted a comfortable little grunt. Shirley took harness and leash back to the house, leaving J.Q. and Allison to deal with the evening feeding. She'd given no thought at all to what people would eat tonight, and she wasn't in the mood to give it any thought, even now. Maybe they'd go out. There was a reasonably good Chinese restaurant in Los Alamos.

She passed the phone. Seeing the number taped to the wall, she tried it again.

Brian answered. "Ms. McClintock? Have you heard something about those papers?"

She told him something, yes, not the expected something, no, and would he prepare himself for a shock. When she finished telling him about the Swaleses, there was only a long empty humming on the wires.

"Brian?"

Still nothing.

"Brian!"

"Yeah," he said. "I'm ... I'm ... I don't know what to say. Phyllis is back in the hospital, Ms. McClintock. That's where I've been all day. My God! A grandmother? A half brother? Mother never said anything about relatives."

"I take it she rejected her mother, but, at least to my mind, her mother, your grandmother, is blameless. Your great-grandfather married her off to an older man named Crowntree when she was only fifteen. Crowntree went off following the oil fields, leaving your grandmother for the most part alone with her child, your mother, whom she went to work to support. Your grandmother was lonely, she took up with someone else, and her husband disowned her. Didn't divorce her, mind you, just disowned her. The way I read that story is that he liked having a wife because it prevented any other woman setting her sights on him, but it didn't prevent his going and doing whatever he pleased."

"What's she like?"

"She's a really nice woman who's terminally ill, Brian. She just wants to see her daughter's children. If you can make time to come down here for a day, it would probably fulfill all her desires."

"They don't want the land? Bridget's and my land?"

"They know about it, Brian. Turns out, it's probably worth a fortune. There's a big copper deposit, and believe me, there'd be plenty to go around, even if you had to share with Bobby. You'd have shared half anyhow, with Bridget."

Another long silence. "I'll see. . . . Phyllis is all doped up. She might not even know I was gone."

"I've got an empty house you can have. No charge."

A sniffle. "I'll call you back."

She hung up. What had she been thinking about? Supper.

The phone rang. Eddy Martinez. Shirley explained about Bridget's buying the house. "She told people she won the money at one of the casinos, but we think she might have blackmailed someone for it."

"Blackmailed who?"

"The man she was having an affair with. It would be worth finding out if she actually did win the money at a casino, wouldn't it?"

"Who was she having an affair with?"

"We don't know. We just know she was. Her neighbors in Madrid know she was. And right after the guy stopped visiting, Bridget bought a house. There could be a connection."

A patient sigh. "Ms. McClintock, that deputy job is still open. . . ."

"Look," she snarled. "I'm not trying to do your job for you, I don't want to be a deputy, but don't you want me to pass on what I learn? Isn't that a citizen's duty?"

A moment's thoughtful silence, then another sigh. "Yes, ma'am, it is. I guess I'm just discouraged. I'm not getting much help on this case, to tell you the truth. There's a TV show wants the sheriff to appear in person, talk about these cattle mutilations, then sort of mention this murder, like it might be connected. Sheriff, he'd like that. He can't quite come out and say it was ETs killed the McCree woman, but he doesn't really want anybody else arrested for it, not just yet."

Shirley gasped in disbelief. Despite all her harangues, despite having met the man herself, she hadn't really believed standards were that low. "Eddy, you must be joking."

"I'm not. Look, I'm career law enforcement. Since I was a kid, this is what I wanted. I've been to school, I've taken courses. Believe it or not, I read books. But my boss, he's elected. He plays it for the cameras, for the microphone. He'd like it to be ETs. He'd get lots of publicity that way." A cough at the other end, a muttered curse. "Forget I said that. Forget I said anything. Listen, we had a look at those tracks and you're right. The vehicle came in from the road down near where the girl was shot, went all the way to the McCree house, then turned around and went out the same way."

"Whoever it was couldn't follow the arroyo the whole way," she said. "There's culverts along the way."

"When he came to a culvert, he went up and over."

"Then why use the arroyo at all?" she cried. "It doesn't make sense."

"I thought the same thing at first, until I looked at it, but it does make sense. Whoever did it drove the whole length of that thing without anybody seeing him, so far as we know. It was foggy as hell Friday night. It was supposed to rain, but it didn't. Maybe he counted on rain wiping the tracks out. There's no houses near where the culverts are. There's no parallel road where you can look down into the arroyo, and there's only a few road crossings. Then, when you get down toward the river, where the water table isn't very far down, there's trees along both sides. Somebody could get in and out down there without anybody seeing him."

"Why?"

"You got me. I haven't any notion. But he drove the vehicle down within fifty yards of that culvert by the McCree house."

"Why are we both saying *he*?"

"Well, ma'am, I don't really want to say *it*. My boss wants to think it's ETs. Three or four of my colleagues, they honest to God do think it's ETs. I had to yell a little bit even to get those tracks checked. Reason we've got nowhere on this thing is, nobody thinks there's anywhere to get. You got aliens shopping for body parts, everybody's thinking about the movies, you know: *Predator I, Predator II*. They don't want to get involved in something out of the *X-Files*. They'd like to close the case. Forget about it."

"Damn," she said feelingly. "I'm sorry, Deputy. Can you find out about the casinos?"

"Ms. McClintock, I'll give it a try."

"Thank you." She hung up. From outside she could hear the voices of Allison and J.Q., their approaching footsteps, the rattle of feed buckets. Damn. Supper!

"Shirley," Allison said, poking her head in the door. "If you haven't started anything, J.Q. and I want pizza for supper. Okay?"

"Are you going to pick it up?"

"Right. We'll call and order it, and be back in about an hour."

"Fine. Sounds great." She watched benignly while they phoned and drove off in the Jeep, then she went purposefully down the hill, where she caught Zeke, saddled him, then let herself and horse through the gate into the bosque, through that into the riverbed, where she turned upstream, toward Bridget McCree's.

In the early-evening light, the river bottom was flat, rosy sand interrupted by patches of low willow and annual weeds, with one silver thread scrolling its way along the far bank where last spring's runoffs had cut a deeper channel. For the most part, there were no riverbanks as such, merely slightly rising ground, grown up in trees that had put on their autumn finery: green gold of cottonwood, bronze gold of tamarisk, copper gold and bloodred of creeping sumac and wild rose, frothing like flame at the foot of the trees. The riverway was a gold-bordered trail, glittering in the early-evening wind. She glanced at her watch, checking the time. She would allow herself one hour.

The arroyo that led past Bridget's house entered the river as a wide, flat gravel road. Up that road a little way, the banks began to rise, and when she came even with the house, Shirley urged the horse up the bank and onto the shelf where the hogan stood. They passed the house, where a window curtain flapped out of an open window, like a lapping tongue. She rode slantingly across the road toward the tall adobe wall, and once past it down into the arroyo once more, upstream of the culverts. Fifty yards along, in a narrow spot among trees, the tire tracks stood plain in slightly damp sand. She dismounted, examining the ground. There was a confusion of footprints. Also a few shiny beads. She picked one of them up and peered at it, a ball of foil, maybe a chewing-gum wrapper. She teased it open. Not a chewing-gum wrapper. This was a more elegant substance, silver on one side, green on the other, with darker green lettering. She had seen something like it somewhere but could not remember where. She sniffed it. Mint. Mint, and perhaps chocolate. A candy wrapper of some kind. A car had parked here long enough for someone to eat a few candies. She put the pellets in her pocket.

Against the bank were three circular depressions in the damp sand. Shallow depressions. Flat. What? Hubcaps? Had someone changed a tire? There was no sign of that, no scuffed sand.

Puzzled, she remounted. Beyond this place the sand was dry and solid enough for a canter. The gelding's ears pricked forward as they went, hooves plopping, slowing as they climbed over the second road, the one that went westward to Rancho del Valle. They were half a mile from Bridget's house at this point, and ahead of them the arroyo bent, hiding the way ahead, then bent again, a long angular Z, disclosing at its end the steep bank that intruded from the right to make a narrow, pointed wall, pockmarked with deep holes. Too late for kingfishers. The bank slanted in a slight overhang, like the prow of a wrecked boat.

She slowed the horse and rode slowly forward until she was even with the jutting clay bank. From here she could look in three directions, behind her, the way she had come, and into the arroyos left and right. There had been no tracks when Allison had walked home. On the following morning, early, there had been. One could not drive the arroyo in the dark. If someone had used headlights, the car might have been seen. Therefore, logically, the car had come in the foggy dusk, or at dawn, and since Ulti had been walking along here at dawn, that left only the dusk.

Someone had driven in all three channels on the night after Bridget was killed. The vehicle had come in by the arroyo to her left, had gone down the route she had just ridden, turned around, and parked near Bridget McCree's. It had stayed there for an unknown amount of time, short or long, then it had returned to this point and turned down the right-hand way. The deputy had said it had turned in the wrong direction. In the dusk, had the driver become confused enough to go in the wrong direction?

After all that planning? The mutilation, the pretense of a UFO landing, the symbols, the whole shebang? Not likely. So meticulous a planner would not have been confused.

She urged the horse forward. So why had he driven into this cul-de-sac? There was nothing along this branch. A few tree limbs washed against the banks. A pile of rusty junk heaped high against one sloping bank, high enough up that no summer flood had buried it. And not far beyond the pile of junk the tracks had reversed. There were no tracks now. The sand had blown over them, or been kicked up by animals. Despite the promised weekend rain, none had fallen, but traffic and the wind had done the erasure.

As she approached the junk pile a lone crow flew up from an edge of rusty metal to perch in a piñon pine at the edge of the arroyo, where it sat cawing at her indignantly. Ulti had seen crows. Tad had seen crows.

She dismounted and went toward the pile. Corroded stuff. Some barbed wire, quite red but still lethally sharp. What looked like an ancient sheet-metal feed bin of some kind, broken into a pair of gaping jaws. Old metal buckets, five-gallon size, that had contained tar or something similar. Gunky black, at any rate. The back half of a Volkswagen Beetle. Some huge, ancient gears. Other stuff, wood and metal, much of it half-buried in the sand. It had been here a long time.

She mounted again, turned the horse, and rode him at the bank, where a collapsed section made a ramp up, onto the prairie. Once there, she turned eastward, then stopped, held fast by the red light of evening, which had painted the eastern mountains a deep magenta. These were the Sangre de Cristos, and this was the light that had given them their name. She went slowly eastward, toward the road. At the intersection of the arroyos, she glanced behind her to see the crow fluttering down onto the pile again, then hop into one of the buckets to peck industriously at the contents.

Abruptly, she gagged. The realization came after the reaction, mind aware after stomach was convinced. She found the first section of collapsed wall, rode down it, and then down the arroyo to the Rancho del Valle road and thence westwardly home, as fast as Zeke could do it without endangering himself or her.

The Jeep was turning into the driveway as she approached it. She waved it ahead, took the horse down to the barn, and unsaddled him. She returned to the house through the back door, went directly to her room, and called Deputy Martinez once more. When she hung up, she sat quietly for a moment, then made another call before joining the family in the kitchen.

"We were giving you up," said J.Q., around a mouthful of pepperoni. "Yours is in the oven."

Shirley glanced at the slice of pizza on his plate, the

bloodlike redness of it, the meaty texture of it. She shook her head. "I . . . may be coming down with something, J.Q. I think I'll just have a cup of tea and go to bed early."

He came to her room about an hour later. "All right. What's going on?"

"I didn't want to say anything in front of Allison."

He shut the door and perched on the side of the bed. "She's doing her homework. Now. What?"

"I rode Zeke along the car tracks, in the arroyo. Just to see if I got any ideas, you know."

He nodded. "And?"

"And when I got to that pile of junk, I looked it over. There were some five-gallon buckets there, J.Q. Metal ones. Three of them, with tar inside, I thought. They were rusty. They looked old. Except the handles were solid, no bends, no . . . well, you know how old wire gets. I guess I saw that subconsciously. Anyhow, I was leaving, and a crow dropped down and began pecking inside the bucket. Crows don't eat tar. And I thought of those three burned places behind Bridget's. And I thought, nobody found the body parts . . . you know. And I thought, why did somebody drive down there that night, late, except maybe to pick up those buckets from where they were hid, and put them somewhere else, where nobody'd even notice them."

"The purloined-letter ploy?" he said softly. "Right out in plain sight?"

"Like that, yes. Junk. In a junk pile. Cans carefully rusted beforehand. With some kind of fuel in them, and then the . . . flesh thrown on that and burned, and then, the whole mess taken . . ." She gulped. "I'd never have noticed, except for the crow."

"Did you call your pet deputy?"

"First thing I got back." She went on to tell him about Deputy Martinez's comments earlier in the day. "The office has it down as extraterrestrials. They weren't even investigating!"

"Will the deputy pick them up? Can he get them tested?"

"I made another call. To Wilson Brett. He's the reporter who covered Bridget's murder. I told him the UFO idea was preventing a proper investigation. I told him the whole story, suggested he camp on the sheriff's doorstep, and force him to deal with it. I told Eddy Martinez I was going to."

"You're not really sure, Shirley."

"No." She said it, not believing it.

"You are sure."

She took a breath like a sob. "I really am, J.Q. I feel it. That's why the crows were there. They wouldn't be pecking at tar, or chemicals, or charcoal. But charred meat, sure."

"Do you suppose there's enough left for a lab to . . ."

She shook her head. "I haven't any idea. I haven't any idea at all. All I know is, I've done everything I can to get someone to deal with it."

6

THE WEDNESDAY-MORNING PAPER detailed the discovery of the buckets, containing, so said Brett's bylined coverage, partially burned organic material that the lab had identified as human flesh. Also, the buckets fit the size and number of the burned circles found at the crime scene. Tests were now being done to find out whether the DNA matched that of the victim. A commentary on the editorial page made several cogent points about the murderer's taking advantage of local credulity to disguise his or her motive.

"That'd be novel," J.Q. asserted, over his morning coffee. "Since when has truth had any status at all?"

The paper also made much of the finding of the second corpse near the place the buckets had been placed. WAS VICTIM WITNESS TO MURDER PLOT? cried a headline.

"At least this will pretty much guarantee we get some

action," Shirley said, casting a worried look over the paper at Allison's face. "Are you all right, All'?"

Allison put down her spoon and stared into her cereal bowl. "When I remember it, I get all . . . I don't know. Mad. Goose-bumpy. Sick to my stomach. But when I realized why she was there, I . . . I actually felt . . ." Her eyes filled and she trembled.

J.Q. put his hand on her shoulder. "You felt glad she was there, dead, instead of her having been there, alive, to spy on you." He patted her heavily, then sat back to unroll his *Wall Street Journal*. "Thinking such a thing makes you feel guilty, as though you might have been responsible."

She nodded, grimacing. "Maybe that's it. If I hadn't agreed to meet Tad . . ."

Shirley put down her paper and poured herself another cup of coffee. "I think it will turn out that Dawn's murderer followed her there. She knew the person who shot her, and if she hadn't been killed there, she'd have been killed somewhere else. Your being or not being there had nothing to do with it."

Allison took a deep breath. "If I'd been there, maybe the murderer wouldn't have done it, because there'd have been another witness."

Shirley shook her head. "Tad's presence didn't stop the killer. In fact, if Tad hadn't been quick and elusive, I rather imagine he'd have ended up dead as well."

"Why do I feel less than grieved at that possibility?" asked J.Q., retreating behind the paper once more.

Shirley said, "Oh, come on, J.Q. He's an amoral brat, but lots of kids are, and most of them outgrow it."

"He ought not to be a brat," Allison cried. "I've met

his mother; she's nice. Tad has a sister, and she's nice. So why is he a brat?"

"Hormones," said J.Q. from behind the barricade. "All those male hormones roiling around and nothing to do with them. Young men need wars and frontiers and tribal raids and stealing horses. They ought to all be sent to military camps when they're thirteen and kept there until they're twenty-five."

"To do what while they're there?" Shirley asked. "Hunt giraffes? You and Newt Gingrich. Funny, though. Mama Swales said something like that. She said women watched soaps and men watched sports, just to pass the time. I guess because they don't have any giraffes to hunt."

"I think women shop," Allison offered. "Women shop and then brag about it just the way men do sports and then brag about it."

"That's an interesting thought," said J.Q., abruptly surfacing once more. "Maybe that explains female fascination with shopping malls. Mankind spent millions of years as hunter and gatherer, much more time than he's spent as a so-called civilized animal, so all the hunter-gatherer instincts are still there, needing to be gratified. So men watch team sports, which is the closest thing to the hunt, and women shop, which is the closest thing to gathering. Write a book about it, Allison."

Shirley grinned. "You left out the bragging part, J.Q. It's hunting, gathering, and counting coup. All of which, according to Mama Swales, doesn't get us anywhere at all." She went to the sink and leaned across it, staring out the window. Mama Swales was not yet in evidence. Her chair was there, a monstrosity by any standard. The thing must be a century old! Like a wicker gurney with hinged head and foot. What they used to call an invalid chair.

"Assuming we've got anywhere to get," J.Q. remarked, burying himself once more. "Allison, you want a ride to school?"

"No," she said around a mouthful of cereal. "I kind of like walking to school with Ulti. Why? Where are you going?"

"To visit the home of Mrs. Dexter French." Shirley returned to the table. "I want to talk to the stable hand over there. The one Tad told me about. Also, now that we have the word on Dawn's pregnancy, her mother will be unable to deny that Dawn was having an affair with someone. Maybe I can find out who."

"You still think whoever killed her had something to do with Bridget's murder."

Shirley shifted, wondering whether, at this juncture, she really did. "I don't know," she said honestly. "It's a coincidence she was there, but then, coincidences happen all the time. It would be silly to think we could all move around in our own lives without sometimes stumbling over other people's."

Allison took her bowl to the sink, rinsed it out, and put it in the dishwasher. "I've got to go."

"How's school?" Shirley asked. "Is there much talk about Dawn?"

Allison made a face, started to speak, stopped. "I guess. Summer and Breeze and Tad all have their heads together, other people are talking in corners. Tad doesn't come near me, and Summer doesn't either. Breeze does, but I'm not sure I like it. There's all kinds of whispering going on." She thrust her arms through the straps of her backpack. "Some of them even drove over to the place during lunch hour yesterday, to see where it happened. Some of them ... some of them think I did it." She clenched her jaw and went out, her back rigid.

"Oh, my God." Shirley shook her head. "I should have seen that coming."

J.Q. put down his paper. "I went past her room last night, she was sitting on the bed crying. We talked. I thought maybe it was that youthful immortality thing, you know, grieving for her own lost innocence. Kids think they're immortal. When one of them dies, they lose that illusion, they are suddenly mortal as well, and the realization hits hard.

"But that wasn't it. I should have known it. Allison came face-to-face with mortality when her mom and dad died. She was crying because people think she might have killed Dawn. Somebody is responsible for that rumor, and I'll bet it's one of those three."

"Summer or Breeze or Tad?" Shirley asked.

"Yes. Despite what you said to Tad, secrets are becoming public, information is bobbing to the top. For instance, Breeze tells Allison that Dawn was attending the local public school as a punishment."

"Punishment?"

"Right. She'd been kicked out of three private schools before she started here, starting when she was thirteen. So her stepfather suggested to her mother that she attend public school, see how the other half lives. She started at the local school in her freshman year. She's been there slightly over a year. When Allison entered, this fall, Dawn took an instant dislike to her."

"Why?" Shirley was outraged.

"For obvious reasons. Allison is sensible, she studies,

she gets good grades, but she's also pleasant and people like her. All of this riled Dawn, so sayeth Breeze. Now Dawn is dead. Allison had nothing to do with it, but still, just deserts and all that, so the student population is focusing on her in a rather unwelcome way."

"And she's grieving over it?"

"She doesn't like being thought a murderess. Who would?"

"We can do something about that misinformation, at least."

"Possibly we should. But let's be careful what we do."

Shirley fumed as she neatened up the kitchen, as she took care of the morning odds and ends, checking that houses were ready for occupancy, that trash had been collected and disposed of, that laundry was not stacking up, that all the bits and pieces of life were properly distributed and attended to. God forfend, she silently demanded as she attended to this minutiae, that Allison should have to care about popularity.

In Shirley's opinion, much of life's trouble resulted from popularity. All those elected officials, like the sheriff of Rio Grande County. All those popular men and women put in office and kept there by people too stunned by life's multiple demands to look beneath the surface, people who didn't care how things got done so long as their private interests were assured. We know you're a liar, they said to a succession of office hopefuls and electees. It's okay to lie to us, so long as you tell us everything's all right.

We know you're a thief, and you can steal from us, so long as you steal only honesty and honor and respect and don't bother those habits, prejudices, and superstitions we call our cultures.

We know you're a hack and a con man, but you can con us out of enlightenment and education and equality so long as we have sports and soaps, talk shows and shoot-'em-ups to distract us.

We know you're superstitious and not too bright, we know you abuse your office, but so long as you pretend to know what you're doing, so long as you smile and wave and tell us you're taking care of things, we'll vote for you.

Shirley snorted. She herself preferred independence, even eccentricity: far better to be incorruptibly obstreperous than to go along; far better to be a quirky individual, however thorny, than to be everyman's ideal. Still, one did not want to be thought a murderess. "Dear God," she prayed, with no sense of mockery, "do not let Allison have to worry too much about being popular."

By the time she and J.Q. set out for the French place, she had talked herself into a better frame of mind.

The French estancia was most visible from across the valley as they descended toward it. The large house was surrounded by a high wall and by so many trees that the branches allowed only glimpses of the house, mostly stretches of adobe with iron grilles covering windows. Several smaller dwellings were scattered uphill from the main house, and a carefully tended polo field lay on the level ground beside the little creek. A lower wall, topped by two feet of jagged coyote fence, shut the entire complex away from the road. When they came to the gate, the five-car garage appeared on the right, open doors disclosing the red sports car Shirley had already seen. On the left stood the stable, a long, low building with its own surround of shrubbery and trees making it virtually invisible from the house.

A man strolled out of the stable and came toward them as they nosed through the gates. J.Q. noted he was in his midforties. Shirley noted that he was quite astonishingly good-looking, wearing highly polished boots and a softly faded flannel shirt.

"My, oh, my," she murmured.

"James Bight," he introduced himself through the car window. "Can I help you with something?"

Shirley introduced herself and J.Q. "I was talking to Mrs. French about Dawn's death, and Mrs. French asked me to continue looking into the matter. I understood there was a young man working here at the stable. . . ."

Bight cast a quick glance up the hill, toward the house. "Come on in here," he suggested quietly, beckoning them out of the car. Shirley parked by the paddock and they followed James Bight through a side door that led into a large tack room. The place smelled of oil and leather and horse; the walls were lined with saddles and festooned with bridles and halters, and bits and pieces of equipment. Their guide gestured at a few bales of straw, a makeshift conversation grouping, as he himself perched on the bale nearest the open door.

"My assistant's name is Isidro. He's from Hopi, by way of San Ildefonso. He's the best help I've had here in ten years, and last Friday he quit."

"Quit? Why?"

Bight gave her a long, level look. "He said he was disgusted, that he couldn't put up with it. I've spent forty years around horses, starting when I was five. I've never seen anyone better than Isidro, though he'd had no experience at all. He took to it as though he understood them, as though they could talk to him and he to them. Dawn French would bring back a mount all lathered up, shivery, eyes going every which way; inside ten minutes Isidro would have it calmed down, eased, gentled. He loves the horses. With her, horses were just something to be controlled, no matter how. She had no respect for them. If she rode one into a wall or crippled it, it didn't matter to her."

"Do you think Isidro killed her, Mr. Bight?"

"Call me James—not Jimmy, please. Do I think Isidro killed her? No. If Isidro ever hurt anyone, he'd do it all at once, suddenly, because he was pushed past where he could stand it, you know? He wouldn't follow anyone and shoot them. That's why I got you in here to talk to you, to tell you that." His eyes were fixed on the house up the hill, and he did not look at them except glancingly.

"It does look suspicious, his quitting one day and her dying the next," Shirley remarked.

He stared her down. "I don't care how it looks. Isidro wouldn't do that."

"You don't want Mrs. French to know you've talked to us?" said J.Q. "You're keeping an eagle eye on the house up there."

"I don't want either of them to know I've talked to anyone, right."

"Why is that?"

"I need this job just now. I've . . ." He turned away from them, then abruptly seated himself once more, leaning forward, confidentially. "Look, I'm a recovering alcoholic. I've been down. I'm on my way back up. I want to put my life and my family back together. When my wife left me, she took everything I had, to keep me from drinking it up, she says. Now she says she'll come back if I stay sober. So right now I need stability. I need this job. I've been here forever; I'm ready to leave, believe me, but for the next few months, I need it. So I'm playing it very cool here. You understand? I don't want waves."

"You think the Frenches wouldn't understand?"

"I don't think they'd even try. The two of them make a good pair. Well, the three of them, if you included the girl. They're slick. Smile, nod, say kind words, and you turn around there's a knife in your back."

"Like?" Shirley asked, shifting on her straw bale.

"I'll give you an example. I have a friend, a faithful friend, who unlike many of my old friends has stayed in touch. He drops by to see me now and then. A few months back he came on my day off, we were leaning on the fence, I was having a soda, he was having a beer, we were talking. Then he, French, drops by, pretending he's looking at the horses. My friend was telling me about a property that he and his sister inherited from his dad, that he wants to sell it, only he hasn't been able to get a good offer. French overheard this, and he asked a few lazy questions as though it didn't matter.

"A few days later my friend got a call from French. French told him he knew someone who might be interested in the property, what's the bottom price he'll take for it? My friend was rather discouraged; he gave French a figure lower than he really wanted, by a good deal, and the next day French brought him a contract for quite a lot less, and he tells him this story about values in that part of town falling, and how they're going to get worse.

"Making a long story short, my friend and his sister sold. A few weeks later the announcement came out that a new highway was going right by the property, and all of a sudden it's worth ten or a hundred times what French paid for it."

"You think French knew?"

"I know he knew. It's the kind of thing he would know."

"So he did a friend a favor."

"Friend, hell. There wasn't any friend. French owns the property. The guy who signed the contract was a stooge for French himself."

"Nothing illegal in it. No law against inside information in real estate," said J.Q. "No law against lying to a buyer."

"Friend, you're wrong there." Bight laughed. "Believe it or not, years ago I was a lawyer, before I drowned the practice in a bottle. If you're a broker, you're required to represent the property honestly. Of course, he could always claim he didn't know. Probably that's exactly what he would do."

"What's a lawyer doing here?" Shirley asked.

"Ex-lawyer, a long time ago. Horses were my hobby, since I was a kid, and now they're my living."

"And you think French is a crook?"

"Oh, I don't think French would do anything illegal. Not where he could get caught, anyhow. I'm just saying he's good at getting what he wants. He can figure a way, you know? And the wife and the girl, they're just like that."

"I've seen them both. Would you say he's broken up about Dawn's death?" Shirley asked.

"Don't know. Haven't seen him. Haven't seen her. Place has been like a morgue since last Saturday."

"Mr. Bight—"

"James."

"James. I'm going to tell you something in confidence. Dawn was three months pregnant when she died. Would you have any idea who the boyfriend might have been? Could it have been Isidro?"

He frowned darkly, making a face. "Not a chance, no. He didn't like her. He treated her like a lit stick of dynamite."

"She was very pretty. I'm surprised he'd be sensible enough to stay away from her."

"He's no kid. He looks young, but he's almost thirty."

"All right. If not Isidro, then who?"

He shook his head, scowling. "Darned if I know. It's not as though she was gone a lot. Her mom kept her on a tight rein after she was expelled from that last private school; that would have been a little over a year ago. Somebody always drove her to and from school— they've got a chauffeur, but when he's off, I fill in as part of my duties. His days off are midweek, so I drove her a lot. She went noplace on weekends unless Mom went along, or French did."

"She went off alone on Saturday."

"Sneaked out, yes. Went over the fence, at the back, and the kid picked her up. That's the way I heard it."

"And the tight rein's been going on for how long?"

"Since a year ago last spring. There was some foofa-raw before that, at Christmastime, then she got sent home from that school in May. With all the yelling and screaming going on around here, the help heard all about it. Her mom told her from here on out, until she's eighteen, she's going to have somebody nannying her."

"Would you know why she was expelled?"

"All I know is her mom was calling her a slut. I figured it had something to do with sex. She was . . . Well, she was a very hot little tamale, put it that way."

"Didn't she make a play for you?"

"She made a play for everyone. I told her I wanted my wife back, I wasn't interested in little girls. Falling for that one would be like falling into the bottle again. After that, she didn't like me much."

Shirley mused, "Would Isidro talk to me? Maybe he heard something from her that would help us."

"You can try. He lives out on the San Pedro Pueblo. There's a trading post out there, Rio Grande Trading Post."

"I know the place."

"Ask them where he is. He works for them sometimes."

"I'd like to go on to the house, talk to Mrs. French, is that possible?"

He shrugged. "I can call." He went through a door into a small room beyond. From where she sat, Shirley could see only the corner of a desk, a small filing cabinet. A door in the far wall opened into a good-sized living room. James Bight's living quarters were right here, by the gate. He would obviously know who came, who went. What did one call his job? Transportation director? In charge of horses and cars? Or was he mostly in charge of security?

She could hear his voice going on and on, explaining.

J.Q. said, "He's catching hell from someone."

A moment later James Bight returned, his face red and his mouth pinched. "Bastard," he said feelingly.

"She doesn't want to talk to me," Shirley suggested.

"Oh, he says she will, at her convenience, if you phone for an appointment." He fumed. "He did all the talking. They're going to St. Thomas next week, says he, and he's not going to waste his valuable time. You should call for an appointment, when they get back."

"Interesting," Shirley opined. "She wanted my help, now suddenly she doesn't. Do they travel a lot?"

"Quite a bit. They go back and forth to her family in Texas. Summers, sometimes, they go to Canada; winters to the Caribbean. They entertain quite a bit. And then he takes his real-estate trips, but those are mostly two-day kinds of things."

"Real-estate trips?" Shirley asked.

"Looking at property. He's got friends here, there, all over. They call him, come look at their house, they want to sell it. So he goes out one day, comes back the next. He used to do it all the time, but not so much lately. Maybe she put a curb on him, too."

"Thanks, Mr. Bight. We'll call Mrs. French at *our* convenience." She grinned at him and rose from her straw bale. "Meantime I think we'll see if we can talk with Isidro."

Bight came to the door with them, still fixed on what could be seen of the house up the hill. He kept on watching it while they turned the car. Only when they went out the gate did Shirley, peering over her shoulder, see him give up this duty as rear guard and go back into the stables. As the road went up the hill she could look down on his domain: stables, paddock, and behind the stables the living quarters extending to the rear, toward the west, with a walled patio at the far end. Pleasant quarters, no doubt, but too large for a single man.

"I don't think he's going to last on that job much longer," J.Q. offered as they went up the hill on the far side of the valley.

"Think they'll fire him?"

"Yes. If he stays sober, he'll be in a position to see too much, know too much. As a drunk, he was okay. If he's prudent, he'll be on the lookout for another job."

"Do you suppose he was disbarred?"

"He said he wanted to put his life back together, not build a new one. Somehow I doubt he was disbarred."

"I think there was something he didn't tell us."

"Maybe Isidro will."

"We can see."

The Rio Grande Trading Post lay deep inside the San Pedro Pueblo at the end of what was either a very long driveway or a fairly short road, near the big river, among the trees of the cottonwood bosque. Outside the door was the truncated remnant of one such tree, an enormously wide stump, fifteen feet tall, with one narrow strip of bark running up the side to produce a tuft of leaves at the top, like hair growing on a corpse. The sheer bulk of the thing had defeated at least two attempts at felling. Deep saw cuts had maimed it, but not quite killed it. Whenever she saw it, Shirley found herself averting her eyes, as from someone badly crippled, wishing they would cut it down and have done with it, wishing they would grind the stump and plant another tree in its place. Or at least fell it and see if it copsed.

"Drains," said J.Q., accurately reading the expression on her face. "They chopped it because the roots were stuffing up the leaching field."

"I know why they did it," she grated. "That doesn't excuse it. I'd have moved the drains. Look at the size of that thing, J.Q. It must be three hundred years old."

Still averting her eyes, Shirley went inside. If the tree outside couldn't be admired, the inside of the trading post certainly could be. The new owners had expanded the original cramped rooms—which had been tacked onto the rear of a dwelling—by adding the dwelling onto the trading post. The airy spaces were newly plastered, floored in a variety of stone, brick, and wood surfaces, with rugs, pottery, and artworks well displayed.

"Isidro?" The trader shook his head. "He's gone on vacation. He has kinfolk in Arizona, at Hano and at Walpi."

"Which is where?" J.Q. asked.

"Hano's the Tewa village near the Hopi on First Mesa. Isidro said he had to get out of New Mexico."

"Why?"

"Someone bothering him."

"Bothering him how?"

"Somebody causing him trouble, that's all I know. It could be a family thing. Or it could be some gang in town he ran afoul of. He brought in a bunch of carvings Friday, late, when I was closing up. He wanted to sell them, all but one, and that one he wanted to pawn. I bought the ones he wanted to sell and lent him money on the pawn. He thanked me, went out, got into his car, and left, headed west. His wife wasn't with him."

"Wife?" asked J.Q.

"Carvings?" Shirley blurted.

The trader regarded them benevolently. "Isidro's Hopi. He's an excellent carver. He's married to a Tewa village woman, and she has kinfolk here in San Pedro. She's a potter, a good one; I have some of her work over there, in the case. It's similar to San Ildefonso style, but with innovative design elements."

"Are these his kachinas?" Shirley asked, pointing at a group of stylized kachinas on one of the side tables.

"Those are the carvings he brought in Friday. Isidro can do traditional-style kachinas, but these are more sculptures than kachinas. He's like his wife; he puts his own twist on things. I didn't want him to leave; he sells too well. At the same time I didn't want him in trouble, or in jail."

"Do you think his wife would talk to us?"

"No idea. She's staying with a cousin named Two Horse Ramirez. Used to be Juan Ramirez, but he's gotten a little militant lately. I can draw you a map." He did so, explaining his cartography as he drew.

Shirley folded the finished product, put it in her pocket, and asked, "Can you get a message to Isidro?"

"I know a guy at a trading post at First Mesa. I can send a fax. They won't go hunting for Isidro, but they'll send word with people who know him."

"Send the message that someone killed Dawn French on Saturday."

The trader was suddenly belligerent. "Isidro was gone by Saturday!"

Shirley shook her head. "I'm not suggesting Isidro had anything to do with it. It's just something he needs to know. Dawn French is the daughter of the family he was working for, and he should know she was killed, that's all."

"What's this really about!"

"Damned if I know. I think Isidro may have gone back to Arizona to keep from getting into trouble with his employers' daughter. By all accounts, she was kind of a . . . what does one say? A troublemaker, I guess. A manipulator. She'd tease men into making an advance, then she'd yell molestation. Something like that."

J.Q., who had been looking over the carvings on the

210

table, picked up one of them and put it on the counter. He pointed to the base, which held a carved stone, with a hollow beneath it from which a spider shape had been carved.

The trader's eyebrows went up. "That's the one he pawned. I never noticed the spider. I didn't really look at them when he brought them in. That spider is totally outside tradition."

He touched it with a forefinger, a tiny arachnid shape, meticulously carved and glossily enameled.

"They don't usually carve spiders?" Shirley asked.

"They don't usually carve anything but the dancer and the appropriate props."

"Look," Shirley said. "Explain this kachina thing to us. It could be important."

"Explain kachinas?"

She nodded.

The trader perched on a corner of his desk. "If the carving is primitive or lifelike, it's a kachina doll, a representation of a kachina dancer who is, in turn, a representation of a spiritual being. That might be the spirit of an ancestor or the spiritual essence of another tribe, or the essence of a species of animal or kind of plant or category of things. There are several hundred kachinas, and they're all guardian spirits, rain bringers. Each one of them has a name and history and a place in the rituals. The spirits are sacred; when the dancers decorate and paint their masks, the masks are inhabited by the spirits, so the masks are sacred; when they put them on, the dancers are also inhabited, so they are also sacred. The Hopi live in a mostly sacred world.

"After the dance, the mask is stripped of paint and decoration, to free the spirit. The person, after the dance,

211

is just a person. After the dance, neither the mask nor the man is sacred. The dolls are not sacred anytime. The dolls are traditionally given to little girls as an educational aid. They bear the same relationship to the sacred dancers as a Bible storybook would bear to the Bible. A Christian, who would treat his Bible with utmost reverence as the actual word of God, wouldn't feel the same way about the storybook. It could be left lying about, or treated casually. A child who would be awed by the kachina dancers can actually play with a kachina doll.

"Sacred things aren't for sale to tourists, but the dolls aren't sacred. So the dolls became a tourist item, and they began to evolve to meet mercantile demand and to provide self-expression for the artists, who responded to that demand by improving the product. Just as the Navajo have improved their weaving and silverwork over the last fifty years, just as the Pueblos have improved their pottery, so the Hopi have improved their carving. The best ones now are fine art, carved all of wood, the feathers and leathers, furs and fabrics all carved in wood, authentically garbed and equipped, meticulously painted and patterned, beautifully done, looking like real persons costumed and wearing a mask. The good ones are expensive.

"Then there are cruder figures carved of wood but dressed up in real feathers, leathers, yarn, bits and pieces of what all. That's beginner's stuff, touristy stuff, much more cheaply done and sometimes without as much regard for authenticity. The Navajos, who don't have kachinas in the way the Hopi do, make a lot of them, strictly for the money.

"There are some similar-looking carvings which are not, strictly speaking, kachinas at all. Occasionally one sees carved figures of deities, and gods are gods, not ancestor spirits. Also, there are carvings of clowns and dancers, who don't wear masks, who aren't representing kachinas, who are performing as people. Still, the representation of a deer dancer or the koyemsi clowns can be fine art. And finally, there are stylized renditions of any of the above which aren't realistic enough to qualify as dolls but may also be fine art.

"You asked what else was carved beside the figure and the costume. A carving of a clown or dancer might allow for a little setting. A clown figure might be shown climbing over the edge of a roof, or he might be seated on a log eating a watermelon, but then, clowns aren't kachinas, strictly speaking.

"As to this spider, I've never seen anything like this one, and since I won't be selling it, I'll ask Isidro what the spider means when he comes to get it back."

"Why would he only pawn it?"

"Because he wants to keep it. It means something to him."

"What is this one?" she asked. "I mean, what kind of kachina?"

"It's one of the exceptions. It isn't one of the usual kachinas. It's not an ancestor or spirit or something earthly. It's a deity, I think, one of the warrior twins. Palo-ngao-hoya . . . paluna-hoya. I'm better at Navajo than at Hopi." He turned the figure in his hands, noting the red moccasins, the mottled skin and shell-decked bandolier, the black-snouted face. Four carved feathers decked the top of its head. "Paluna-hoya is one of the warrior twins. He'd be a deity you'd call on if everything else had failed."

"Not a kachina?"

He frowned. "Sort of a Hopi St. Jude, only more militant."

Shirley concentrated. "Deities preexist man?"

The trader nodded.

"Then the carving would be more like St. Michael," she said. "Who presumably antedated mankind."

"I guess an archangel would be more similar. Anyhow, this is a divine warrior twin, killer of monsters. The warrior twins are important deities all over the Southwest and down into Mexico. The Mayan legends have warrior twins also."

"Both male, I suppose," said Shirley sourly.

"Among the Zuni, yes. But among the Hopi, the younger is sometimes female, and the Mayan name translates as female. The elder is god of the sun, the younger of the moon. The Navajo call them Monster Slayer and Born of Water, and they were raised by their grandmother, Spider Woman."

"Which is this one, the elder or the younger?"

"This one is male."

Shirley took the figure, turned it, set it down, and thanked the trader for his time.

When they were outside and out of earshot, she said musingly to J.Q., "You did notice what kind of spider that was."

"Black widow, wasn't it?"

"Sort of interesting. She's the spider who eats her mate, or rather, eats the male who tries to mate with her."

"You see some connection?"

"In the figure, the dancer's foot is raised. The next time he puts that foot down, the spider is going to be right under it. If these images are intended as prayers or evocations, one might think the warrior god was being asked to do away with a particularly venomous critter."

When they arrived home, Brian McCree's car was in the drive and Brian himself was sitting on a chair beside Mrs. Swales. On the ground beside her chair were several leather cases, and Mrs. Swales beckoned to Shirley, nodding and smiling.

"A new grandson," she said as Shirley approached. "It's so wonderful to meet Beatrice's other boy. Such a pity his wife is sick. He's told me all about the hospital bills and all. We've got to get going on that property, Shirley. Brian says Beatrice didn't leave a will. They've got a court document of some kind that says they inherited her property. The land wasn't even worth enough for them to have to pay inheritance taxes on. I can't imagine what Bridget did with the papers."

"The house was ransacked. Didn't Brian tell you? It could be someone found them and took them."

"What good would that do? According to Brian, the property's still recorded in Beatrice's name."

"You're quite sure?" Shirley asked sharply.

Brian nodded. "Yes, I'm sure. When Mother died, I took care of things, the funeral and all, and the lawyer said we should get the deeds recorded in our names, Bridget's and mine, but we just never got around to it. It's still recorded in Mama's name, but Bridget had the probate papers. Somewhere."

"Look, my lawyer is very good, Pascal Yesney, Yesney and Peake. If you want to consult someone while you're here, he'd be an excellent person, and unlike some of his colleagues, he does not charge several hundred dollars an hour for simple things."

215

"I guess it's about time we see to this," Brian said. "Maybe Bobby and I will go see him together, if he can see us before I have to go back."

"How long can you stay?"

"Two or three days. Phyllis said stay as long as I need to, but if they release her from the hospital, I'll have to go back. My boss's been really good about my being gone so much, but that kind of thing only stretches so far."

"Brian's an underwriter for an insurance company. I think it's so interesting." Mrs. Swales reached out a dainty hand and patted Brian's arm. "Bobby manages a hardware store, back in Oklahoma."

"I thought you were from Chicago?" Shirley said, confused.

"Oh, no. We were just visiting kinfolk in Chicago. We're from Oklahoma. Oklahoma's big rodeo country. I guess I told you I was brought up rodeo. We all had to ride and rope and shoot by the time we were four or five. Daddy wouldn't have it any other way. I brought my kit out here to show Brian."

"It's so interesting," said Brian, kneeling on the gravel beside the leather case and throwing the top back. He lifted up a fringed leather skirt; Shirley estimated it as size ten.

"Wasn't I a skinny little thing?" Mama bubbled. "I can hardly remember what it was like being little like that. Look at my gun belt, Shirley."

Brian lifted out the gun belt, white leather with silver studs and two holsters, each containing a pearl-mounted revolver.

"I did a trick-shooting act," Mama said. "Shot balloons off the backs of trotting horses, shot a cigarette out

216

of the trainer's mouth. They wouldn't let you do that stuff today. Too many people suing each other when something goes wrong. My whole family, we was all rodeo."

"How many of you were there?"

"Ten. Daddy was part Comanche." She giggled, a girlish giggle. "He always said we Indians had to have bigger families, push you white folks back a little."

"I think everybody could stand pushing back a little," Shirley remarked soberly. "There's too damn many of us."

"That's the truth," she agreed. "I told Ella, you stop at two. Don't let Bobby bamboozle you into having six or ten, the way my daddy did my ma. He was a strutter, my daddy."

Shirley left them to their conversation and went on into the kitchen, where she found J.Q. taking care of phone messages. "What did we miss?"

"Nothing very significant."

"I want to tell Brian to be careful while he's here, but I didn't want to upset Mrs. Swales. See if you can catch him alone, J.Q."

"Where's he staying?"

"I told him he could have Frog House, no charge."

"Eating up the profits again."

"He needs it worse than we do. I also suggested he visit Pascal Yesney and get that Montana business straightened out. I can't understand what happened to the papers Bridget had. They wouldn't do anyone else any good, not if the property is recorded as belonging to Bridget's mother. Not so long as . . ." Her voice faded away thoughtfully.

"Um." J.Q. sat down with a thump and finished the

sentence for her. "Not so long as Bridget had a brother. She couldn't have sold the property, could she?"

"She couldn't legally have sold his interest, though she could have sold her share, I suppose. She bought that house with money from somewhere. She told Brian it was casino winnings, but we haven't verified that."

"If she did sell her interest to someone who didn't know she had a brother, that person might assume she'd sold the whole thing."

"That person might try to get rid of the brother, you mean?"

"It's a thought." J.Q. nodded to himself.

Shirley objected, "But now there are two brothers. And two wives, and grandchildren."

"There's also a grandmother. But we're really the only ones who know that, aren't we?"

"If the killer knew it, would it make him back off?"

"Or her."

"Would it make a human interest story?"

"You're thinking of getting it into the paper, by that reporter? What's his name, Brett?"

Shirley got up and went to the window and looked out at Mrs. Swales and Brian, still deep in conversation. "I am. Something along the lines of 'Tragedy Brings Sundered Family Together.' "

"Sundered?"

"Why not?"

"It wasn't exactly sundered. More separated. Or maybe lost."

"I started this conversation by suggesting that Brian ought to be careful. Lost, separated, or sundered, he should still be careful."

"Agreed." J.Q. got to his feet, stretched, looked at his

watch and headed for the door. "It has suddenly occurred to my stomach that we haven't had lunch."

"Oh, right. I'll fix us some sandwiches or something."

She was busily slicing tomatoes when Brian knocked, then stuck his head in the door.

"I've called your lawyer. He says he'll make time to see us if we come into town right now. Bobby's driving me. Ella and the kids are staying with Mama."

"You and Bobby had better move her inside before you leave. It's supposed to rain this afternoon."

"We will. What are you making?"

"DNP sandwiches." She grinned. "Damn-near-perfect sandwiches. It's basically a BLT on dark pumpernickel bread, with guacamole, white cheese, and sprouts. You want one?"

"Oh, that'd be grand."

"I'll make you a full-size one. You can share it with Bobby." The middle slices of the round loaf were huge. Shirley slathered together a sandwich, piling it with bacon, and then pushing down firmly to meld the ingredients. "The trick is to let the cheese warm up a little. I used the microwave." She cut the massive construction into halves, wrapped them in foil, and sent him away with the two packets. A moment later she heard the car leaving. Damn. She'd been so busy feeding him she'd forgotten to tell him to be careful.

J.Q. returned with the mail, mostly magazines. They sat down to their late lunch, munching and sorting the mail, browsing through the *New Yorker*—J.Q.'s—and *Natural History* magazine—Shirley's.

"What's Stephen J. Gould in an uproar about this month?" J.Q. asked around a mouthful of sandwich.

"People who would rather believe in superstition than

science," she replied. "Creationists. People who still believe the earth is the center of the universe."

"All you have to do to disbelieve that is stand out under the stars," he said.

She put down *Natural History* and picked up *Scientific American*: an article on bonabos, how they used sex as a social bond. An article about the age of the universe. It seemed the Hubble Telescope had determined that the stars were older than the universe was. Cosmologists in a pickle. Standing out under the stars wouldn't solve that confusion.

Under the stars. Bridget said something about under the stars. She put the magazine down with a fretful sound.

J.Q. asked, "What's wrong?"

"I'm remembering something. Bridget said she wrote it all down in her journal, under the stars."

"So, she wrote at night."

"You can't write under the stars at night, J.Q. You can't see what you're writing. And if you have a light, you can't see the stars."

He looked up from the page. "So?"

"So . . . I suddenly thought, maybe she meant some other stars, that is, the pentacles. In her hogan."

"On the floor?"

"Right. That doesn't make sense. Now wait, maybe it does. She said it was in her journal, *set* down under the stars."

"Set. Meaning placed. Put."

"Put. Yes. She put it under the stars. J.Q. Hurry up and finish your sandwich. We need to go over to Bridget's house right away."

J.Q. refused to be hurried, and it was almost two

when they turned into the side road. Clouds had gathered, and a light cool wind had come up, but there was no rain as yet. They parked in the drive, where Shirley had parked before, then went around to the back where the hogan was. The blanket covering the opening had been jerked loose and lay on the ground in a dusty heap, but nothing was much changed inside. The pentacle painted on the dirt floor had been trampled and worn, but its outline still showed clearly. To get inside, Shirley had to get down on hands and knees, and her knee protested. She turned about at the center of the little hive-shaped space, examining the floor.

She turned toward the opening. "The dirt was wet," she said, pointing to the star point nearest the opening. "Right there. As though she might have dampened it to make it smooth."

"I'll see if there's a spade in the garage." He left her and she continued kneeling upright, looking out through the opening and up through the smoke hole. This structure had to be fairly new. The mud construction wouldn't stand up to much rain or snow. Unless Bridget had replastered it, at intervals.

J.Q. returned. "No spade. This is the best I could do." He pushed a large, rather rusty trowel toward her. Shirley reached for the pillow lying against the wall and put it under her steel knee. Thus padded, she dug into the soil at the tip of the star.

"I shouldn't think it would be very deep," J.Q. opined. "She wouldn't want to dig a deep hole, not if she had to dig it up very often."

"Four inches," Shirley muttered as the trowel scraped across a metallic surface. She shoveled industriously, uncovering a metal box about eight-by-thirteen inches,

221

wrapped inside a plastic sack that she had ripped to shreds with the trowel.

She levered it out of its resting place, thrust it out the door at J.Q., then put the dirt back in the hole. "J.Q., find me some more dirt. I don't want this to look hollow. And there's some paint inside the kitchen door, in the nicho."

"You're putting it back the way it was?"

"Well, I have this hint of an idea, and I think we ought to make it look undisturbed."

He went away, returned with a flowerpot full of soil, then departed again. Shirley filled the hole, thumped it with her fist, then scraped it smooth with the side of the trowel. The surface was different from the rest of the area. She was about to yell at J.Q. when he returned and handed her a glass of water.

"Right," she said, sprinkling it on the disturbed soil, then repeating the thumping-and-smoothing procedure.

"The house was locked," J.Q. said, "but the kitchen window was open. Here's the paint, but the brush is hopeless. It's dried completely stiff."

"Maybe there's another one in the garage," she suggested, crawling out of the confined space and using J.Q.'s proffered hand to haul herself upright. He went away again while she examined the box. It, too, was locked. After a time J.Q. returned with a brushy bit of fiber in his hand.

"The Indians use yucca fiber," he remarked. "There's yucca in back of the garage. If this won't do, we'll have to bring something from home."

She tried the dried leaves, using a small stone to pulverize the connective tissue at the base of the leaves. The result was not exactly artist's material, but she supposed it would do. She put some paint into the glass of water, thinned it well down, then used the yucca leaves to brush the tinted liquid onto the soil, recreating the tip of the star.

"Too white," opined J.Q.

"Give it a minute to soak in. We'll throw dust on it."

They did throw dust on it. When they left it, the floor looked undisturbed.

"You're taking this to Brian, of course," J.Q. said, all innocence.

"Of course," Shirley agreed. "After I've seen what's in it."

The box yielded to persuasion in the form of a chisel. Perhaps not surprisingly, it contained videotapes, ones Shirley had already seen: Bridget with her unknown partner. The tape of the same unknown man and the younger woman was not included. Shirley checked the contents in the privacy of her bedroom, running them on fast forward, then put them away with the ones she'd bought from Pete Merwiczi. She described them briefly to J.Q., but she thought Brian didn't need to see them, and neither did anyone else.

Also in the metal box was the deed to the Montana land; a journal written in so minuscule a hand that any attempt to decipher it resulted in immediate migraine; and a copy of a bill of sale in which Bridget McCree turned over her entire interest in certain specified land in Montana in return for a house near Santa Fe. The legal descriptions of both pieces of property were appended.

The name of the other party to the sale was not.

"It would explain the attack on Brian," J.Q. remarked.

"I don't want to give him this journal until I've had

223

a chance to read it," Shirley complained. "But we've got to give him this bill of sale and deed immediately."

"So, we'll tell him we found the box, and the bill of sale was in it. If you want to give him the journal later, we'll have to have found it somewhere else."

"You don't think it's too dishonest. . . ."

"Of course it's dishonest. But I presume you're trying to save him pain. You may have to give it to him anyhow, but if it's painful and not relevant, the minor dishonesty is excusable."

She grinned ruefully. "Right, J.Q. Put the bill of sale back in the box, along with the deed. Give it to Brian and Bobby as soon as they get back. Meantime I'm going to get a magnifying glass and see how far I can get reading this thing."

Back in her bedroom, she flipped through the pages. At the end of the book was a section devoted to patients, their names, in some cases their addresses and phone numbers, a brief description of their troubles and the amount they had paid. The section was undated but was presumably written in chronological order.

The front of the book was like a diary, with entries made every few days, or on successive days. The entries weren't dated by year. Each one was headed with a day of the week, sometimes with the month mentioned. Starting at the last entry, which Shirley thought would probably have been made in the days or weeks immediately preceding Bridget's death, she worked her way back through the pages, making faint pencil notes at the bottom corner of pages: minus one, minus two, minus three, minus four years. The first entries had been made in the spring, four years before.

Autumn, four years past. Bridget was in love. She

224

bubbled and chortled on the page. She had met him through her business; he had come in and asked her to prepare a report for him. She recorded erotic details that made Shirley feel like a consummate voyeur. Bridget recorded everything about the man, his looks, his style, his mannerisms, his words—he had what Shirley regarded as an excessively earthy vocabulary—everything but his name. They went on vacation together. They camped out in the forest together. They swore undying fidelity. They went to a tattoo parlor together. They each had a tattoo, the same tattoo.

Shirley made a note. *Bridget, tattoo?*

Winter, four years past. Tragedy. The lover was being threatened by his wife. Someone had seen him and Bridget, or seen his car, or seen something. His wife was now suspicious and had issued an ultimatum. Cease or I divorce you. All the lover's money had been invested in his wife's business. He no longer had access to his own funds. For the time being they must play a waiting game, until he could extricate himself. Much wailing, much sorrow. They must not risk discovery; the only way they could continue to be together would be if she moved out of Santa Fe.

What should she do with her business, the business it had taken her years to build? What did her business matter in the face of this great passion? She would sell the business; she would use the funds to live in some small town, not too far away, where he could visit her. Then, when he had extricated himself and his money from his wife's clutches, they would run away together, far away, where no one would ever bother either of them again. This rhapsody went on for paragraphs.

There then followed a listing of towns, people's

names, the search for a rental house in Mora, in Penasco, in Dixon, in Espanola, in Madrid. Madrid was chosen. It was out of the way. She had found a house that could be rented cheaply. She was moving to Madrid.

At that point Shirley's eyes gave out. She took off her glasses, lay back on the bed, eyes closed, and promptly fell asleep.

She woke to a tug and an insistent voice. "Shirley? Wake up."

She sat up, rather groggily. "J.Q.? What's the matter?"

"Nothing's the matter, except Brian's back, and he has a tale."

Brian was waiting in the kitchen to tell them that Pascal Yesney had called the recorder's office in Montana. Yes, the property was still recorded in Beatrice's name, but also recorded was a bill of sale, to the Western Mountain Land Development Corporation, at a post office box in Albuquerque.

"I called information," said J.Q. "They have no listing."

Brian ran his hand through his thinning hair. "Mr. Yesney's starting a process to clear the title. He says Bridget could sell her interest, all right, but that's not the same as selling the property. Legally, it's more like a lien against the property. We have to clarify that claim before we can put the property up for sale."

"If she'd been the only heir . . ." Shirley mused.

"Then it could have been equivalent to selling the property, he says. But since Beatrice had three of us kids, and since she left no will, then Bridget never really had title to it. She had only a one-third interest. Mr. Yesney says so long as she wasn't married and had no children of her own, there should be no question about who owns the property. Bobby and I do."

"How does something calling itself the Western Mountain Land Development Corporation fit into all this?" Shirley demanded. "And how and when did Bridget get involved with them?"

"It had to be when she moved from Madrid," said J.Q.

"How? Bridget didn't know the land was valuable, did she?"

"I didn't know until you told me." Brian rotated his head on his neck, trying to work out the kinks. "I don't believe Bridget would have cheated me on purpose. I don't think she knew it was worth anything."

"Let's try this scenario," Shirley suggested. "Suppose Bridget thought the property in Montana was worth around fifty or sixty thousand. Suppose somebody offered to give her the house here in exchange, and she knew the house was worth at least four times that. Mightn't she have sold the land, intending to leave you the house or give you a half interest? She might think she'd done you a favor."

Brian nodded slowly. "Bridget might, yes. She might have thought that way."

"So then, when you came to her, asking her for the papers so the property could be sold, what would she do?"

"Well, she couldn't give me any money, because she didn't have any. She couldn't sell the house . . . or maybe she just didn't want to sell the house. So, she'd . . ."

"She'd go to the person she'd sold to, call him X, and she'd tell X that her brother was part owner? She'd

227

say that X had to lend her some money for the brother? Or that X had to give her back half the property? Something of the kind?"

"Right. Probably."

"At which point, the person who traded her the house kills her and tries to kill you? Which means that person undoubtedly knows what's going on in Montana."

"Now we all know!" said J.Q. "And that knowledge ought to be widely disseminated. It's important we let the world know that Brian isn't the only other heir."

"You think Mr. X really tried to kill me off the other day by cutting my brakes?" Brian shook his head in disbelief.

"I think somebody might have tried to do you some harm, yes. Did you tell Bobby about that?"

"I told him everything I know. J.Q. says you're the one who figured out where the deed was."

"I did. Something Bridget said made me think where it might be, and the two of us went over and got it. Did he give it to you?"

J.Q. said, "It's over there on the counter."

Brian shook his head. "Funny. Why would she hide it like that?"

Shirley, well aware why Bridget would have hidden the contents of the box, merely shook her head to indicate bafflement.

"How did you figure it out?" Brian asked.

"She said something to me once, about setting something under the stars."

"Under the star! Of course!" he crowed. "When we were kids! We lived in this house with a kind of patio out at the side. It was made out of concrete pavers, set in sand, in patterns—hexagons and triangles that made

228

six-pointed stars. We used to hide things under the tiles, and we'd hint to each other, I set it under the triangle, I set it under the star. Where was there a star at Bridget's?"

"In the hogan. Painted on the floor," said J.Q.

He paled. "I never went out there. I didn't want to see. . . ."

"Just a tiny room with a dirt floor. It's where she did her healing," Shirley said soothingly. "She painted a star on the floor."

"I didn't believe in it. Phyl, she didn't believe in it. I wonder if she really did. . . . Bridget, I mean."

"She healed heartache. That's all Buffalo Man healed either, heartache. His daughter told me. When Bridget and her . . . friend broke up, Buffalo Man helped her, and then when he died, Bridget decided to do it herself. She was a loving woman, Brian. Just listening to somebody's troubles often helps them."

"That bastard."

"What bastard?"

"Him, whoever he was. I never knew Bridget to be that way before, the way she was when he was around. Like a kid, all lit up on Christmas Eve, you know? Gave up her business, gave up her life, moved out there where she didn't know anybody, kept him a secret. Why did it have to be such a secret?"

Shirley bit her tongue firmly. "I don't know. Didn't you ever get a hint of who he might be?"

"Never a hint. According to Bridget, he was perfect. He was educated, he had taste, he was sophisticated, and he was madly in love with her. I think it was that last bit that really mattered. She wanted someone to be madly in love with her." He sighed and rubbed at his eyes. "She knew he was married, but it didn't matter to her. Bastard. I want to get her house on the market, too. Mr. Yesney is helping me with that. That realtor, Crabbe, he never dropped a card by, did he?"

Shirley stared at him, a long moment, then turned wordlessly to the desk. She took out the phone book, looked up Realtors in the Yellow Pages, and ran her finger down the Santa Fe listing. Then she turned to the business listings in the white pages and repeated the search. "No Crabbe," she said in an expressionless voice. "Not in Santa Fe, not in Espanola, not in Los Alamos. He might have been from somewhere else, but that doesn't make much sense."

"Maybe he just moved here?"

"Maybe," she said, not believing it for a moment. It was entirely too coincidental. "What did he look like, Brian?"

Brian frowned in an attempt to remember. "Tall. Very blond. Nice looking. Very . . . professional. He had a briefcase."

"Tycoon," said J.Q. "The one Kip and Joana mentioned."

"Probably so," Shirley agreed. Crabbe, whoever he had been, had not been a local realtor looking for listings. Whoever he was, he didn't want them to know who he was. And there could be no virtuous reason for that.

7

"WE KNOW WHO killed Dawn," Breeze said, in an almost whisper to Allison as she stowed her books in her locker, shut the door, then leaned against it, awaiting Allison's response.

Allison noted the watchful faces here and there down the hall. Summer, and Tad, and a half-dozen other kids who had always been more or less in Dawn's camp.

"Really?" she said, in what she hoped was an uninterested voice. "Who told you?"

"Nobody had to tell us." Breeze's voice was louder now, and the others in the hall had moved somewhat nearer. "It's obvious. Those people you live with killed her because they were mad about what Dawn and Tad planned to do. They probably intended to kill Tad, too, but he got away."

Allison felt herself quaking, felt her face go cold and pale. Damn Breeze. "Unless Tad is a liar, that wouldn't

231

be possible, Breeze. Shirley and J.Q. and I were at a neighbor's house when Dawn was killed."

"So you say," said Summer, from down the hall.

"Yeah," echoed Tad. "That's what you say. You can't prove it."

The others in the hall had moved closer. There was something in their manner that Allison did not like. They'd planned this. What did they plan to do? Assault her? Right here in the hall at school? With teachers still in their rooms where they could hear?

"The sheriff's deputies are satisfied that we weren't involved," Allison said stiffly. "None of us. We have witnesses to that."

"Yeah, well, we think maybe the sheriff ought to take another look at you, because you and your people are the only ones who had something against Dawn. You didn't like her, and probably you told your folks, so they didn't like her."

"How did my folks know she was there?" Allison surprised herself by asking. "Since she'd sneaked there, since I didn't know, how did they know?"

"They followed you." Tad spoke up gloatingly. "They followed you, then they stopped you, and they came on and shot Dawn. Or maybe they didn't stop you, and you came with them and helped shoot her!"

Allison held her books protectively before her, feeling her face burn with anger. They'd planned this. There were nine or ten of them, at least, and they had already decided to do something nasty. It wouldn't matter what she said. They were like a dog that decided to nip at you, or a horse that decided to try to kill you, just for the hell of it.

"What's going on?" asked a new voice.

She looked up. Close behind Tad was a familiar face. Ulti.

"None of your business," said Tad.

Ulti moved so fast that Allison couldn't even see what happened, except that Tad was on the floor and Ulti was standing over him. "I don't mind hitting women," he said to the wall. "When they're bitches who need hitting. You want to clear out of here, Smythe? You, Watkins? Or you want me to help you clear out of here."

Summer and Breeze melted away. Down the hall, a door opened, and Jeremy Patterson stuck his head out into the hallway.

"Allison?" he called. "What's going on?"

"Go tell him," Ulti instructed, looking down at Tad. "Right now."

"I don't want to. . . . I'll get them in trouble," she objected.

Ulti snorted. "Right. That's sort of the idea."

Half-reluctantly, she went down the hall to tell Mr. Patterson what had happened.

"Now that's interesting," he said, when Allison had finished a play-by-play account. "Breeze and Summer. Heirs apparent for the role of chief bitch. They really are nasty little shits, aren't they? Don't quote me, Allison. I could lose my job."

Allison flushed, nodded. She knew enough to keep her mouth shut. "They know I didn't have anything to do with it, or Shirley or J.Q. What do they think they're doing?"

"I doubt they even know," he said. "Their whole lives are lived by soap-opera standards, and they're not

233

worth worrying about. Is Ulti going to walk you home?"

"I think so."

"If you want to walk with him, fine. I'll give you a ride if you like."

"I think they're gone."

"Well, go drag Ulti off Tad. I'll take care of Tad."

She didn't need to drag him. Ulti stepped contemptuously over Tad Pole and went out the front door with her while Mr. Patterson moved in from down the hall. No one was waiting outside. No one was waiting in the parking lot. The incipient mob had evaporated.

"Who put them up to that?" Ulti wanted to know.

"Breeze, I think."

"She's a bitch, that one."

"Why do people call ... women bitches? Women they don't like? I mean, a bitch is a female dog, but we like dogs, mostly."

"It doesn't have anything to do with dogs," he replied as they went across the parking lot to the edge of the arroyo and down the bank into the arroyo bottom.

"It honestly doesn't," he went on as they reached the path. "It's what we call a woman who doesn't fit our idea of what a woman ought to be. So, one guy calls a woman a bitch because she works instead of staying home with the kids. Another guy calls a woman a bitch because she yaps at him all the time. Another guy calls her a bitch because she likes sex, and his idea is women shouldn't like it. It's just a word. I call Breeze a bitch because she doesn't have any ... ethics."

"Ethics?"

"No ... no system. Nothing she believes in. I like people to have something they believe in. It usually

234

doesn't matter what, just so long as they stick to what they believe in."

The day was gray, with a chilly wind, and Allison shivered as a gust of it came around a corner, blowing sand into her face. They walked for a time in silence, but a glance at Ulti's face told her he was still angry.

"It's all right," she said, not meaning it.

"It isn't all right," he muttered. "They know damn well your . . . well, she's not your mom, so what do you call her?"

"Shirley? I call her Shirley. She's my guardian. Sometimes she calls me her foster child."

"Well, whatever she is, those kids know damn well she didn't do anything to Dawn."

"Did you know about Dawn and the teachers?"

"What about them?"

"Dawn kept trying to get the men teachers in trouble. She'd pretend something was wrong with her neck or back, to get them to touch her. And she'd have Breeze or Summer watch so they could say they saw it."

He stopped, glaring. "That's rotten. I mean, sure, some men are like Tad the Frog, they think women are some kind of game you make points on. But it's rotten to do that to a teacher. I wonder how come I never heard about it."

"Mr. Patterson told Shirley. He said he had to lure Dawn away, down the hall to Susan Williams's room."

"Who?"

"Susan Williams?"

"Is she a teacher?"

"I . . . I don't know. The way Mr. Patterson told it, I thought so."

235

"Funny," he said, shaking his head. "I don't know any Susan Williams who's a teacher."

Shirley, after a mostly silent supper with Allison and J.Q. plus a solitary hour in her bedroom reading Bridget's journal, leaned back on her pillows, shut her eyes, and tried to reprise what she had read in less breathless tones than Bridget had used.

After Bridget's move to Madrid, her journal account was solely dedicated to her extremely erotic love affair. As a matter of fact, eroticism seemed to be its sole component. Even when the journal mentioned a trip the two of them had taken together, what was set down on paper did not reveal the surroundings, did not detail the conversations, did not disclose any shared experience except the time spent alone together. Whether in a motel room or a forest glade or a hot spring, what they did and all they did was sex it up like crazy.

It was not routine. Either or both of them had been remarkably inventive. Most such chronicles would quickly become repetitive, but Bridget's accounts remained unflaggingly novel. Each episode was designed, like a drama, with a great deal of costuming and role-playing. Evidently Bridget's lover scripted these encounters, telling her precisely what she was to do, and it seemed she had no problem following his direction, no matter how demeaning—as it frequently was—or painful—as it sometimes was. Either the man had a library full of porn that he was living out, or he had one hell of an imagination.

In Bridget's accounts, she spoke only of *he*, or *him*. There was no mention of a name or of any identifying detail. The journal was structured like fiction, and if

236

Bridget had had nothing else to live on, she could have made her living as a pornographer.

On the final pages Shirley had read tonight, Bridget had been a slave girl, singled out to be given to some pagan deity. That particular plot had lasted for several sessions of bathing and oiling and incensing and dressing in erotic clothing, first a costume of silk, then one of leather, then one made mostly of beads. *Where does he get these wonderful clothes?* Bridget bubbled onto the page. *He says he makes them. I wonder if he really does.*

Was it possible to think of this man, this unflagging lover, this imaginative paramour as a murderer? So far he was one of only two suspects in Shirley's mind, neither of them with a name. This man, the Lover, had killed her for some unknown reason; or the other man, Tycoon, had killed her for profit, assuming he was part of Western Mountain Development Corp.

But why stop there? With all this role-playing going on, why not assume that other persons might also have played games? Perhaps Brian had been playing a part. Perhaps Brian had known all along about the copper strike and had, himself, inveigled Bridget into selling him the property before he killed her. All this grief and horror he was expressing could be pure drama. Perhaps even the drained brake line had been pretense. Far-fetched, but remotely possible. In that case, lover and murderer were, probably, two different men.

Or, what about Bobby? They had only Bobby's word that he had just recently learned of Bridget and Brian's existence. Perhaps he had found out about them a year or two before, without letting Mama or Ella know about it. Perhaps he had approached Bridget, without ever saying who he was, and offered to trade house for land. If he had not had enough money to buy the house, perhaps he had taken a partner who had the necessary capital, and he and his partner were Western Mountain etc. In which case Brian's brake line was readily explained, for Bobby knew all along that Bridget had a brother.

To eliminate them as murderer, one would need to know where they were, each of them, last Friday, and since two of her postulated suspects were totally anonymous, that seemed to be impossible.

Was there anyone else she could suspect? Buffalo Man was dead, so he was out of it. Did it have to be a man? Suppose Buffalo Man had been Western Mountain Development, and had then been accidentally killed? His daughter, Lydia, would inherit, and she would have no way of knowing Bridget had a brother until Shirley told her. Or suppose father and daughter had been in it together?

Going at it that way, allowing for the unlikely, anybody could be a suspect. Including Kip and Joana from next door. Perhaps Kip was the unflagging lover, and Joana a complacent accomplice. What it really came down to was that anyone who could have known about the discovery of copper in Montana was a suspect.

If it was any one of these people, however, what did they have to do with Dawn French?

Not a damn thing. There was no way Bridget's Tycoon or Bridget's Lover could tie to Dawn French, and no way Bobby or Brian or Buffalo Man's daughter could either.

"Shirley." A sad little voice.

She sat up. "Allison? What is it?"

"I'm just . . . Can I sit on the bed with you for a while?"

"Of course, child. Come tell me what's the matter."

"I'm just . . . sick of those kids is all. Summer. And Breeze. And Tad. Today, after school, they ganged up on me. They accused you and J.Q. of killing Dawn, because of what she was going to do to me, and they said I might be involved in it, and if Ulti hadn't come along and knocked Tad on his butt, they might have—I don't know—they might have hurt me."

"You're saying there was a group? That they all knew what Dawn was planning? I told Tad to keep his filthy little mouth shut."

Allison wiped at her eyes. "I think they knew before it ever happened. Summer knew, and Summer couldn't keep a secret if her throat was slit. And I don't think Breeze would even try. And let's face it, Dawn may have spread it around. She always had a lot of fun whispering in corners. I think the whole school knew what the plan was, maybe last week, before Tad even called me."

"So who thought up this idea that J.Q. and I did the deed?"

"Breeze, I think. They were all waiting in the hall, around ten of them, and Breeze accused me and they all started to kind of gang up on me. Then Ulti came. He was so mad."

"This group, you know who the kids are?"

"Yeah. I know their names."

"Write them down for me. Here, take this pad."

Allison scribbled, remembering nine names. Shirley read them over slowly.

"What would you like to do about it?" she asked.

"I'd like to bury them all about ten feet deep."

"Particularly Breeze and Summer and Tad?"

"Particularly them."

"I think we can start with them." Shirley scooted to the side of the bed next to the phone, picked it up, and dialed the sheriff's office. "May I speak to Eddy Martinez, please?"

She smiled at Allison, waiting.

"Deputy Martinez? Shirley McClintock. I have some additional information for you. Breeze Watkins and Summer Smythe, two of Dawn's friends from school, are telling people that they know who killed her. Tad Pole has some information as well; he was actually there when she was shot. Also, there are six more young people who may have information. Shall I read their names?" She did so, slowly, spelling them. She listened, said yes and no a few times, then wished them a good day and hung up.

"What'll happen?" asked Allison.

"The sheriff's office will pick them up for interviews. Which should be unpleasant for them. Particularly inasmuch as I'm about to make some additional calls." She took the phone book from the table drawer and opened it to the *W*s. Walter, Wanamaker, Wanslow, Waters, Watkins. "They live in Tesuque, right?"

She dialed. "Mrs. Watkins. You're Breeze's mother? My name is Shirley McClintock; my foster daughter is in school with your daughter; and I'm afraid your daughter has made some rather serious allegations against me personally. I consider them slanderous. Prior to calling my attorney, I thought I'd call you and ask whether you care to intervene before the child gets herself in real trouble."

"_____!"

"That's right. Pertaining to the death of Dawn French."

"_____?"

"Quite. Her mouth seems to have outrun her good sense." Aside to Allison: "Assuming she has any."

"_____!"

"Thank you so much for discussing the matter with her. I'll be expecting her personal apology, Mrs. Watkins. I'll expect to receive it at the school, in front of the same people who were there when she made her accusation, tomorrow afternoon at three-thirty."

And the disconnect.

"Shirley!"

"Never too early, Allison, to let people learn about responsibility. Next stop, Summer's mama. Then Tad's father, and I'm really looking forward to that one."

Summer's mama was a fluttery type who had elevated incomprehension to an art form. Shirley had to get rather nasty before Mrs. Smythe woke up to what was happening. Once she did, however, her reaction was gratifying. Mr. Pole, by his astonishment, let it be known that he had been kept completely in the dark about his son's involvement in anything more serious than bird-watching.

Shirley said loftily, "He was actually there when Dawn was shot, Mr. Pole. As to why he was there, I believe it may have been a juvenile attempt at blackmail. Certainly it was a conspiracy to ruin my daughter's reputation. Not the kind of thing one would expect from the son of an officer of the court. Boys will be boys, we all know that, but malice of this kind is exceptional, don't you agree?"

241

The words that came were stiff, shocked, not quite apologetic. Shirley didn't push it. Mr. Pole would warm up by the time Tad was on the receiving end.

"I will be expecting his personal, public apology," said Shirley, as she had to Mrs. Watkins and Mrs. Smythe. "I will be at the school tomorrow afternoon at three-thirty, to receive it.

"There," said Shirley, reaching out to lift Allison's chin. "Does that make you feel any better?"

"It . . . it shouldn't, should it? I mean, it's being really nasty." Still, she was trying not to grin.

"Well, it's fighting fire with fire, Allison. It isn't always a good idea; sometimes, if it leads to escalation, it's actually a bad idea; but in this particular case, I think the kids involved need to learn something about real life. Such as: actions have consequences. In this case, the consequence is me on the warpath."

"You don't think this will lead to escalation?"

"I don't think they have anything to escalate with. Besides, I have an ulterior motive. Put Summer and Breeze under a little pressure, like the wine grape, they may suddenly produce juice. Informative juice, one hopes. Do you feel better or worse?"

"Better, I guess. They had me all worried. Let them worry awhile."

"Right."

"I did want to ask you one thing. Didn't Mr. Patterson tell you something about Dawn, about his taking her to another teacher's room?"

"He did. Susan Williams, he said."

"Ulti says he doesn't know any Susan Williams, and he's been going to school there forever."

Shirley stared at the wall, considering. Had it been

Susan Williams? She was sure it had. Why would Patterson have told her a tale? Was the whole story a fib, or merely the part about the other teacher? And if the whole story was made up, why?

"That's interesting," she murmured. "It might mean something. Or it might not. Now, is there homework waiting doing?"

"Not much. I'm almost finished."

"I suggest you finish it, but first . . ." Shirley glanced at her watch. "It's only ten on the East Coast. Why don't you call Mingy and talk to her for a few minutes. Tell her about this whole thing. Her advice on interpersonal matters is always good. Be sure to tell her what I did. She'll think it was dreadful. You can tell her I'm on the warpath and let her tsk at you."

"Can I? Oh, that'd be great. I miss her."

So did Shirley. At the moment she missed Mingy very much. "Go do it."

Allison left. Shirley fumed, stretched, reached for Bridget's journal, then put it down fretfully. She really didn't need any more of Bridget's erotic euphoria. What else instead? Dawn's notebook. Maybe Dawn had written something about her attempts on the teachers. Maybe she, too, had kept a kind of diary.

Shirley had put it in the top drawer of her dresser, from which she retrieved it. Sitting at her desk, under a good light, she began going through it page by page. Notes on classes. English. Algebra. Social studies. French. Biology. Nothing there of any interest whatsoever except a unique eccentricity in spelling and punctuation. If this was the best Dawn could do, pity the poor teacher who had to read her papers!

There followed a few pages containing lists of names.

One list, beginning with Dawn's name, contained Summer and Breeze's names plus a few others. Another list, headed *Possibles*, on which Tad was listed, and a third headed *Impossibles*. Among the impossibles, Allison's name was prominent. As was Jeremy Patterson's. Were there other teachers on Dawn's list? Shirley glanced down the list, seeing a couple of names that seemed familiar, but not able to identify them. Susan Williams was nowhere mentioned. Of course, Allison had been in the school for only a couple of months, and Jeremy Patterson was the only teacher Shirley had actually met.

The next section was a folder that had been taped top and bottom, turned backward, and hole-punched on the open side to fit the three-ring binder. Whatever was inside was protected against peeking and could only be seen if the folder itself was removed. Sighing, Shirley removed it and dumped the loose pages on the desk.

They were numbered. They were full. They were in code.

Shit. Shirley snarled to herself. Then she looked again, stared, jotted rapidly with a pencil, and grinned. Silly little twit. All she'd done was write the words with spaces between each two letters, then filled the spaces with random letters. Shirley took the first half-dozen pages to the library, where there was a copier. She ran two pages, took them back to her desk, and began whiting out every other letter. The result read:

There's this music, from some old play. "Baubles, Bangles and Beads." He put it on the record player. The dress has beads all over it, inside, and when you lie on it, it feels . . . strange. He had gloves with beads all over them, and when he put his hands on me . . .

Shirley sat back. Well, well. She skipped to the next page. *He has this underwear made out of leather, and.* . . .

Gritting her teeth, she searched the space between, finding the references she had halfway expected. Baths and fragrant oils and silk clothing. Bridget's erotic slave-girl scenario, all over again.

For the love of God, who was *he*?

She started out of the room, stopped suddenly, then went back to unearth the tape she had received from Pete Merwiczi. She put it in the VCR and ran it fast forward, settling on the last sequence, the one with the younger woman. Then slowly, she started and stopped until she came to a short section where all was in shadow except for the girl's face. She stopped it there and went to get Allison.

"Who?" she asked, when they returned to her room. "Do you know who this is?"

"It's Dawn French," Allison replied. "What's she doing? Where did you get that?"

Shirley sat down with a thump. "I thought it might be. At first, that is, when I first saw it, I thought the girl was older than Dawn. But . . . she has notes in her notebook about her relationship with this 'older man.' On the tape, she is having sex with the 'older man.' Unfortunately, his face is so heavily painted that it's impossible to see who he is."

"Can you see how much older he is?"

"Not really. He's a grown man. He's fairly hairy."

"Can I see?"

245

"No, Allison. I don't think that's appropriate. And despite your schoolmates' nastiness, I wouldn't tell them about it." Shirley shooed her away, then came back to remove the tape, put it back in the envelope, and hid the envelope once again, this time in an old shoe box at the back of her closet. She trusted Allison, but curiosity was a powerful goad.

Ignoring the papers on the desk and the journal on the bedside table, she lay on the bed, wondering if *he* might not have had a whole stable of young girls. Who was to say Dawn had been alone in his regard? Maybe Breeze and Summer had been part of this whole thing.

Also, there was the matter of Bridget's journal, and this one. Surely it was not coincidental that both this man's paramours had written detailed accounts of their encounters. Perhaps the man in question gave the writing as homework, as an "assignment"? Did *he* enjoy reading of his own activities, using that to spur him on to ever greater effort and imagination?

It gave her, literally, a bad taste in her mouth. She got up, put on her pajamas, brushed her teeth, then fetched a favorite book from the library. However long it took to get to sleep, she was not going to spend any more time tonight wondering about *him*.

When Shirley went into the kitchen Thursday morning, she found Tabasco once more in residence.

"His ear's cut." J.Q. was digging out the iodine. "I think he got shoved up against the fence by one of his brothers."

Shirley leaned over to rub the kid's neck, and he leaned into her leg. "Is he missing being petted?"

"I pet him, three times a day when he gets his bottle.

246

What he misses is this nice warm kitchen. Now that we've put a heat lamp down there, all the kids try to sleep under it."

"I've noticed they like to sleep under the mangers."

"Right."

"So couldn't we make a long, low kind of four-sided box and put a heated pad under it. There are those heated pads they make for dog kennels."

J.Q. emerged from the closet with the iodine and a wad of cotton. "Hold on to him while I dab his ear."

They were thuswise engaged when the knock came at the door, followed by the opening of the door and Allison's voice, saying, "They're in here, Mrs. Watkins."

Shirley did not bother to straighten up until the task was finished, and when she did so, it was to go to the sink to wash her hands.

"Mrs. McClintock?" the woman asked. The silent girl behind her said nothing.

"Ms.," said Shirley. "McClintock is my family's name. And you're Breeze's mother."

"I am. Could I . . . could I impose on you to give me a cup of coffee and a couple of minutes?"

J.Q. said, "I'll take this baby back down the hill." He went out, taking Allison with him.

The woman sat down at the table, almost collapsing into a chair. The girl still stood by the door, head down. Shirley decided to ignore her, though she gave the mother a slightly sympathetic look.

"You take it black?" She poured one black, one with milk and sugar, and sat down across from the other woman, an olive-skinned, dark-haired, rather plain person with an expression somewhere between shame and fury.

"Breeze and I have had a talk," she began. "Actually, we've had about six talks, starting last night and going on until very early this morning. I made Breeze tell me everything about Dawn, everything she knew, everything the girl had ever said to her. Of course, I can't vouch for the truth of any of it. I don't think Breeze can vouch for the truth of it either."

"She said something important enough to bring you here?"

"No. I would have come here to apologize to you in any case. Breeze has behaved badly. A friend of hers— well, an acquaintance, at any rate—has been killed, and instead of doing everything she could to help find the murderer, she's been involved in these evil little conspiracies. Making up stories. Telling lies. Being a bully. I'm ashamed of her." She glared across the room at her daughter before lifting the cup to her lips and drinking deeply from it.

Shirley put her own cup to her lips, giving herself time to think. "Perhaps she was aping behavior that seemed to have paid off for Dawn?"

"Paid off how? By getting her killed?"

Shirley thought this over. "I doubt it was anything she did at school that got Dawn killed, but I take your point."

"It took me hours to get the whole story out of Breeze. I made her tell me everything. I didn't think you should have to put up with all her excuses and evasions, so I've brought her, to make sure she gives you the whole story.

"Come over here," she said to Breeze. "Sit down."

Breeze came. Breeze sat. Her hair was a mess, her face was tearstained. Her mother did not seem to care.

"Tell Ms. McClintock what you told me."

"Dawn had a lover," she whispered.

"I'm sure you already knew that much," Mrs. Watkins remarked.

"We did. Yes. But we don't know who."

"Go on," the mother said in an imperative tone. "Tell her!"

"When Dawn first met him, he had another woman. Mistress. Dawn told us she seduced him away from the other woman. Dawn told us she made him stop seeing the other woman. Then, on Friday, she told us she overheard him making a phone call to the other woman, and Dawn was really mad, because he'd promised her he'd never see the woman again."

"When did she overhear the phone call?" Shirley demanded.

"I don't know. She told us Friday, but she didn't say when. Dawn said she was going to go see the other woman and tell her what was what."

"She told you this Friday. When on Friday?"

"Before English. That's right before lunch."

Shirley drank, thinking over the implications of this. A young woman could have killed Bridget, but not a young woman who was at the time sitting in English class several miles away.

"Did you have lunch together?"

Breeze nodded.

"Anything else?"

The girl sighed, looking piteously at her mother.

"Tell her!" Mrs. Watkins demanded.

A sniffle. "Dawn said they were making plans, her

and the man. As soon as she was eighteen, they were going to run away together, because then she'd be old enough not to get arrested for it, or for him not to get arrested for it."

There was a long, thoughtful pause, accompanied only by the clink of cups in saucers. "Do you have any idea when this phone call was overheard?" Shirley asked at last.

The girl made a face. Her mother said, "Speak! When Ms. McClintock asks you a question, you give her an answer."

"Summer and me—I—we thought it must have just happened, because she was really mad."

Shirley got up, fetched the coffeepot, and warmed their cups, saying to Mrs. Watkins, "I'm grateful for this information, of course, but has Breeze told any of this to the sheriff's people?"

"She hasn't. She will, today. Dawn, of course, pledged her to secrecy, and there may be some stupid idea of loyalty playing a part in all this."

Shirley asked the girl directly, "Don't you want to know who killed your friend?"

Breeze made the face again. This time Shirley recognized it. It was the rejection face. The face that accompanied a refusal to think about unpleasant things.

Shirley set down her cup and said in a conversational tone, "You know, Breeze, dead is dead. She's not coming back."

The girl burst into tears.

Shirley nodded. "You're not too young to realize what death means. Of course, the media don't help. Kill somebody on TV, the next day he's playing another part

250

in another show. This is real, however. Dawn is really gone."

No response except the steady tears.

Shirley sighed. "I really do expect a public apology, this afternoon, at the school. The same applies to Summer and Tad. Leave that aside for the moment. I think you should take her to sheriff's office, Rio Grande County, not Santa Fe, and have her tell one of the investigators everything she heard from Dawn, but I'd be sure to speak only to them. The one responsible for this case is Eddy Martinez. He's a sensible man. I have no idea if any of this information will help them, but they should have it, nonetheless."

"Breeze, go on out to the car." The girl went, closing the door very softly behind her. Mrs. Watkins got up, pulling her coat around her.

"Mrs. Watkins . . ."

She stopped, waiting.

Shirley frowned. "Do you know most of the teachers at the school?"

"Most of them."

"Is there a Susan Williams among them?"

She looked puzzled. "No. Not to my knowledge."

"How well do you know Jeremy Patterson?"

"Oh, I'm one of the parents on the faculty review committee, so I know most of the teachers quite well, or know about them, at least. He's an excellent English teacher. Married. His wife is a businesswoman, and they never had children. I remember one of the committee members asking if this meant they didn't like children, and Jeremy said no, he liked them too well to saddle a child with a genetic disability. I don't remember what it was, cystic fibrosis or something. I guess

251

they sank everything either of them had into her business. There for a while it was touch and go, and Jeremy worked two jobs, teaching in the daytime and driving limos at night. I guess things have much improved now, though, and he's gone back to working on his doctorate. He's rare in his ability to get young people to write well."

"Good reputation?"

"Excellent. Why?"

"Just fumbling," Shirley said, moving toward the door. "Last few days, all I've seemed to do is fumble."

Mrs. Watkins offered her hand, drew her collar up around her ears, and went out to the car, where Breeze sat like a statue, eyes down. Their car moved off slowly.

J.Q. and Allison materialized from around the corner, both of them eager to hear what had happened. They went into the kitchen, where J.Q. made toast and scrambled eggs while Shirley went point by point over Breeze's information.

"Dawn's lover had another woman, and she made him give her up?" said J.Q. "Now, who does that remind you of."

"Bridget?" asked Allison. "When Rolls-Royce stopped seeing her?"

"The thought crossed my mind," said Shirley. "So then, she turns to Buffalo Man. And Buffalo Man somehow ends up with tapes of Bridget, and of Dawn, both involved with the same man. That can spell only blackmail, particularly if there was some reason the man in question didn't want his affair publicized."

"Bridget's lover was married," said J.Q. as he portioned out the eggs onto three plates.

Allison carried two of them to the table, and Shirley brought the third.

"Was Dawn's boyfriend married?" Allison asked. "How do you know they were both the same person? You said you couldn't see his face."

"They had ... they had the same tattoo," said Shirley. "In the same place. I can't be positive, of course, though I think some sort of computer graphic analysis could probably determine whether they're the same man."

"So, do I go to school today?" Allison asked around a mouthful of egg. "What's going to happen?"

Shirley put marmalade on her toast and thought it over. "I know Breeze is going to be there. Summer and Tad will probably be there; I'll have to check with their parents. They are going to be somewhat chastened, I should think. This afternoon, about three-thirty, I will arrive at the school, and I expect the three of them to make a public, loud apology, right out in front of the world."

"I guess I'll do what Mingy suggested. I'll pay attention to my schoolwork and politely ignore them."

"That's probably an excellent idea."

"What are you going to do until then?" J.Q. asked, reaching for the marmalade.

"Not sure," Shirley murmured. "Not sure at all. There are a few little things. . . ."

"I'm going to clean the barn," he said. "That's where I'll be if you need me for any of those little things."

The little thing that Shirley found herself doing was wandering rather aimlessly about. The Swales family

253

still occupied the Big House, and Brian was staying in Frog House. Little House was empty until later in the week. Garden House held a middle-aged couple who disappeared before light each morning and did not return until after dark. Ditch House was not occupied, which was giving the new maintenance man, Batisto, time to mend the plaster and repaint it as needed.

After much thought and no little procrastination, Shirley had gently pushed her hired couple, Alberta and Vincente, toward resigning. They were nearing retirement age anyhow, and the list of things they didn't like about the job had grown with each passing week. Mostly, what Vincente didn't like was work. And mostly what Alberta didn't like was his not liking work, because it increased the burdens on her. They had been given a nice severance check and a weasel-worded recommendation, and had at once found other work for *dos gringos ricos con poquito trabajo solamente*, as they had put it, somewhat gleefully. More power to them. In her opinion, no *trabajo* would be *poquito* enough for Vincente.

When she decided to let them go, Shirley had also decided not to try for another couple. Couples were, on the average, not worth it. If he was good, she was terrible. If she was good, he was a crook. And often, both were not only terrible but united in their mutual destructiveness, feeding off one another's every little ire and anguish. Shirley had suffered one such couple as managers of a property in Washington, years ago. The female half had been a closet hysteric with neurotic tendencies and he had been a man so full of barely suppressed anger he had visibly boiled each time she asked him to do something. During their final interview, both of them had let go with verbal blasts straight off the analyst's couch, and it turned out they had indeed both been in therapy for years. In Shirley's opinion, they were walking indictments of the mental-health profession.

So, she had not advertised for a couple but for two employees, a maintenance man with broadly based skills, plus an excellent and well-recommended housekeeper. Batisto seemed to be doing well, if one allowed for certain language difficulties. J.Q. had come further with his Spanish than Shirley had, at this point. Batisto was truly a man of all work, flexible, and thus far reliable. The housekeeper had been harder to find, but after interviewing for the better part of a month, Shirley had found Genevieve Stephens, called Jennie, who had proven to be scrupulously clean, indefatigably energetic, and totally reliable. On all counts, a find.

Shirley stopped in Ditch House to check on progress and found Jennie cleaning the rooms Batisto had finished repainting. They chatted for a while, mostly about the Swaleses, whom Jennie found interesting, and Brian, whom she felt sorry for. "That lupus, that's an awful disease," she said. "I had a niece with that. Poor thing. But he says they're trying some new medicine on her, and it looks like it might improve things. We'll just hope so." And with that she went back to her mop.

Shirley wandered over to the Big House in time to meet Mama, who was being brought out to her chair by the two boys, Brian and Bobby. Moved by some obscure impulse at do-goodery, wanting to relieve Ella, who looked even wearier than when she'd arrived, Shirley fetched a chair of her own from the portal and set about keeping Mama company. Only when she was launched on the story of Bridget's life, as disclosed by the journal, did she realize her own motive, which was to find out where Brian and Bobby had been on Friday last.

"That poor child," said Mama, tears in her eyes. "When Brian told us how she was killed, how they cut on her after she was killed, we just cried. And you know, it was such a funny thing: Bobby, he had her phone number, but he'd never called her yet. And we started out driving on Friday, you know, so he thought maybe we'd warn her we was coming, but since she was an hour earlier, he waited to call until we stopped for lunch. Noon, he called. That was eleven o'clock, your time, and there wasn't no answer because she was already dead."

"Where'd you call from?" Shirley asked, trying not to sound overly interested.

"Well, we was on our way to St. Louis, that's where we stopped Friday night. We talked about going through Peoria, but it wasn't Peoria. No, I'll tell you, it was Normal! Isn't that a silly name for a town? Then we went on to Kansas City, Saturday, and we got to Oklahoma City on Sunday night. I can't go too far at one go without having lots of pain, so Bobby and Ella, they took it real easy. Monday night we was in Amarillo, and then Tuesday we got here, and all that time she was dead and we didn't even know."

"Bobby and Ella spell each other driving?" Shirley asked idly.

"No. Bobby, he won't let Ella drive. Says she goes too fast. He did all the driving."

"I think that's really strange, your calling on Friday."

"I thought so, too. Almost like we should've known.

256

But"—she heaved a gigantic sigh—"we didn't know. Wish I had. Wish somehow I could have stopped it. It just makes me real angry."

"We'll find out who," Shirley said, unthinkingly.

"Oh, let me help. You started to tell me about Bridget. Tell me the rest about her, tell me everything you know."

Which, at first unwillingly, Shirley found herself doing, telling not only about Bridget but about Dawn, and all the ins and outs of the case thus far.

When she wound down, some half hour later, Mama said in an awed voice, "So these two dead, our Bridget and this Dawn girl, they was both bedding down with this same man. Lordy me. What I wouldn't have give for a man like that once on a time."

Shirley's jaw dropped.

Mama laughed. "Well, we can remember, can't we?" Her face crumpled. "No excusing him, mind you. He's a villain, that one. I thought my first husband was a bad one with the women, but this one is worse. And whoever did it tried to make it look like aliens, just because of that newspaper story."

"He almost succeeded," said Shirley.

"What're you going to do next?"

"Go talk to Pete Merwiczi," Shirley said, glancing at her watch. "If I can find him. I want to know what he knows about his old friend. I figure I've got just about time to get there and back before the apology ceremony."

"Well, you come tell me if you find out anything," Mama said, patting Shirley's hand. "One thing about all this, it's interesting, and that's what makes it worthwhile to keep going."

It was interesting. Personally, however, Shirley felt she could have kept going just as well with a lot less of it. She went down to the barn to tell J.Q. she was leaving, then called Lydia Wafferneusse about Pete, combed her hair, found her hat, and started for Madrid, using the time to build a sequence of events regarding Bridget's death.

Bridget and—call him X again—had a love affair in Santa Fe. X's wife threatened the affair. For financial reasons, X didn't want to break with his wife just at that time. So Bridget gave up her business and moved to Madrid, where X could come and go, if not unnoticed, at least unscathed. Bridget used all her free time trying to be a writer, a writer of both fiction and fact. Assuming the journal was fact.

Then, about a year and a half ago, Dawn bombed out of her private school and was brought back home. Somehow Dawn hooked up with X. X made his trips to Madrid less frequently. This may have been because of Dawn, or he may simply have run out of sexy stories to playact. Maybe his scenarios worked better if he had a new partner. It worked that way with rats. Rats get tired of their usual mates, but put a new rat in the cage— whoa, Nellie. On the other hand, rat sex is not known for innovation.

So Bridget goes to Buffalo Man and tells him about her false and wicked lover who got her to sell her business and then cheated on her. And Buffalo Man says, well, we'll get some tapes of the guy and make him pay for them or we'll tell his wife. So Bridget cooperates and they get tapes.

Meantime Buffalo Man has maybe done some detective work. Or maybe Bridget just out and out told him who the guy was. She probably did. So Buffalo Man follows the guy when he leaves Madrid, and Buffalo spies on him, and sees him with his new, young partner, and he arranges to get some tapes of that session, too.

So then . . . then what? Bridget tells X that he'll have to repay her for what she lost selling her business, because he's a cheating bastard. Maybe she mentions the tapes, maybe not. And he says, okay, he'll give her thus and so, and she says no, he should buy her a house in Santa Fe. Which he does. But somehow, he ends up with her share of the Montana land? That didn't fit. If he was buying the house . . . Wait a minute, Bridget didn't know the land was valuable. She thought it was close to worthless—well, fifty thousand, but that's hardly anything for three thousand acres—less than twenty bucks an acre.

Maybe he says, yes, I'll buy you the house, but just in case my wife finds out, I'll have to prove it was business, like a trade. What've you got to trade? He knows damn well what she's got to trade. She's told him everything about herself over the last couple of years except, maybe, that she has a brother. So, she makes out a bill of sale and gives him fifty thousand dollars' worth of land in return for a quarter-million-dollar property.

Then Bridget moves into Shirley's neighborhood and starts doing healing, picking up where Buffalo Man left off.

Buffalo Man. Who got killed by a hit-and-run. And why did he get killed? Because he had a tape of X's current underage girlfriend, and he tried to blackmail X with it, which would be easy because she was only fifteen. So Buffalo Man was murdered, maybe. Maybe he was the first murder victim. And no doubt X looked for the tape, but he couldn't find it because it was in the buffalo head and the originals of X and Bridget were somewhere else, in an envelope with Bridget's name on it.

Okay so far. Then what happens? Then what happens is brother Brian's wife gets sick, and he has to have money. So he tells Bridget, we need to separate this property so I can sell my half. So Bridget calls X and says, hey, I need the land back, because my brother is up against it. And X says, oh, you never told me about a brother, we need to talk about this. Or maybe he says, no, let's just pay your brother off, I'll bring you the money for his half.

So he comes to Bridget's house for some such ostensible purpose, and Bridget ends up dead. Why?

Because X can't afford to have his real relationship with Bridget known. He can't afford there to be any questions asked about the Montana land. Maybe because X had already used the bill of sale for something. He had ... borrowed against it, maybe? Something. Maybe he meant to use it to finance his elopement with his new, young partner. Maybe he didn't want to wait until she was eighteen.

So he killed Bridget, and since there'd been such a foofaraw in the papers about cattle mutilations, he got the bright idea to make it look like aliens did it. Which, for a wonder, people actually did believe, and if Shirley hadn't messed in, they probably still would believe.

But meantime Dawn heard X make the date with his former girlfriend. Dawn doesn't know what it's all about, so she gets mad. She ... what? Threatens X? Threatens to tell somebody? His wife, for example? Or the law?

Something like that. At any rate, she takes off with Tad to play a nasty trick on Allison. X has been hanging around, just looking for an opportunity to get her alone but well away from whatever location they normally meet in. He follows her to the arroyo, and bingo, dead Dawn. Now the only connection between X and the murders is the Western Mountain Development Corporation, which X is fairly confident about because X doesn't know that Mama Swales exists, or that Bobby Swales exists, and he for sure doesn't know that both of them already know about the copper.

That's the way she'd laid it out for Mama Swales, and that's just about the way she figured it had happened. If Pete gave her some verification, or if Lydia could, she'd present the case to the law-enforcement men and hope they did something with it!

There was an accident on the highway, tying up all lanes of traffic. Shirley sat and steamed for twenty minutes until the tow truck arrived to pull the wreckage to the side of the road. When she arrived at the bottom of the tailings pile, she knew she couldn't spend much time there and was pleasantly surprised to find that Lydia had collected Pete and had, at least partially, sobered him up.

The three of them sat in the three chairs; Lydia provided coffee; Shirley gave a rapid-fire presentation of the scenario she'd worked out. When she was finished, she asked, "I need verification. What can you give me?"

Lydia said in an interested tone, "The place was all torn up the day after Dad died. Somebody had been here, hunting. That envelope I took to Bridget? That was in Dad's car, and his car was parked down behind the first house on this road. He usually left it there. Sometimes it snows and you can't get out, or it snows and you can't get in. It was easier for him just to park there and walk."

Pete nodded unwillingly. "I don't think Hiram was blackmailing anybody. Hiram, he just offered to sell the tape to the man. Or, anyhow, that's what he told me he was gonna do."

"What man?" Shirley asked.

"The guy that was screwing Bridget. That guy."

"His name, Pete?"

"I dunno. Hiram, he never said. He said he had some hot stuff on the tape, but he never said who."

"Was there any suspicion that your dad was murdered?" Shirley asked.

Lydia shook her head. "Why would there have been? He was hit by a car. He was dead and backed over by the side of the road. Here in New Mexico, every day people get killed by cars. It's this whole Mexican-Southwestern thing about getting drunk, which is very similar to a Southern-redneck thing about getting drunk. They think it's recreation. They think it's fun, or funny. The drunker they are, the more fun it is. And the Indians are even worse; staying drunk is a whole way of life with them. Plus the Anglos who move here because they like the local attitude. It's going to go on that way until we start putting them in the stocks in public. Until we start holding them up to ridicule."

"Until we stop allowing drunkenness to be a defense against killing or hurting people," Shirley suggested. "Until we start increasing the penalties for people who are drunk or high instead of letting alcohol or drug use be extenuating circumstances."

"Well now," said Pete, getting angrily to his feet. "Well now, ain't you the plaster saints." He slammed out.

"Ignore him." Lydia wiped an angry tear. "Pete's one of the ones I'm talking about. He'll kill somebody one of these days, and then he'll argue he didn't mean it, he was drunk. Anyhow. They did an autopsy on Dad. His death was consistent with being hit by a car that then backed up to see what they'd hit and ran over him again. They ran a story, asking people to report repairs made to a car of such and such a type. I forget what. There was headlight glass and some paint on Dad's clothes. Nothing ever came of it."

"What color?"

"Black, I think. I'm pretty sure, black."

"You never reported the place being torn apart?"

"I never gave it a thought. I figured somebody local had heard Dad was dead and decided to pick up what they could. I thought, well, hell, more power to them. I never connected it to anything. I wish I didn't now. It was a lot easier just thinking he was dead by accident."

"I know what you mean." Shirley looked at her watch. Time to head back. She got herself under way with a muttered prayer for no more roads closed to traffic. As it was, if she kept to a steady fifty-five, she would be at the school just in time.

8

SHIRLEY ARRIVED AT the school at three twenty-three. She recognized the Watkins car in the parking lot, Mrs. Watkins ensconced therein. A fluffy someone accompanied by a saturnine someone occupied the front seat of a Range Rover. A dour-looking man occupied the front seat of a new and very shiny minivan. Summer's parents; Tad's father. Well, all very nice.

Shirley got out of the car, stretched, nodded in kindly satisfaction at each of the occupied cars, receiving a return nod from Breeze's mama, a quick look away by fluffy, a sour stare from saturnine, and a somewhat frosty nod from dour. All present and accounted for. Presumably Tad's mama couldn't get off work, or Tad's papa had decided to handle it himself.

The surprise was the sheriff's car, with Eddy and a colleague leaning on either side of it. They came over to her.

"We thought we'd talk to this teacher," said Eddy. "Now that we're sure it's not ETs anymore, we're getting a little cooperation."

"The DNA from the buckets matched Bridget's?"

"We'd sent it to the state lab. It matched. That sort of took the wind out of the sheriff, kind of eliminated extraterrestrials. We sent the fetal tissue there, too, from the French girl. Now if we can just get somebody to match it to. We came to ask some questions when school was out. This Tad kid, maybe some of the others."

They walked together to the school steps, arriving just in time to hear the clangor of a bell from within. Young people poured out, the flow gradually diminishing to a trickle. When it had all but dried up, the three miscreants arrived, arranged themselves in a ragged little line, and looked at their feet. Breeze mumbled, Tad fidgeted, Summer seemed incapable of speech.

"I can't hear you," Shirley said loudly.

"Breeze!" came her mother's voice from across the lot.

"Ms. McClintock, we're very sorry for what we did and we won't do it again," gabbled Breeze, breaking and running for her mother's car.

Tad, who had meant to say something smart-ass, took a good look at the uniforms on either side of Shirley and decided not to. He repeated Breeze's formula in a surly voice and departed in what he obviously hoped was a dignified manner, only to be nabbed by the deputy. Together they went to the car where Tad's father sat. After a short discussion, Tad returned with escort to the deputies' car.

Shirley and Eddy had to move closer to hear Summer, who was unable to speak for the tears. "Didn't mean to," she mumbled. "Didn't think it . . . didn't want to . . . Mother's really mad. . . ."

"You're a silly child," Shirley said finally, realizing that no sense would be forthcoming. "Go home. Try to grow up."

Cars moved away. Shirley watched them go, then turned to see Jeremy Patterson watching through the glass doors. He came out. Shirley murmured to Eddy and went up the stairs to meet him.

"I wondered if the other teacher is here," she asked. "The one who massaged Dawn's neck for you. Susan Williams?"

"Did I say Williams?" he asked. "You'd think I'd remember; she's been married almost four years! She was Susan Williams, my neighbor, from the time we were ten years old. She's now Susan McCarthy, called Sissy by most. Sure, she's here. Does the deputy want to talk to her?"

Shirley nodded, feeling a wave of relief. She had absolutely not wanted to think ill of Jeremy Patterson.

"While you're here," she murmured to Eddy, before he went inside, "can you tell me who informed Bridget McCree's brother that she was dead."

"I did," the deputy replied. "There was a list of phone numbers by the phone, in the kitchen. It said Brian McCree, and the number was a Colorado number. I phoned from right there."

"What time, Eddy?"

"Oh, not long after we got there. It was his house number. I got his wife, and she gave me his work number. I called that, he was there. It was before three."

She thanked him and strolled back to her car while

Eddy went in to speak with Patterson and McCarthy. No way Brian could have killed his sister and been back in Denver before three. Not unless he flew from Santa Fe itself. The airport was small and was not heavily used; a charter flight would be remembered. Also, it was unlikely he would have returned to Denver and then shown up late for work. From the way Brian talked about his boss, the man knew where he was every minute.

Shirley got into her car and started to pull away when she saw Ulti and Allison emerge from around the corner of the school.

"We wanted to watch," said Allison. "We were just inside, back where they couldn't see us. Summer's a real wuss-ass, isn't she? Do you mind if we drop Ulti? I told him we'd take him halfway."

"What was the law doing here?" Ulti asked as he climbed into the backseat.

"They want to talk to Mr. Patterson and Mrs. McCarthy about Dawn. Mrs. McCarthy is Susan Williams, or was, before she got married."

"Oh, was that it?" Allison commented. "I thought last night maybe it was somebody who'd gotten married or changed their name, like Bridget did."

Cross off three suspects, Shirley told herself, admitting for the first time that she had suspected Jeremy. Cross off Jeremy. Cross off Bobby. Probably cross off Brian, though it would be worth a call to the airport or to his boss to be sure. Which left her right where she'd been to begin with. With Lover. Or Tycoon.

They dropped Ulti off halfway, Shirley dropped Allison off at the head of the drive. "I'm going to the San Pedro Pueblo," she said. "Tell J.Q. I'll be back in time to fix supper. I'm going to see if I can find Isidro's wife."

The directions the trader had given her were still in her jacket pocket. Two Horse Ramirez lived away from the pueblo center, on a dirt road. She found the road without trouble, but thereafter had some trouble staying on it. Tracks went away from it here and there, and since the road was only tracks itself, it was difficult to know which was which. After several false tries that ended up in informal dump sites along the riverbed, Shirley came to a lone house that looked very much as the trader had described it. An open water tank by the corral, shaded by a couple of cottonwoods watered by the tank overflow. A shed by the corral, now occupied by two horses. A small house, with a clothesline and an arbor. A spinning windmill. A length of pipe running into the roof of the house from the windmill. There'd be a water tank in there, up on a pipe frame, one that stayed warm enough not to freeze in the winter. They probably filled it every day, or whenever the wind allowed. A hundred gallons, maybe. Two hundred. Maybe a water heater. Maybe only one pipe to the kitchen, one to the toilet. She inferred the toilet from the fact that there was no outhouse.

She parked and got out. A man came out of the shed and stared at her. She did not approach. She had been told it was politer to wait.

He came over after a moment. "You lookin' for somebody?"

"I'm looking for Isidro's wife."

"She don't want no trouble with you people."

"I'm not you people. Are you Mr. Two Horse Ramirez?"

"So what?"

"The trader told me she might be here. I only wanted to ask a couple of very short questions."

"You the mother?"

"Mother?"

"Of that girl. The one that got killed."

"No. I'm not her mother. I'm the mother of the girl who found her body."

He stared at her for a moment, then stomped his way into the small house. Shirley merely stood, looking about her.

A woman came from around the house. She was round-faced, stocky, hair in plaits at either side of her head. Her hands were clay-covered. "You come around the side," she said, going back there herself.

Around the side was under the arbor, bigger than it had looked from the road. A half-built pot sat on a flat stone; beside it, a lump of clay protruded from a plastic sack. The woman sat down and resumed her work, pulling wads of clay into her hands, rolling them into worms between her fingers, smoothing each clay worm into the one before, spiraling around the pot, building it higher.

"My brother says you want to know about Isidro?"

Shirley shook her head, then, aware the woman wasn't looking at her, said, "No. I wanted to tell him about the girl who was giving him trouble."

"She's dead," said the woman. "We saw that on TV."

"Does he know?"

"Maybe."

She went on coiling. Shirley waited, silent.

"I was there once, in her house," the woman said. "One of my pots won a ribbon at Indian Market. It was a very large pot, very beautiful. It was the blue ribbon. The woman bought it for a lot of money. I went there with Isidro, I took it there, put it there, in the nicho. I saw that place."

"The house."

"The house. The rooms. So many rooms. She showed us, the girl."

"A girl who was trouble."

"Isidro, he wanted the warrior god to step on her." A ghost of a smile fled across her face and was gone.

What did one say to that? "I saw the carving," Shirley admitted.

"That carving is not our way," she said. "It is not Isidro's way. Our gods perhaps do not want their business carved in wood. I told Isidro it was perhaps not a good thing to do, but he said she was white and it is the white man's way, in their church."

"What white man's church?" Shirley asked.

"Where the god with wings has a spear," she said. "Where he kills the monster."

The god with wings. An angel. And the monster would be Satan. A stained-glass window, perhaps. Or a carving. "St. Michael's Church?" Shirley guessed.

"That church." She rolled the clay, twined it, smoothed it, scraped it with a curved piece of gourd shell into an almost organic smoothness, dipping her fingers into a can of water beside her. "Isidro says, if the white people do it, then he can do it, she is white. Then he went away, to be far from here when the god steps on her."

Shirley crouched down. "She bothered Isidro? She threatened him."

"She said she would tell stories about him, to the sheriff, to the tribal police, to the FBI. She said she would tell them he raped her. If he did not do as she said."

"She wanted him to go to bed with her."

The woman turned her head and spat. "In that house. In her room. The room where she took us, Isidro and me. Where the holy ones dance and watch."

"Thank you for telling me." Shirley rose to her feet and stayed bent forward for a moment, rubbing the knee. "She was very wicked, but I don't think the god killed her. I think a man did, a very wicked man."

The woman glanced past her with veiled eyes. "A man can be full of the god, sometimes, when he dances. He can pull people, like the god. So a god might fill up a man. If the god wanted."

Shirley stood for a moment, stunned. He can pull people, like the god. Pulling people, pulling things. And the holy ones watching! Suddenly those words, telling her something she hadn't realized she knew. She gulped and turned to go. When she got to the car, Two Horse was waiting.

"Do they know who killed her?" he asked.

"They don't," said Shirley. "But I do."

J.Q. was coming up the hill when she got home, a feed bucket in each hand. She leaned on the wall and told him all about it.

"What are you going to use for proof?" J.Q. asked.

"Bridget's journal, Dawn's notebook, both describe the man and his sexual impedimenta. All those costumes and paraphernalia have to be somewhere. Don't you think a search warrant will find them? And remember, she was three months pregnant! There'll be DNA. There's the tape, with the tattoo. They can probably blow that up and make something of it. There may even be something they can find that will tie to Buffalo Man's death, though that was a long time ago."

"And records," he mused. "Somewhere. Tying him to the Western Mountain Development Corporation. Are you going to the deputies?"

"I think I must, don't you?"

He heaved a deep breath. "Yes. I just hope they don't foul it up."

"You think now?"

"I think the sooner the better."

"I'll make the call from my room."

She tried, but Eddy wasn't there. Would he be there? No, off duty tonight. Back tomorrow. What was tomorrow? Friday. The end of the week. The Swaleses' last day. They were leaving Saturday morning. Brian's last day. He was going home as well.

She had time to make a few phone calls, verifying things. One to Brett, at the paper. One to a guy up in the northeast corner of the state.

And then it was suppertime. What tonight? Something quick. Maybe a huge chef's salad. Cheese. Ham. Chicken. Lettuce, tomatoes, some garbanzos. Croutons. Why not?

She heaved herself erect and stalked off to the kitchen, where she found J.Q. finishing up a large pot of menudo.

"When did you do all this?" she cried, nose widening in pleasure.

"I had the day free," he said stiffly. "You being off by yourself on all kinds of detecting."

"Oh, J.Q., I'm sorry. I didn't think you'd necessarily want to go along."

"Didn't," he said. "Necessarily."

"I should have asked," she said contritely. "But then, if I had, we might not have had menudo."

"There is that," he said, with only the hint of a smile.

She took the lid off the pot and bent over it, floating on the steam. Wafted, she reminded herself. Pulled by chilies anchos, and onion and garlic; tripe and pigs' feet; posole, not too much. Oregano. More garlic. Salt, of course. A deep red-brown liquid surging with flavorful bits. Wafted and pulled.

She dipped up a spoonful and blew on it, then sipped. "People wouldn't kill each other nearly so often if they all got nice bowls of this soup every day," she said.

J.Q. began dishing up: hot tortillas and soup, and who needed anything else? Allison came in, looking calmer and in a better frame of mind than she had for some days. They sat down at the table.

The phone rang.

Shirley answered it. Eddy Martinez. "I came into the office and got this message. You need me?"

"Yes," she said, somewhat guardedly. Oh, what the hell. "Eddy, I know who killed them."

"I can be there in half, three quarters of an hour."

"Fine. We'll be here."

Outside, in the driveway, Mama Swales was also having supper, something from the barbecue. Shirley could see the smoke from where she sat.

They ate in virtual silence. Allison was sleepy-eyed, and Shirley guessed she would be in bed early tonight.

J.Q. looked out the window and said, "Mama's showing Jesre her costumes."

"Her costumes?" Allison asked.

"She used to be a little bit of a thing, a trick rider in

273

a rodeo. Do you believe that?" Shirley said, draining the last spoonful.

"I want to see," said Allison, tipping her bowl to get the last drop.

They put their bowls into the sink and went out into the evening. Not dusk yet, though getting close, the light turning red. Mama beckoned at them from across the wall, and they went to join her.

"Jesre doesn't believe I was ever your size," she said to Allison. "He thinks I was born like this."

Jesre looked at his feet and mumbled something. Allison grinned at him, and his face lit up. Lonesome, Shirley thought. The kid was just lonesome. No fun being hauled around the country in company with mom and dad and dying grandma.

"Can I see?" Allison asked.

Shirley lifted the case onto the bench beside Mama's chair, and Mama began showing Allison the contents. Costumes and hats, fancy lassos and gun belt. Dog barked throatily from beside the wall. Car coming.

That would be Eddy. Shirley moved away from the others, waiting, seeing the car only by the glints of sun that reflected from it. It didn't look like a sheriff's car.

It pulled into the drive, and the man inside extracted himself and stood up, staring at her.

"Good evening," she said in a noncommittal voice.

"Ms. McClintock," he replied. "I just got a call from the sheriff. He says you've found out who killed Dawn."

In the quiet of the evening, his voice had a metallic quality, a trumpet voice.

"I had some information I wanted to give the deputy, yes," she said.

"And what might that be?"

She didn't want to tell him. What she really wanted was for him to go away, now, before something untoward happened. She was all too aware of Mama Swales, behind her. Of Allison and Jesre.

"Just some information I got down in Madrid," she said. "There was evidently some evidence that a man from down there was murdered instead of accidentally killed. I think it ties into another case up here. Which might tie into Dawn's murder, though I'm not at all sure." Which was a lie. She was dead sure. "The deputies will be here in a minute, and I'll give it to them."

"I think you should give it to me," he said.

Behind her, Mama Swales's voice fell silent. Allison and Jesre were quiet. They had heard the threat in that voice, just as she had.

"Why would I do that?" she asked.

"Because I need to know," he said. His voice was quite implacable. He wasn't going to be sidetracked.

"Dawn was pregnant," Shirley said, playing for time. "Did you know that?"

The man across from her did not move, did not shift, stayed where he was, fixed, his left hand dangling negligently at his side, the right hand in the pocket of his jacket. Still, something changed about him. Something had stiffened and drawn away, into some other place. "Was she?"

"Three months pregnant, yes. The deputies have sent samples of fetal tissue to the state lab. The state lab has also matched the DNA from Bridget's body to the flesh found in those buckets out in the arroyo. So it isn't extraterrestrials, whatever else it may be."

"How did anyone find the buckets?" he asked mildly, curiously.

"Crows," she said. "They can smell flesh, even charred flesh."

"Crows," he repeated. "Sticking their noses in, quite literally. And you, of course. You, who had to stick your nose in, too. You, who had to interfere."

Shirley drew a deep, sobbing breath. "Why did you do it? We know why you killed Bridget, but why did you kill Dawn?"

"You know?" He laughed, hackingly. "You know why I killed Bridget?"

"Oh, yes. You killed her because she wanted the Montana land back, or she wanted it split, or she wanted money for Brian's half of it. Bridget was naive. She didn't know how valuable the land was; she never thought you might know more about it than she did; but of course you did, from the beginning. From the very beginning. Five years ago, was it?"

"Before I ever met her," he said. "Before I ever found her, here in Santa Fe, almost on my doorstep. Right."

"How did you find out she was the heir to the property?"

"As soon as I heard about the copper strike, I went to the recorder's office, in Montana. They had a letter she'd written about the taxes. Her name and address. In Santa Fe. But she never told me she had a brother."

"Two brothers," said Shirley.

"Two!" His face creased into a kind of satanic amusement. "Think of that. Two."

"You tried to kill one of them, didn't you?"

"Now, why would you think that?"

"You visited Bridget openly, in the daylight when you were arranging for her to move to this house down the road. In your role as real-estate agent, you didn't need to hide. But previously, you had visited her often at night, in your role as lover."

"And if I did?"

"You got her out of Santa Fe. You kept her where she was isolated while you figured out how to dispose of her, how to get her to sign over the land to you. Then your grip slipped, didn't it? You fell for . . . a much younger woman."

He didn't reply. He merely stared, eyes glinting slightly red in the sunset glow.

"She seduced you. Usually I would blame the older man in a case like this, but in this case, I think Dawn actually did seduce you. Perhaps around Christmastime, two years ago. Definitely when she was kicked out of her private school and had to go to school here, live here. She was very pretty. Very . . . nubile. And extremely sexy."

"Yes," he said. "You have no idea."

Where was Eddy? Her throat was dry. "She found out about Bridget. She made you give up visiting Bridget. But it worked out well for you. It actually gave you a reason to get your hands on the Montana land. Bridget blackmailed you, and you gave her a house in return for the worthless land. To protect yourself, you said. So it could appear to be only a business deal. And then, for a while, you let your plans . . . rusticate. You didn't think much about Montana for a while, did you? You didn't go on with your plans. You were having too much fun."

"Yes. For a while."

277

"But, of course, that couldn't go on. Buffalo Man got some pictures. I think he took them through a window. He already had some pictures of you with Bridget, taken before you completely broke with her, and he got some of you with Dawn. In her bed, in her house, where the holy people were dancing and watching."

"What are you talking about?"

"A painting. Probably a very valuable one, a prize-winner at Indian Market. A line of kachina dancers. They appear on the tape, with Dawn, with you."

"I want that tape," he said. "You give it to me." His hand came out of his jacket pocket, holding, as Shirley had assumed it would, a gun.

A tiny sound from behind her, perhaps an indrawn breath.

"I don't have it," she lied. "I put it in a safety-deposit box."

"That's very similar to what Dawn said about her boyfriend," he said bitterly. "She told me she didn't have one. But I'd overheard her, I didn't believe her. And I don't believe you." The hand holding the gun came up, pointed at her. A target pistol. Quite lethal at this range, for all that. He was aiming at her face, and his calm expression had changed to one of cold rage. "And now it doesn't matter. It's all fucked up. But I'm going to take a few of you meddling fools with me!"

She saw his finger tighten. She heard the shot. She waited for the bullet, for life to shatter into nothing, time stretching into an aching silence. Slowly, so very slowly, he crumpled and fell. The little hole in the side of his head was barely visible.

Shirley turned. Mama was sitting there, quite upright, one of her pearl-handled pistols still in her hand. It was still smoking slightly. No smokeless powder for Mama. Wild West riders wanted a lot of dramatic smoke.

"He killed that girl?" Mama asked. "He shot her?"

"Yes."

"He would have killed us, too. And he tried to kill Brian?"

"Yes."

"He killed Bridget? He cut on her?"

"Yes."

The enormous woman heaved a huge sigh. "Then there was a reason for my hanging on, after all. And it all kind of winds up, just the way I wanted. All those loose ends . . ."

She sighed again, lying back, smiling. "Who was he?"

"Dawn's stepfather," said Shirley. "Dexter French."

Eddy's arrival a few minutes later was anticlimactic. The people at Rancho del Valle were accustomed to preserving crime scenes. Luckily, there were no guests present except for the Swaleses.

"He said the sheriff called him," Shirley told Eddy. "That's how he knew."

Eddy shook his head, started to say something, then shook his head again. "As if life isn't hard enough," he said. "We have to try to do our jobs with that . . . that . . ." Words failed him. "I told the sheriff where I was going. I never thought for a minute he'd be stupid enough to call someone and tell them." He sighed again. "He's sucked up to those people ever since the girl got killed. Pranced around like a pet pony."

Eddy called for help from the state. When other law enforcement arrived, Shirley took Eddy into the library and gave him the tapes. He came out half an hour later looking sour. She had Bridget's journal ready for him, and Dawn's notebook, and the letters and the cassette of the sound effects.

He took a lengthy statement.

And finally he asked, "How did you know?"

"It was a silly little thing," she said. "Last week, a week ago today, there was a story in the Santa Fe paper about cattle mutilations. That same morning, when I was talking to Bridget, she mentioned the story, but she also mentioned a gravity ray. At the time I thought I'd just missed it on Friday, but it actually hadn't been mentioned in the first story. It did appear in the Sunday paper, but she had known about it on Friday. Dexter French wrote the story. I checked with the people at the paper; he brought the gravity-ray story in on Saturday afternoon. The man he quoted in the story lives way the hell up near Clayton, the incident hadn't been reported anywhere else, and the man in Clayton never heard of Bridget. Where did she hear about the gravity ray? She had to have heard it from French. And if she heard it from French, it meant French was in contact with her. If he was in contact with her, there had to be a reason. The only unusual thing that Bridget was doing at that time that any of us knew about was the attempt to get some money for Brian.

"And everything fit. How could Dawn have been having this affair with an older man when she wasn't allowed to go out? Answer: she didn't need to go out. Why was Dawn included in the tape? Answer: because Buffalo Man wanted to blackmail French. Why was Buffalo Man killed? Same reason. French couldn't realize any money on the Montana land as long as anyone was left alive to

280

question his possession. He didn't have title to it, he just had Bridget's interest. With Bridget dead, he thought he could get title, but that's before he knew about Brian. And Bobby."

"And you remembered this little thing, just out of the air?"

"Not quite. I was talking with a potter, over at San Pedro Pueblo. She said something about the French house, about Dawn's room, where the holy ones danced and watched. That made me remember the painting on the tape. And she spoke of the kachinas being holy, how they can pull a man, or words to that effect. I got this flash, those cows floating into the woods. Wafted on gravity rays . . ."

"How do we pin this?"

"DNA," she said. "If he's responsible for Dawn's pregnancy, you've got your case. If the painting on the tape is the same as the one in Dawn's room, you've got your case. If Western Mountain Development turns out to be tied to French, you've got your case."

"God. What's her mother going to say?"

"Dawn's mother? She's going to be absolutely out of her skull. When you go over there, assuming you do, take a couple of female deputies with you, and have somebody standing by to take over. I'm sure they've got a housekeeper. Maybe it'd be a good idea to talk to her first."

"Did Dawn actually have a boyfriend from UNM? Tad told us Dexter French asked him if he knew who Dawn's boyfriend from UNM was."

"That was Dawn, hinting, teasing. French overheard a phone call between Dawn and one of her friends. Dawn may even have pretended to have another lover, just to drive him nuts. It would be in character. When she told him the truth, he didn't believe her. He was strung out on the Bridget murder, which, thanks to you, wasn't going the way he wanted it to, the way he'd planned on. He had the murder of Buffalo Man on his mind, and he thought it might come home to roost. He had to keep Anne Pelton-French happy. Dawn's unfaithfulness was the last straw. He was besotted with her. When she went over the fence to go with Tad, he thought she was sneaking out to meet her lover, which sent him right over the edge. He followed her, and he killed her."

"All nicely wrapped. I don't guess we'll even charge that fat woman with anything."

"Mama Swales fired to prevent my being killed. I was surprised as hell. I had no idea she kept those guns loaded. I asked her, afterward, and she said, 'Of course, dear. What good are they without bullets?' By the way, she fired within a foot of my head to hit him. When I figured that out, I got rather queasy."

They had been sitting at the patio table during this interchange. They heard the *whoop, whoop* of the ambulance moving away, a dwindling sound of men, car doors slamming, then the gate latch clanking to let J.Q. come through.

"All finished out there," he said. "There wasn't even any blood on the gravel. Bobby and Brian just arrived back from town. Ella's explaining everything to them."

Shirley put the heels of her hands into her closed eyes and pushed, rubbing her forehead with her fingers. "I feel like I'd been running a race. I thought I was going to die."

"I was washing the menudo pot," J.Q. said apologetically. "I missed it all."

"I ought to tell Lydia Wafferneusse," Shirley said. "I ought to—"

"What you ought to do," said Eddy, very seriously, "is run for sheriff of Rio Grande County."

She laughed, throwing back her head, enjoying the humor of it.

It wasn't until she was through being amused that she noticed Eddy and J.Q. weren't laughing.

The Shirley McClintock series

by Anthony and Edgar Awards nominee

B. J. Oliphant